ILLNESS

Jodie M. Swanson

ISBN:1533033730
ISBN-13:978-1533033734

DEDICATION

To Kyle,
for making me read futuristic,
and keeping my creative spark going.
Love you, Dude!

Special thanks to:
Awesome Writers of the North
for all the input and suggestions

To be able to rise from the earth;
to be able, from a station in outer space,
to see the relationship of the planet earth to other planets;
to be able to contemplate the billions of factors in
precise and beautiful combination that make
human existence possible;
to be able to dwell on an encounter of the human
brain and spirit with the universe
all this enlarges the human horizon..

-Norman Cousins, 1973

Sirius, the brightest star in the heavens....
My grandfather would say that we're part of something
incredibly wonderful – more marvelous than we
imagine. My grandfather would say we ought to
go out and look at it once and a while so we don't
lose our place in it.

-Robert Fulghum

Log-in: JessReynoldi18851
Date/Time: 22 Mar 2203/2203hrs
Subject: cult journal entry (and I hope to forward my journal back home to Earth)

I don't really know what I want to say, other than I am afraid. I think I may be the next person to die. To be the victim of what I have witnessed. To be eaten. I know this may be my first, last, only entry I transmit on this subject. I am not sure I will last the night.

Where to begin? What can I do to share this plot in case I am indeed next?

God. What if this is my last chance? My only chance to tell this and let the truths I have discovered be known. My one and only opportunity to save my name.

I want my family to know that I do not regret my decision to attend this elite campus. My first year was fun-filled and I learned all that I had hoped to. I know you have been forwarded my academic results of my first 2 semesters and letters from my Head Professor and Academic Master. Please remember me as that kind of student: Eager, Promising, Talented, Charismatic, Leader, Brilliant.

God. I'm going to die. That is what I was thinking when I looked at the time on the wall next to my sleeping cot in my quarters. It was the same time as it is the day and month, as well as year. It freaked me out and I knew I had to start writing.

Where to begin? Do I start with what I now know? Or do I start with my first day? My arrival?

I will try to start at the beginning, to answer questions I am sure a lot of family members have had this past year, and longer still. *Lord. Has it been going on this whole academic year? How have I lasted this long?*

If I never get to finish...he is NOT who I thought he was.   He is ill and deceitful. The things I have seen!

But now, before they kill me...I will start with when I arrived here at Interstellar Discipline and Exploration Academy. I will forward my relevant personal journals. (It may look like I have tried to send them to you, but I never did. It was easier to start them that way and I just kept on doing it since I have been here.) Read my diary. So odd that they, that he, encouraged us to write everything down. Hopefully it brings him down.

I love you. Before I die, know I love you.

Mom, I was true to your list (you'll see).

Dad, I hope my last few weeks here make you the most proud.

I have to hurry and find the entries and put them in order before they show up.

I'm afraid. And I can't stop the tears.

I love you!

Jess

ENTRY END

Start TRANSMISSION/SEND

Log-in: JessReynoldi18851
Date/Time: 18 Aug 2201/2041hrs
Subject: I have ARRIVED!!!!!

Oh my GOODNESS! I cannot believe that I am here! All the interviews and tests to get accepted! All the hours worked for the deposit. Scholarship interviews and begging family and friends for the money to get here. And I made it! I am now officially a cadet studying at IDEA! This Interstellar Discipline and Exploration Academy (IDEA) is still the most prestigious of all space studies universities, and I AM IN! It's hard to believe that at sixteen, I am a member of an advanced and accelerated program for being gifted academically. I'm to get specialized and real-world training a minimum of two full years ahead of my old high school classmates. I'm part of an elite group now.

I'm excited to report that my Head Professor is even cooler than I thought from his letters to us. Director Michael Forshay came to each of our rooms to personally welcome us newbies, or plebes. He gave me my identity badge, data pod, and my chip card, and reiterated the need to carry it with me at all times. It tracks our location while on IDEA and allows us entry to rooms, monitors our activity/patterns, and allows us meals, and acts as our line of credit at the Shoppette. He let me know when our academic orientation would be this evening (which was at 1900hrs, and very boring). With that, he showed me my uniforms and name badge/pin, which were already in my closet and dresser drawers. (It's official, I'm Cadet Jessica M. Reynoldi.) Then he said he hoped my time here would stretch me and make me reach my full potential, and left for the next cadet.

ENTRY END

All of us new cadets were given some time to unpack and settle in after being brought to our personal little rooms. However, I was too exhausted to do that. I just listened to some oldie tunes and then slept, for about four hours, until someone knocked on my door. When I opened it, oh my goodness, "HEAVEN at 6 foot something!" He had liquid blue eyes and a soft smile. Standing before me was Cadet James T. Bennett! *Mee-yow!* Sure he had a bunch of other new cadets with him, but I only saw him. I'm sure I looked less than awesome. I swiped at any drool and errant hairs but he seemed to not notice. He must have seen a dozen of us plebes in my tired "condition" to not even flinch or wince at my appearance. Or maybe James' just as nice on the inside as he seems on the outside.

Cadet Bennett, he insisted that we call him James, introduced himself as our House Aide. After introductions, he gave us the big tour to stretch our muscles from the long trip here and to quiz us on any signs of space sickness, and what to look for, and to assure us that no one would judge us if we display any signs: shakiness, slurred speech, either too much sleep or deprivation (weird it can be either/or), depression, and aggression. He did stress to seek any advisor or medical staff right away. "Better to be safe than spacey," he said. I was not the only one who laughed, though I may have been the loudest.

I thought it sounded like someone without caffeine. The cadet next to me, a petite red-head named Tori Buchanan, laughed out loud when I said it. People stared at us. James included. Well, at least I got his attention. Though from the look everyone gave us, I silently vowed try to curb myself and make my achievements more noteworthy than my outbursts of humor.

James took us to the Commons to point out a scale model of IDEA rising off the floor opposite the chow line. Some cadet had made it about twelve years previous out of recycled items during his stay at the academy. The huge structure rested in a shallow cradle and was supported by cables from the two-level high ceiling above it to prevent toppling. He said that both Directors had smaller versions made of bronze in display cases in their offices as well, and that is where the young designer had taken the measurements and recreated the Commons sculpture. James pointed out how "The Donut" (as James calls our circular academy) is divided by houses between Director Forshay and his counter-part, Director Brent Bradley, and the Academic Quarter versus the Maintenance Quarter. James explained that there are many floors which separate the students by their respective academic years: Plebes, Trekkers, Journeymen, and Firsties. He also spoke to the aquatic pools being on the outer most part of the donut due to the generated gravity of our sphere. Someone really smart did an amazing job designing this place which was originally supposed to be a military outpost that went outdated prior to completion. And the cadet did a fantastic job showing us the casing of our new home away from home.

I really liked looking at the eighteen foot tall reconstruction of IDEA. What a beautiful creation, for starters. The detail in it is amazing with various colors depicting sections of the structure we now live in. And to know that this cadet had built it all himself during free time after he sought the permission to construct it permanently. It is just too cool. I admired that he even had put all the detail of the few space portal windows in with little figures looking out. I hope I can do something like that, leave something cool behind for other cadets coming here. (Note to self, start thinking what I want to leave behind as part of my legacy and possibly empower and excite future cadets.)

This place has everything a city has. Next to the Commons is the Shoppette for all our toiletries and gadgets. And there is small theater mostly used for classes but occasionally they show a film or newscast there. There are four medic stations evenly spaced on IDEA, at every juncture between Quarters. It reminds me of attending that military base where I had my physical before I was allowed to come here.

We briefly toured the first floor of each House (and the respective doors to the Director's Quarters) and the Academic Quarter before venturing into the Maintenance Quarter on our level. Most of the cadets of Director Bradley smiled as we were introduced. Some gave me the hee-be-gee-bies (yeah, I may not know how to spell it, but I sure know how I felt), but they were ranking cadets, mostly guys eyeing us down like we are fresh meat.

We were shown the gardening chambers, but we weren't allowed to go in. But there were big tinted windows that we could look in and "See what's on the menu," as James said. I saw rows and rows of tiered shelved fixtures holding plants and irrigation hoses. I could recognize some of the vegetables and fruits that were closer to us. In the distance I saw trees bearing bananas and other species, like papayas. Someone made a crack about being monkeys up in space, and I was able to control my mirth better this time. But looking too long at all that made my eyes hurt as the UV lights being used were very bright, despite the tinting. (Side note: Someone asked what the plants ate. James simply said, "We eat the plants' by-products. They eat ours." Of course, some people were doing the famous, "EEEEWWW!" I thought it's cool that nothing is wasted here, including our "by-products.")

There is a UV room to combat Seasonal Affective Disorder (SAD) with a mock sandy beach and piped in sounds of waves crashing and seagulls. Especially important to be shown this space since James said it's mandatory that we get some UV time at least once a week for a minimum of fifteen minutes. You won't find me complaining and I definitely am going to check that out later. I wondered if they restrict the amount of times you can go tanning here as I am pretty pale.

Along the outermost hull wall is a huge series of enclosed tanks filled with fish stock, like that of an aquarium back on Earth. The brochure and website only show bits, but these vats are ginormous. James showed us just some of the bass and trout ones. It seemed like thousands of fish were in each of the vats: four for bass, and four for trout, and two for salmon to travel back and forth between in their in-bred migratory pattern. Apparently we eat a lot of fish here, which explains why they asked all the allergy questions on the applications and during the interviews. James said something about CoQ10 and Omega-3 levels and that it's naturally found in fatty fish.

We were taken to an inner layer of IDEA which has various gymnasiums set up for sports, complete with steep stadium seating overhead so spectators can look down on the play. There is a football-slash-soccer field, and we saw some people scrimmaging each other with fancy footwork, so I knew they were playing soccer. In the next spectator corridor, we saw a running track. James said there was a dojo and volleyball court and gymnastics arena as well. Mind you, these are smaller scale than the Olympic venues, but they are still functional and every semester there are various events scheduled for us to watch.

We were also shown one of two large classrooms done in a steep seating style where training and in-house theatre productions can happen.

Just as I was wondering if we get steak or chicken or pork, we passed The Coop. Yes, a chicken coop, for eggs, and Lord there better be, BBQ chicken! (At least it won't always be fish.) Another large window shows a variety of levels housing "loose chickens" (not small cages, but larger ones). Apparently, according to James, they only allow twenty roosters at any given time, and sometimes they "cycle up fresh incubating eggs" to keep the genetic pool strong...for chickens.

I don't care, as long as they taste good. And I like my eggs over-easy with a side of hash browns.

We finished the tour about half an hour before dinner. James strongly recommended that we be in our Class As, our academic uniforms, and tidied up for dinner. Then he dismissed us, and just like in the video clip we watched about this place, cadets scattered and scurried to their rooms.

I laughed as I closed the door to mine, and then I looked in the mirror from across the room. I hustled over to get a better look.

Had I really looked that hideous the WHOLE tour? Red

splotches under my eyes. Hair *all* in a disarray. Clothing wrinkled from sleeping in it. Yep. Wretched was an understatement. So, I took a quick rinse off, after figuring out how the showers worked. And then I reached for that uniform, my uniform. Ran my fingers over the fabric of the soft jacket. Yes, I teared up before I geared up. I wore the pant suit version, not sure what everyone else would choose. I sat and easily slipped my black soft-soled mid-calf boots on. Then, the infamous shoulder shrug jacket of silver with navy cording. I can't even begin to explain my reaction as I finally saw myself in the white shirt and navy pants trimmed with silver threads, and finished with that cool poor-excuse-for-a-jacket jacket. Quickly I pulled my brush through my long brown hair and turned it into a confined, soft bun. I may not be a stunning beauty, but I pulled off this professional cadet look like no one's business.

When I looked at the time, I was already two minutes late. Hustling through my door, I found myself in a throng of other cadets scrambling towards the Commons. We must have sounded like cattle stampeding because everyone was looking at us as we burst through into the room, and slowed to find our respective Houses and seats. Embarrassing doesn't even begin to touch what I guess we all must have felt. But we quickly took our assigned seats and looked innocently around until the Blessing of the Meal was given by a rather cute cadet who was introduced as Journeyman Marshall Hammond of Director Bradley's House. Then we filed into our House's lines for the cafeteria-style serving of dinner.

The brochures did not even come close to describing just how awesome everything tasted! A simple grilled filet of salmon with a pineapple and onion salsa served with brown rice, and I was Pavlov's dog. It was all so very good. Fresh strawberry juice was our drink. I had never had it before, but I definitely could get used to it, blended seeds and all.

So healthy and fresh, so Mom, yes I'm eating well. Don't worry.

Like I said earlier, the Academic Meeting with Director Forshay was just "Do this" and "Don't do that" kind of stuff. Do make a name for yourself. Don't leave your chip card behind. Do your homework. Don't traverse upper classmen levels without permission and escort. Do eat all three meals served. Don't hesitate to come to him with concerns. Do get rest and brush your teeth. Don't go someplace you shouldn't. Do your best. We were reminded that after the first semester, we would be assigned chores on IDEA, based on our aptitude, course of study, and the needs of the academy. We were reminded more than once that we represented the top sixteen and seventeen year olds from Earth. The discussion seemed to last for hours, but apparently it was only about thirty minutes. Then we were given some free time in the Commons to meet the other cadets from both Quarters.

Although we are all a select group of young individuals, it was nice to see that we could have some down time. Some of the other cadets are really haughty and stuffy. I know well over ninety percent of the cadets at IDEA have photographic memory or are tested using a updated Mensa which required an intelligence level of a minimum of 132. I have neither a photographic memory, nor a noteworthy 132. My results landed me a solid 125, but my extra efforts and letters have helped me acquire my slot. That and grandpa's money. I guess we are all on IDEA for a reason, but I want to enjoy the next four years of my life here. I'm glad that I brought my music along to insert into my issued data pod. It's going to make it easier.

Though I tried to get close to James, I found that the bond made earlier with the red-headed cadet, Tori Buchanan, was apparently the one with which I am stuck. Unfortunately, she too thought James is gorgeous, and she is at IDEA for the same thing I am, Military Exploration and Expansion, but not with my secondary emphasis in Leadership and Command of Remote Civilizations. Who knew? But I guess she came from money and her brothers (Timothy and David) had both been here, and David graduated just last year. I also met a scraggily young Doug Burrows, a beefy black guy named Lincoln Townes, and some silent and reclusive blonde Adam Fuller. A few girls, some pretty, some plain, rattled off their names quickly, and I only caught one, Kimberly Hess, a pretty blonde with a sunshine personality, so I don't know if I want to hate her or befriend her.

Lots to do tomorrow. Lots more to see. More cadets to meet.

I practiced names so I would remember everyone's names without having to gawk at their name badges or pins. Or at least that was the plan. I might not be classified as a genius or "photo" but I can remember faces and conversations very well.

Log-in: JessReynoldi18851
Date/Time: 20 Aug 2201/2102hrs
Subject: Breaking that Space Lag thing

I am not sure I have had enough sleep to beat this adjustment to

IDEA yet. I overslept and missed breakfast. James came to my room to check on me. He brought a girl I met last night, Cecile Jacobs, with him. Talk about embarrassing and intruding. She's just that perfect combination of oh-so pretty and so-very snide. She makes you wish you could disappear when she looks at you and does that slanty eyebrow lift thing. Ugh!

Anyway, I told them both (yes, I addressed them both) that I was fine, just tired.

ENTRY END

James asked if I remembered the signs of Space Illness and I cited them all, and reluctantly confirmed them that I hadn't slept properly the past two nights.

Cecile hadn't really looked concerned as she asked, "Why ever not? Home sick?"

Gag me, or gag her. "No, I have been away from home many times, for months at a time. My pillow just didn't smell like mine and I couldn't sleep. I used to have to spray mine with perfume, even at other lodgings. As perfumes aren't allowed here, I'm sure it will just take me some time to adjust." I hoped I didn't sound as bitter as I felt. She rubbed me the wrong way...and I knew it might just be because I thought she had James' eye, but still.

James suggested I ask at the Medic Station for a sleep aid to put me on a schedule. He said we didn't need any mental illness on IDEA.

I nodded and said I would go later today.

Cecile suggested I use a little deodorant on my sheets so it wouldn't smell so foreign.

I agreed to try it. I secretly hoped it won't work so I can throw it in her face, in a nice sugar-sweet-vinegar way of course.

Despite my not really feeling like going anywhere I did venture to the UV Room and bumped into...you guessed it, Miss Know-it-all Cecile...and that Tori, who were just showing off their bodies in their cute, little two-piece suits for the male students gawking through windows. Great. Just great. I felt super uncomfortable, but I did do my mandatory fifteen minutes and split as fast as I could, pulling on my loose-fitting comfy shirt over my modest one-piece as I exited.

I decided to wander the corridors and found myself peeking in the observation decks of the various gymnasiums. No one really seemed to be out and about. A couple guys looked like they were boxing with some guys around them cheering them on, but as boxing isn't my thing, I kept moving.

James' words had kept trickling into my thoughts while I had been in the UV room, so I stopped by the Medic Station. After a quick written quiz testing to see if I was displaying Space Illness they said they didn't think I had it, but they would note it in my records and monitor me. They also suggested putting some familiar items that smelled like me in my bedding and prescribed a sleeping aid for three nights to help get me on a schedule.

"Don't worry," the medic had said. "About thirty percent of you need something to help you adjust to up here. But familiar smells tend to help more."

Dang Cecile for being right (but maybe it won't work).

"Thanks James," for the suggestion.

On my way back to my quarters, I passed the Commons where dinner was mostly over. I hoped I wasn't going to get into trouble for being late, but after explaining why, the server presented me with a tray. After swiping my identification card and securing whatever little bites I thought I could hold down, I took a seat next to the sculpture of IDEA versus my assigned seat as most of the tables had already been cleared.

Bet I must have looked down-right melancholy and probably a tad ridiculous all by myself in that big room next to that dwarfing sculpture but I didn't care. I just continued with my tasty vittles. As I was just taking in the piece before me, I sighed, probably a little too loud. Some loud laughter from across the room drew my attention. A group of guys from the Bradley House were all looking at me, and I guessed they found my behavior humorous. I offered a weak smile and went back to looking at the miniature IDEA.

I hadn't even noticed that they crossed the huge expanse of the room. But when one spoke right behind me, I guessed I probably jumped a good ten inches out of my chair as I bumped the table and tipped the last bit of my strawberry juice.

"Easy ma'am," came a smooth voice from my right.

Looking around at the five males around me, I felt just a moment of alarm. Part of me doesn't know why, as everyone here is special, gifted, and determined. But still, looking at their faces, I forced a smile before I offered, "Sorry. I was deep in thought." All snickered, and I just nodded my head along knowing how foolish I must have looked to these guys. A quick glance I and recognize the year-insignias for a Trekker, two Journeymen, and two Firsties. "Ha, ha," I bit out, not unaccustomed to my peers heckling me back in my Earthly academic years.

"No, Miss…" he looked at my name badge, "Reynoldi. You have us all wrong," one of the third-years chuckled as he spoke. "Name's Dan Adams. You are sitting in the Faculty section, and Jackson here was thinking you were a new instructor." He smiled in an infectious way, one that breeds harmless mischief. "I bet him dessert for a week that you are actually a medic."

I smiled, and shook my head. "Sorry. No dessert for you." I met Adams' eyes, "Not a medic."

"Bummer," Adams lost his grin. "So you are a new faculty member?"

Again I indicate the negative, "No, sorry." I found Jackson, then look at his face, "I'm not faculty."

"Why are you sitting over here then," said a brawny Journeyman with a nametag of Hanson.

"I didn't know this was for faculty only," I answered honestly.

"So you aren't faculty?" Hanson squinted his eyes.

"No. I'm not."

Hanson whistled low, "Out of uniform for dinner?"

Quickly, I looked around those still finishing their meals. Sure enough, all the rest were in their class As, except me.

I know my jaw must have dropped as Hanson quickly spoke, "Hurry, but not to draw attention. I have your tray. Next time, be dressed for dinner." With that, the five guys each grabbed parts of my tray and silverware and headed towards the revolving portal where we placed our used utensils. Once the guys had finished depositing my used flatware and tray, Hanson turned my way one last time, and offered me a wink and a smile. Then they all filed out of the Commons to Bradley's side of IDEA.

After they all had filed out, I casually stood and proceeded to my side of IDEA, humbled and appreciative of their coaching, even if done in a playful way.

So much to still learn.

"Going somewhere, *plebe*?"

I had sucked in my breath in surprise as before me was one of the Bradley cadets who had just used the traditional naval name for a first year. My eyes followed his stiff movements as he orbited to stand beside me. "I...I'm sorry. You startled me," I stammered. "I was just finishing dinner and heading back to my room." My eyes found his nametag. "Can I do something for you, Cadet Williams?"

His eyes flickered for a moment. "You were sitting in the faculty section."

Knowing I was busted, I admitted my mistake and apologized if I had offended him.

"Offend me?" His eyes shifted again as he looked around, "Nope. Not offended." He started to walk away and tossed over his shoulder, "Be careful who you become friends with...and where you sit. You can't afford to make mistakes here, *plebe*." I wasn't sure but the last thing he said before he went around the corner sounded like, "It could cost you your life."

Confused if I really had heard that, I continued on to my quarters at my slow pace, wondering what had just happened. Had I just been threatened?

Log-in: JessReynoldi18851
Date/Time: 22 Aug 2201/2109hrs
Subject: Space/Jet Lag...what?!

I'm so acclimated to this place. The pills the medics prescribed did work wonders. I took advantage of the last day before courses begin. I went with Cecile, Tara Rogers (Cecile's best friend), and Tori to the UV room for about half an hour. Leaving that room, I admit that I felt a bit different, happier, more at peace. Don't know why more people wouldn't want more than the fifteen mandatory minutes.

We also went to the solarium to smell the fresh flora that grows here this far away from Earth. Oh, the fresh, heavy green smell of the solarium...AWESOME! I can't believe I will miss mowing our little patch of grass or pulling weeds in that organic garden of Mom's. But the ferns and trees here are far more than therapeutic. It is also very cool to know that the plants kept in that room help sustain the oxygen levels that we need out here. Some of the plants bear simple fruits and veggies which we can pick and eat. In the far corner, I saw a smaller wall showing part of another huge, glass-enclosed pool stocked with large fish, possibly the salmon track between vats. I didn't notice it when we had our tour earlier in the week.

I think my favorite place here has to be a toss-up between the UV room and Solarium. Both are SO peaceful. Sometimes I just listen to the sounds there. Other times I listen to my oldies faves like Lincoln Park, 3 Doors Down, Daughtry, Pink, and Evanescence, or even the vintage classical masters while relaxing in the atmosphere of either room.

It's hard to believe we only get to live here for four academic years. I could live here for the rest of my life. Maybe I should become a faculty member. That would leave other cadets with that lasting contribution, an inspiration and enticement for the future IDEA cadets. But then, I wanted to help set up outposts on the horizon. I wonder what chore or chores I will be assigned.

Time would tell.

ENTRY END

Director Forshay had a private dinner for all of us new cadets in a big conference room to prepare us for what will happen tomorrow and the rest of our time here. What cuisine we were offered. Fresh bass with a carrot and papaya relish on a fluffy rice pilaf. Oh my God, so yummy. And then the rolls we had were so light and flaky, I ate four. Someone said the signs said they were called popovers. If they were popovers, they were like having a dessert during the meal.

Then the real dessert came. Slivers of various flavors of cheesecakes arrived, as wells as a decadent chocolate cake. I had to try them all! They were all sublime and I wished for seconds on the desserts alone despite feeling like my pants would burst at the seams.

Clearly I would have to use the exercise rooms and find a way to combat all the fantastic meals in a positive way. I have been exercising some in my room, still shy of my physique unlike Cecile and Tara. You can tell those who have been here a while. They are all more trimmed and toned versus us first year plebes. And I'm not strong enough of a runner to make use of the track or treadmills, of which, I am sure they are skilled at as well. Maybe I would prove better in the lesser gravity gyms than those back on Earth.

While at dinner I saw more of some of those I met that first day. Miss Kimberly Hess has taken to Lincoln Town. Tori fawns over Adam Fuller. Others seems to be melding just swimmingly with the other students, and...I still feel out of place. Sweet Doug Burrows seems to be finding his niche with some of the other guys while still keeping an eye on me to make sure I'm "not alone."

Gee, thanks. I went from being excited to be here, to being the one everyone was worried about.

I guess I won't worry about the friends and relationships everyone else was making right now Then again, I didn't pay all of this money to make friends.

I'm here for my own professional advancement.

I will focus on my academics.

I will push aside any thoughts of liking guys.

I will keep my quarters clean, and make Dad proud with my decisions and academic successes.

I will strive for excellence and positive endorsements for when my time here is done.

That being said, as cool as this place is, with as many things to learn, and experience and see, I'm lonely. With the two thousand cadets here, and approximately three hundred staff members that work here, I feel alone. Utterly, and completely...ALONE.

I started playing some of my music.

I hope I don't have the Space Illness.

Maybe I just need to sleep.

Wake up with a new attitude.

I'll try.

Night.

But tonight I can't sleep. It wasn't the medicine's fault. Or maybe it was.

So, I sat on my cot and looked out the two foot square window of my room into the darkness of space that shows as the academy rotates our view. Every minute the hoped for glimpse of Earth is visible. It had been a calming thought I have likened to counting sheep. *How many times will home pass by before sleep claims me?*

Holy crap! What the...? I just...I swear that I just saw someone float by my window as I was sitting on my bed. Not like a peeping tom type, but more like a "Freak-me-out, there is a weird, bloody body floating sightless past my portal!" But when I flipped on the lights by my cot and went racing to my square window to look out to see if I could see it or if I was imagining things, I didn't see anything except the blackness sprinkled with pinpoints of lights representing distant stars, then Earth. I had to peel my face from the many-layered glass and kept looking into the stillness beyond.

How long I had continued to look I do not know. I lost count as to how many times our blue oasis appeared and disappeared from my view as my lids grew heavy. When I head-bobbed and bounced my head off the paned portal, I decided enough was enough, that I must have imagine it. I made my way to my sleeping cot and dimmed my room's lights.

Despite my fatigue sleep tried to elude me...the images of a body lost in space bothering me. I eventually got up and closed the shield on my portal to block the view.

It didn't help.

The clock announced very early morning hours, and I groaned, dreading a full academic workload on no sleep.

Please, don't let it be Space Illness.

Log-in: JessReynoldi18851

Date/Time: 23 Aug 2201/2148hrs
Subject: And so classes begin

First day of class and I am feeling swamped and drained already.
There is so much homework. In each of my classes the lectures
seemed to drag on for hours every class. But...I made it through
what Hanson (yes, I have seen more of him lately) and James said
has been termed the Day of Gauntlets. All-in-all, I guess it wasn't
so bad. Gym, or as they term it, "exercise hour" wasn't horrible.
And I have kept up with the assignments during class periods, so I
hope that I will have more free time than some of the others.
Before supper I finished what little homework I had left.

Dinner tonight is to be casual, meaning not assigned seating, and I
have been invited to join some of the Bradley House cadets. The
five guys who saw me the other night have taken me in and I feel
more welcome, comfortable, the past few days. I'm not sure why
they want to hang out with me though. I would have put money
on Kimberly Hess being more Hanson's style.

Still having visions of that body floating by my window. Did I
hallucinate? Am I suffering from Space Illness?

ENTRY END

"What are you thinking about?" Ian Hanson questioned me as we all ate together on the Bradley side of the Commons.

My fresh pineapple juice glass tipped over as I jumped. "Oh my gosh! I am...I'm so sorry." I reached out with my napkin in hand, and tried to mop up the liquid spreading across the table. "I can't believe...wow," I tripped over my tongue as I try to not knock anything else over while cleaning up my mess. "Don't think I have ever been this clumsy."

"Calm down, Jess," Adams said as he threw his napkin into the war zone. "Don't cry over spilt juice."

While the guys chuckled, one of their friends, a Journeyman named Elizabeth Daggel, or Ellie as she preferred to be called, joined us. "Having fun without me? I'm hurt." She took her customary seat and smiled at me, "How goes it tonight, Jess?"

The smile that came to my lips had been genuine. "Doing well, Ellie-Beth. You?"

Ellie rolled her eyes as she drawled, "Super freak-tastic." She started playing with the surprising lack-luster green beans. "I see the quality of the cuisine is going back to normal."

Wide-eyed, I took in the rest of the table's tenured occupants. Seeing their saddened expressions I looked down at the simple broiled salmon and soft roll. "I thought it was the head cook's night off or something."

Ian laughed and patted me on the shoulder like I was one of the guys. "Isn't she adorable? Night off." His eyes shone as loud as his audible mirth. "Seriously, you crack me up."

"What?" My question lingered in the air only a second.

"Guess they aren't interested in keeping up to the photos and promises of the brochures," Ian mumbled.

"Hey, plebe," came a voice from behind.

My blood chilled in that instant, and I looked across the table over Bryce's shoulders. There he was again. The cadet who was cute, creepy, and condescending in one sentence. I forced away the shiver as he sized me up. "Williams," I offered casually with a careful smile.

Bryce looked over his shoulder and whispered, "Stalk much?"

But to his credit, Ben Williams just countered with, "Apparently not as much as you. Didn't realize I had a follower of my own."

Ian kept shoveling his dinner in with disinterest.

Ellie wasn't as silent, "Ben, need a table tonight?"

He squinted his eyes for a quick second. "No thanks, Ellie. Just was going to ask if anyone has seen the plebe that has the room below mine. I think his name is Jacobs."

My interest piqued, no denying it. The vision of the body floating outside my portal flashed before my eyes as I listened. But I looked around the table, and no one else seemed as taken.

Ellie answered him anyway, "No. Why?"

Ben Williams' eyes shifted again before he answered. "We talked his first day. Then he asked if he could borrow something from me. I haven't seen him since. I have the rest of what he was asking for."

Bryce didn't bother to turn around, "What did you lend him?"

Ben shrugged, "My notes from Advanced Geometry. He said he was taking that so I offered."

Bryce shook his head. "Giving first years notes. Not really cheating, Ben, but wow. Couldn't wait to share how smart you are with the new-blood?" Bryce looked at me and rolled his eyes, "Another genius."

My eyes flew to Ben's flushed face.

But Ian was the one who spoke. "Bryce, who is acting jealous now?" Ian elbowed me. "Bryce has had to settle with being second best to Ben almost every class."

Jackson piped in, "And worst was Advanced Engineering II last semester."

"Thanks guys," Bryce said. "Lay off the lemon juice, will ya?"

My eyes looked into Ben's shifty ones. *"You're* a genius?"

All faces swiveled to mine.

"Slam!" Ellie burst into a fit of laughter and pointed at Bryce. "Do you have some burn cream for Ben?" Tears appeared at the corners of her eyes.

"Ellie," Ben admonished. He shook his head. "Anyway, if you see him. Could you see if my notes helped and if he wants the rest?" With that he walked away with his nearly empty tray.

After several tense seconds, eating resumed.

Except for me.

Coincidence that someone was missing?

Or was he? Thoughts ricocheted around my skull as my fork played with the limp green veggies on my plate.

"Has anyone gone missing before?" I heard the words before I realized I was the one who had said them.

"Missing?" Ellie snorted. "Just because one someone can't find another someone doesn't mean someone is missing." She stabbed at her salmon before she added, "This place is deceptively big. And we're trapped here. Where could someone really go?" And then she stuffed the fish into her mouth.

Jackson chortled, "Nice vocab. Nice grammar. Can't believe you passed on the final that first year." He took a sip of his pineapple juice. "Oh wait! You did because of me!"

Ellie sputtered and dropped an obscenity. "And you wouldn't have passed Linguistics without my help last semester!"

Despite myself, I was drawn into the new bantering. So unlike I would have expected to find here in this elite university. Here we were, two thousand smart and talented teenaged cadets, talking like we were back in high school. It was enough to reinforce my need to stay professional in the classroom, yet find that way to relax and let go to keep my sanity.

When dinner was over, I saw Ben was still approaching other tables. I could only guess what he was asking.

As I walked the corridor back to my quarters, I passed people I recognized from this or that class, but had not taken time to get to know yet. As they went by I tried to smile and note their faces and ranks.

So many people here.

So many places people could be at any given time.

"Jess!"

The shrillness brought me up short. Holding back a groan, I turned and plastered a smile on my face. "Tori!" I'm not sure my tone matched her enthusiast one.

She barreled into me like we were best buds from forever and ever ago, with a big girly bear hug. "I have been looking for you everywhere!"

Two thoughts fought being first. "Oh? Why?" And almost in the same breath came out, "This place isn't that big." *Is it?* If Tori picked up on my nerves, she didn't show it. "They're playing a movie tonight in the Commons at eight. Wanna watch it with me?"

I'd rather not. "Me? Why not Fuller?"

Pouty lips greeted me. "It's a girly movie. He's not interested." She sidled up next to me and clutched my left arm. "So? Want to go? Have your homework done?" Tori batted her sad puppy-dog eyes, "PULLLEEEEEASE?"

"Ugh...fine," I gave over.

Instantly Tori's face went terse. "Well! Don't sound so excited."

I shook my head. "I apologize. I just haven't seen much of you since the first day or so, and now you act like were best friends. I'm not sure what that all means. And now I feel like... you're upset because someone stole your dessert." I saw my words land. "But I am happy to go, sure." I put a smile on my face and gave her a gentle squeeze. "You just surprised me."

Tori still looked hurt and very unconvinced.

"And then you did the whole big-sad-eyes thing," I waved my hand. "That's why I said 'Ugh.'"

Tori slanted me a look. "Tell you what...if you're there, great. If not, I understand...that I'm a nuisance." She sashayed off in a huff.

"Wait! Tori!"

Crap. Finally asked to do something by one of my own house, and I blow it. Real smooth, Jess.

"Evening, plebe."

A shiver threatened but I kept it in check. I turned towards him, "Williams."

He looked uncomfortable.

"You okay?" I couldn't help but ask as the guy looked positively ill.

He nodded and kept his head down. "Ian, Hanson scolded me for disrupting dinner with my questions." Ben peeked at me, "I'm sorry, plebe. I didn't mean to...be a problem."

Confused, I offered, "Oh, phfft...it's okay." He just stood there, making both of us more uncomfortable, "So, you *really* are a genius?"

Ben just nodded. "Certified. There are quite a few of us here."

His discomfort seemed stronger than my own, and despite his oddness I felt a softening for this cadet. "Is Bryce always that mean towards you?"

Ben gave me a funny eye-shift before he glanced around. "We're friends. I think that's the way he shows it. He and I play cards, chess, or marbles almost every week."

My jaw must have dropped.

The edge of Ben's mouth curled. "He's my toughest competition here."

Remembering when Ben first interacted with me, I asked, "Why did you warn me to stay away from them then?"

"Who? Bryce?" The look on his face was priceless.

"Yes," I challenged. "That day in the corridor."

He shook his head. "I never warned you about Bryce." Then he turned and walked away.

I watched him go. He stopped a couple of other students and asked if they had seen the first year he'd been asking about all evening.

As I reached my door, I pulled out my chip card and swiped it for entry to my quarter. I looked around my small domicile and sighed.

Earth chose that moment to come into view with all its brilliant contrast to the darkness. Then it was gone for another minute's rotation.

After several glimpses of that beautiful orb, I sought a distraction.

I decided to meet up with Tori for the chick flick. I needed a break from my acquaintances of Bradley house.

With a quick change of clothes from Class As to casual, I made my way back to the Commons. Tori was waiting with a pathetic pout and looking down at the table. Her dejection ate at my gut and I hung my head in shame for my earlier behavior. I crossed the large room and took the seat next to her. I elbowed her slightly, "Made it."

Tori turned, elbowed me back, and smiled. "You did."

To ease the tension, I pursed my lips. "If I don't get my homework done, I blame you."

Her laughter was contagious.

Log-in: JessReynoldi18851
Date/Time: 25 Aug 2201/2057hrs
Subject: lectures

Wow. That is all I can say after today's classes with both Director Bradley and Director Forshay. Information overload.

ENTRY END

I hadn't really looked back too much into the history of space exploration and habitation before the opportunity to attend this academy arose. I had loved the thought of living beyond Earth's realm, but didn't ever really believe I could make it here. It had been an understood that what happened over two hundred years ago was obsolete, thus unstudied.

But today, that was not the case.

Director Bradley used detailed holograms and led the class lecture for us plebes today on the origins of NASA and its work on space habitation. The presentation also included images of early test modules, some of which were still maintained on Earth. Even early samples of different living nodes and practice living spaces were still on exhibit, as I could attest. In these mock futuristic homes, vegetation grew on the walls to produce the air that the early Mars habitation homes would eventually use. That was fascinating to me, especially as we found that the vegetable and fruit garden we witnessed, with shelves upon shelves, and rows upon rows, lined the innermost ring of the sphere we live on, where there was less gravity. But those vegetables were not all that offered our oxygen supply. Several walls similar to those that had been on display two hundred years ago in what had been a beautiful state called Florida, had been also put to use here.

Bradley stressed how our chores would benefit both IDEA and all of her cadets because of her hands-on needs and academic training. He said some plebes may be selected may be assigned their tasks before the end of the semester, depending on aptitude and need.

Due to the nature of space and asteroid-to-meteor showers, multiple locations and "cells" resided in the inner part of the ring where less gravity was necessary, and produced the air supply we breathed. Storage of any excess oxygen was always being processed in case of emergency, such as a temporary loss of a cell. The stored oxygen tanks were dispersed throughout the interior and exterior of our academy, which meant they were accessible whenever needed. These were only placed and retrieved by professional members of the staff, most of whom we would never see during our stay. Each storage tank could maintain IDEA's oxygen level for a day with the current number of occupants and the systems being brought down to minimal.

Bradley also went into detail on the items grown here, as wells as the mass quantities produced. It was fascinating to hear how much we grew and then consumed. Approximately ninety percent of what we ate was grown on IDEA. The other ten percent was transported in with new recruits every year and again at mid-year as a fresh rotation of dry goods. He assured us that on IDEA nothing went to waste.

A smiling blonde asked if it was true that our waste was recycled.

Director Bradley nodded and spoke to the compost areas on IDEA.

Snickers sounded.

"I mean...our waste," she tried again.

Undaunted, Bradley changed to the capture of any methane, which helped in the generation of required electric energy, as well as the use of water conversion into energy, like mills from five hundred plus years ago. He said the miniature hydro-mills use the same "river" that the salmon traverse as part of their migration.

The same young lady asked for clarification on waste being fed to the previously mentioned plants. After a few snickers and "Gross!" floating through the lecture hall, the room quieted down. Unflustered, Bradley addressed her question by stating that it was indeed true. "Processed by-products, from some of animals dying for our consumption, human waste and refuse, and plant decay, are composted and repurposed as fertilizers for maximum nutrient sustainability for the vegetation on this station. Some of the fish stock are refed to other tanks upon expiring, thus aiding in sustaining their nutrition and food sources with the vegetation in their specific habitats."

A guy next to me said, "I don't know if he was talking down to us, or if that's just how scientifically he always speaks."

I had to nod in agreement, like the other cadets around. "I bet he has that little speech planned for as many times as he has to answer that kind of question."

He masked his chuckle as a cough.

The rest of Director Bradley's oration was less climactic and informative. I remember something more about the recycling processes of the various water, but I have to be honest, I wasn't really paying attention. I was looking around the room to see almost every seat was occupied, and we were all beginning to doze off, whether induced by the warmth of close quarters or in boredom.

Many of us cadets were more than grateful for the doors to finally open. But we groaned because of the stiffness from sitting through such a long two hours. We were encouraged to partake of the refreshments in the Commons to aid in our "mental lethargic state" by the verbose Bradley.

Part of me liked his verbiage and banter, but I was certain not many others did.

What I did appreciate, like most of those around me, was the fresh fruit displayed on the buffet line. The one blonde girl just shook her head in disbelief before she added, "Tell us how you feed what feeds us, then you feed us it. Gross." The Commons erupted in chuckles.

In the next class, Director Forshay discussed the construction of our facility. "A History in the IDEA Making," as he called it. IDEA had originally been an expensive experiment on space habitation. It took twelve years longer to finish than was expected and was obsolete upon its completion. Due to other habitation ships being constructed for travelling purposes, IDEA was sold with an agreement that the military still have jurisdiction in the need of the orbiting space craft.

We learned that each quarter of our academic home, had been built separately and in five pieces, and then joined together out in space. Each of the quarters had then positioned and joined to another quarter until all four were melded into a cohesive and precise whole. Years and years of planning and shuttle missions were needed to get all the plans and parts up into orbit, then to bring electrical and biological specialists for inhabiting. That process was what had taken the longest. The sheer size of IDEA had proven that life could survive for masses if catastrophe befell Earth. IDEA could safely house almost five thousand people, and maintain them for six months before food would start to deplete with no means to replenish. IDEA as a campus was more scholarly in nature and wouldn't need to be subject to such stressful management of resources. By limiting the number of cadets it allowed for more efficient hands-on training and excess in food production. Any salvageable extra food was frozen and sent on the shuttle for sending on to other outposts that were facing agricultural issues.

Forshay also spoke to the evasive maneuvering of our home in the event of asteroids, comet tail particles, et cetera. He explained, like we had to understand prior to our arrival, that each of the cadets' living quarters were independent, meaning if the hull was compromised in a particular cadet's quarter, the ship would not leak valuable air. He stressed that so far, thankfully, only one cell had been lost, the cadet in it as well. I had never heard that before.

Forshay also spoke to what to do in the event of a fire or an accident. He showed us how to activate a fire alarm, contact our respective house director or maintenance, and find a secure location said evasive maneuvering protocol had been initiated, all using our issued data pods.

Also, I did not know this, but protective shields came over our portal windows automatically with the alert of a potential threat or collision. These shields helped repel serious damage to the portal's panes. That made me feel better about the amount of cosmic debris Forshay quantified as "in our neighborhood."

Apparently, exterior service work was routinely done on IDEA to ensure hull integrity and functionality of all protective measures. Repairs were constantly being executed by forty maintenance personnel, and sometimes cadets for real-world experience, as needed without our knowledge. At the same time the oxygen tanks are recycled for freshness and checked for leakage.

The vision of the body going past my portal prompted my hand to raise. When called upon, I asked how often did this happen, and what do they wear or use when the service work is done outside.

Someone else blurted out about the worry of being peeped upon.

Forshay calmly reassured the now humming lecture hall that the shields would close prior to anyone passing that section of portals. That quieted the masses.

But not my mind. My hand went up again. "Has anyone ever been lost outside?"

Again the whir of noise filled the room.

Forshay smiled and shook his head. "As far as I know, no one has become lost in space from IDEA." He pointed his finger, "Except for that one cadet previously mentioned with the loss of his cell."

My darned hand raised again.

"Yes, Cadet Reynoldi?"

"Sir, how do you know that? How can you know there haven't been any more losses?"

Forshay blinked, and then pulled out a familiar object. "See this? You were told to keep your identification card on you. This is tracking each and every one of us as we go through our days and nights. It opens the doors to your respective cabins and into your classes. It tracks your logging in for chow. The cards are also used for Shoppette purposes. If a card were to go inactive, meaning it isn't being used or moving, we House Directors would be notified within twenty hours of inactivity."

Thank goodness someone else asked as to why twenty hours because my mind was still racing with questions and I didn't want to be the only one with them.

"Because if someone is ill, or misplaces a card," Forshay answered. "It gives someone time to report and locate it." As the buzz of talking resounded, Forshay put up his hands, "Would you all feel better with a mock maintenance drill?" Sounds of affirmation made him grin again. "Good thing you are all so agreeable. We always schedule a drill within the first couple of weeks of the new cadets' arrival."

Again the hall erupted with sounds of students and their thoughts.

Director Forshay waited all of ten seconds before his voice boomed, "Cadets!" Immediately the hall of five hundred fell silent as he looked us over with a hard glare. "Silence please, so we may continue our lecture."

And carry on it did, for the full two hours. He spoke to the size of our academy and the spin required to maintain a gravity. He lectured on our orbit, above the moon to use some of her gravitational sway to help prevent our decent into Earth's. Forshay discussed how the engineers thought that plant placement and growth could be in lesser gravity, hence the inner ring of IDEA, while the fish tanks had to have realistic gravity and thus the myriad of tanks that lined the outer most ring.

A red-head cadet from down the row from me asked if the lesser amount of gravity on the inner compartments was why the UV treatment room was on "that half of the circle of life."

Forshay eyed the male for a second before he tossed, "You feel better leaving there, yes? Lighter in mood and spirit?"

I was glad I was not the only one who laughed.

At the end of the lecture, I had found I was not the only one doing a head bob trying to stay awake. Once again, relief flowed when the hall doors opened wide. The freshness of the outside air recharged our tired minds as we pried ourselves from our seats. Many snaps and pops filled the air as we all worked out the tightness and kinks.

"I will never complain about sitting through an hour of math again," Tori hissed as she came up beside me as we made our way out of the room.

A smile played at the corners of my mouth. "Bet you dessert for three days that you complain before the end of this week."

The glint of determination met my challenge. She typed something on her data pod. A second later, a message displayed on mine. "Challenge accepted."

Log-in: JessReynoldi18851
Date/Time: 7 Sept 2201/2221hrs
Subject: chess

I have survived yet another late night. I even found some exercise time as I limped my way through the four laps to make a mile. But, I promise, my homework is getting done. Dad you'd be proud because unlike everyone else, I complete it before dinner so I can try to enjoy some of my evenings.

Tonight something made my earlier conversations with Ben more interesting. I was invited to watch a chess match between Ben and Bryce, the Bradley Boys, as they were called. Apparently it was considered, on the Bradley House side of IDEA, to be a big sporting event. The Commons was divided in half by supporters for both Bryce and Ben. I don't know why the thought of Ben having supporters surprised me, but I found myself smiling seeing them all there cat-calling "the other guys". It's hard to believe, especially when you are just sitting there for HOURS, but it was a lot of fun.

ENTRY END

I saw Director Brent Bradley sitting across the Commons watching the festivities of the chess challenge. A slight curve representing a smile stayed upon his face for the first hour of the competition. And as the pawns were laid to waste for both contenders, I found myself watching Bradley to see any inkling for whom he was rooting. If he was favoring one of them, he masked it well.

He kept sipping from his steaming mug of something. As the game went on, he'd refill it from a nearby carafe. As soon as he finished his sip, Bradley would bring his left hand to his face, index finger across his lips. Sometimes that finger would move either side-to-side, or up-and-down on his lip, and I tried to pinpoint some sort of correlation with his movements and those of the chess players. Apparently there were none.

It occurred to me that Bradley couldn't possibly view very well from his vantage point. Even though there was a huge three dimensional board representing the game being projected, Bradely wasn't even facing it. And he was even farther away from the young men than I was, and I could barely make out the figures of the pieces. I guessed that he was making a mental note of what pieces were moved and followed the game that way. Either way, I fought a smile every time Bradley would allow that lip to curl a little more, or he'd rub his lip back-and-forth with his pointer finger, then stop with a move before the room would comprehend what the move meant.

"People watching, Cadet Reynoldi?"

With a sharp intake of breath, I turned and faced Director Forshay. I knew I couldn't deny it, so I nodded and tried to stand, ashamed. "Sorry."

Forshay creased his brow. "Sorry? For what?" And he waved his hand, "Sit. Please enjoy the match."

I shrugged and looked around to see who was watching me be admonished. A couple people glanced our direction and nodded at the Director. James was one of them, but I hadn't realized he was here for the match. Beside him sat a bemused Cecile and unamused Tara. A quick glance around the Commons confirmed a few other Forshay House members were in attendance.

"Cadet?"

"I...I'm sorry for not paying attention to what we were here for, sir," I stammered. "I hadn't meant to be rude. I was just trying to figure out who Director Bradley supported. His mannerisms weren't giving him away."

"Yes, he has an excellent Poker face," Director Forshay agreed. He sat next to me like a trusted friend, "So he's also excellent in Poker. I owe him dessert more often than not."

I couldn't help the burst of laughter than blurted forth. Some of the attendees turned our way with a look of annoyance and a "Ssh!" until they saw the House Director, then turned back nonplussed. "I'm sorry," I squeezed out trying to hold in the mirth.

"You tend to do a lot of apologizing, Reynoldi," Forshay chastised.

I opened my mouth, but the look he gave with his eyebrow raised, stopped me mid-mouth. I snapped it shut, which drew more looks and head shakes. After a couple of seconds, I regrouped, "I will work on that, sir."

Forshay smiled and patted my shoulder, "Good." Then he turned back to watch the competition.

My eyes darted to where Director Bradley sat, still alone. His eyes were on us, then back to the match, finger still on his lips. After a few seconds of my watching him, Bradley's eyes landed back on mine. No look of amusement, or interest. It was a bland, hollow look that made me shiver. When I did, his eyebrow lifted just a tinged. Then he was back to watching the chess players.

I turned and took in the match just before Bryce's knight lost his position and ended on the table next to Ben.

"Crap!" exploded Bryce as he pushed back the hair on his forehead. Then he hunched over the board with purpose, or rather more purpose.

But Ben was cool as ice and still looking at the place where he had captured the knight. "Check."

It was said so quietly, I thought I had imagined Ben's voice.

"I freaking *know* it's Check, Ben," Bryce growled ten times louder.

The whole Commons erupted when Ben tossed back, "So do something about it."

"Time is ten o'clock Cadets," Director Forshay blurted. "Time to retire to your quarters. Match is to continue tomorrow evening, gentleman. Bryce's turn on the 'morrow."

I watched the spectators rise and congratulate their favorite, each of whom were eyes-locked on the board in front of them. Both had little ticks as they hid their smiles as the bantering of supporters continued.

Movement across the way had me turn and see Director Bradley making his way to the competition table. "Well done, Bryce, Ben. Another great round." He shook each of their hands. "Should be a great end tomorrow. Now off you go."

With the mob of fans dwindling I made my way to the table. "Wow. Fun!" Okay, I know, lame, but I couldn't think of anything else to say. When both guys turned to look at me, I just shrugged.

Bryce laughed, "Haven't watched much chess before, huh, Jess?"

I shook my head and added, "Can't say that I have."

Bryce stood and bent his head near mine, "Maybe we can play sometime?"

I backed up a half-step, "Maybe." I took in his serious look, "Are...are you flirting with me?"

Ben stifled a cough, or maybe a laugh.

My look went between the two, then fixed on Bryce. I couldn't tell if he was serious, so I played along, "Shame, shame. I thought you were on IDEA to study."

Ben stood and stretched. "Shame, shame, Bryce. Lost a knight, stopped in check, and got turned down." With that, quiet and reserved Ben shook Bryce's hand and left.

Bryce burst out laughing, causing the people departing to look back. "Night Ben. I'll come by to tuck you in later. You're going to need your genius sleep to beat me in this game tomorrow."

Ben just nodded and waved him off, "Yep." And without looking my way, "Night, plebe."

Bryce chuckled, "It's nice that Ben takes to you. He's such a loner."

"Takes to me? I don't understand," I challenged.

Bryce smiled down. "Ben doesn't talk to females, much less female *plebes*. I have no other choice but to think that he must be interested in you."

"Wow. Just wow, Bryce," I throw a soft shoulder punch.

"Careful, *plebe*, or you're going to make Ben jealous," Bryce caroled as he stepped away in a fit of laughter.

So I stomped that boys-can-be-so stupid stomp all the way to my quarters and secured myself safely inside. A passing blue filled my portal as I looked out it, and before I flung myself onto my cot. "Boys!"

My cabin lights went completely out, replaced seconds later by a deep red light. Something loudly groaned as it slid over my portal blocking the view of the stars. I swung my feet to the cool floor as panic hit me just before the sound of a klaxon.

Then the intercom crackled with a recorded female voice saying, "Attention, Cadets. Attention, Cadets. Please remain calm. This is a test. This is only a test of the emergency preparedness system. Please check to ensure the protective shield has completely covered your portal. Please contact your House Director if your shield did not completely cover your portal. This was only a test. Had this been an actual emergency, you would be advised with further instructions. This completes the test."

My data pod lit up with a dramatic message from Tori about how she had freaked out.

I was startled when the lights abruptly resumed their normal tone.

And the portal shield moaned open just in time for the Earth to come into view.

Log-in: JessReynoldi18851
Date/Time: 9 Sept 2201/2147hrs
Subject: bonds thicker than blood

People are still talking about the portal test today. Seems like all of us plebes really were startled, with the guys dramatizing it just as much as the girls. It makes me laugh.

I decided to walk through Bradley House after class today. Ellie and I were done using the UV room and thought I might catch some of the guys and ask them about some homework problems.

I have heard about male bonding, but what I saw this afternoon... guys really have a special bond, I'm tellin' ya.

ENTRY END

After watching some exciting wall-ball, an atheletic version that combines both soccer and football, I walked with Ellie to her door. We really hadn't spoken as we each had our own music piping into our ear pieces, but it was nice to not be walking solo. At her cabin, Ellie waved and presented her card so her door opened. Without a backwards glance she danced into her living space and left me in the hall.

I didn't mind. I put in my music buds as I walked away. I hoped to catch up to some of the guys to see what they were all up to.

As I came around a corner I saw Ian Hanson, James, Jackson, and a few other Bradley cadets way ahead of me, with arms linked over each other's shoulders, in a line, and bending at the waist with a swooping left-to-right, and then right-to-left motion. I knew they were some of the players tonight, and I was sure they were still in their euphoric high after a cool save and phenomenally kicked goal. To hear them better, I took out the music buds in my ears. They were chanting something low, but their posturing brought a smile to my lips. It reminded me of when the team members of different sports were getting all hyped before a game. I could only imagine what hoopla these guys were worked up about after that win.

As I neared, Ian smiled and waved his fingertips my way. Jackson was a few guys down the line and gave me a stern nod, and then soft-edged smile. Then with a big "Hoowah!" the guys dispersed. James and Ian headed my direction with one of the other guys, to pick up their satchels of class notes and homework. Jackson went with two of the others in the opposite direction.

"Hi," I offered casually.

Ian and James just nodded and kept right on going.

So I did the same and put in my ear buds again.

As I continued walking, I found some droplets on the floor

that looked like blood. A few more steps and I saw some more. I glanced back over my shoulder and confirmed that the mini puddles where getting bigger the direction I was headed. Not seeing anyone else around, I took out my ear buds and brought out the cloth I used to wipe sweat from my face when I use the UV room, and wiped at the red splotches.

"Whatcha doin'?"

Glancing up I found the face of the cadet who had said grace over our first meal at IDEA. "Cadet Hammond?"

He smiled, "Marshall."

I returned his pleasant look before I continued. "Looks like someone had a nosebleed. I just thought I'd wipe it up before someone stepped in it, tracked it around." I shrugged, "Slipped."

Marshall laughed, "That'd be kinda gross." Then he pulled out a tissue from his pocket and crouched down next to me. "Let me help."

And as we collected the biohazard I looked ahead. "There's more." I pointed and Marshall's gaze followed my fingers.

A frown creased his features. "Why don't you let me worry about cleaning all this up? I will get some of the maintenance people to do this. I mean, this *is* blood, right?" At my nod, "So I'm sure they have stuff to do this properly. I'll be right back with Phil."

"Maybe I should wait here to make sure no one walks through it until they come," I offered.

Marshall nodded and went off to find reinforcements. After several long minutes he came around a corner with someone with gloves, spray bottle, and a mop bucket. But they were both spritzing and mopping up as they approached. "Sorry," he grimaced. "There was a lot more stuff we were cleaning up as we came back."

"Oh my gosh," I whispered. "Did you find the person?"

Marshall shook his head. "Blood trail ended by the men's public latrines. I called inside, but no one answered. I didn't see anyone when I went in though. Probably already done with the nosebleed or whatever."

I bobbed my head in understanding and after a few seconds of uncomfortable silence, "Well, I guess I better get back to my quarters. Thanks for the help."

Marshall gave me a thumbs up and watched the maintenance member finish taking care of the spots around us. "There's some, Phil."

Dismissed, I decided to head to the solarium for fresh air and a view of greenery, and to see if anyone I knew was lurking there. Upon arrival I noticed a few drops of blood on the floor there and proceeded to swipe them up with my already soiled cloth.

I brought out my electronic data pod to read while I sat by the fish tank.

After a while, someone finally came into the area, but I didn't know her. She asked if she could be in there or if it would distract me. She was holding a vintage drawing unit, and I smiled.

I told her she certainly could, that I didn't mind.

She sat across the way and looked at the tank, and began to drag her art pencil across the flat electronic board. For several minutes she worked away. Then she sighed loudly.

I looked up and smiled, but she was watching the fish in the tank. "What's the matter? Not in the mood to draw?"

She shook her head. "No, that's not it. The fish...they're moving funny. Guess I have never seen them feeding before. Hard to draw them when they are moving like that. Oh well."

I glanced at the tank, and sure enough, the big salmon and some other fish were hunkered down around something in the water by the rocks. They all took turns working at whatever it was, then swam off, and back for another go.

I offered a small grin and as she got up to leave, I went back to my book. But after a bit, curious as to the kinds I saw in the tank, I pulled up my research guide and scrolled fish that inhabited IDEA. Catfish and other bottom feeders that helped keep tanks clean, along with fresh and salt-water crustaceans, were listed, and sometimes on the menu.

By the time I was ready to call it a night, the fish that swam in the tank near me were done eating. I took a deep breath and left the quietness of the solarium for my room.

Ben was sitting alone in the Commons working, and saw me as I passed. "Evening, plebe."

"Evening, Ben," I returned. I made it almost all the way to my hallway before I came back to ask, "Did they find the guy with the nosebleed?"

Ben was clearly confused, so I filled him in on what Marshall and I had seen. His eyes did that creepy eye-shift thing, and then he furrowed his brow. "Didn't hear anything about it. Doesn't surprise me though."

In the silence I started to turn away, but decided to continue with questions. "Oh, and did you ever run into that cadet you were looking for?"

Another eye-shift movement. "No. Guess he's avoiding me. Most do, so I'm used to it."

"Hmmph," I tossed out. "You seem harmless enough...for a genius."

Ben offered a small hint of a smile. "Thanks, plebe."

"You're welcome. Night." And I finished the long trek through the Commons and off towards my room.

I don't think I will ever tire of seeing that beautiful orb pass my window.

But the mental replay of tonight's game, then that body floating past wars for my attention. *Darn it*!

Maybe I need to go to the Medic Station and take another test. Maybe I should ask them if anyone else had seen the body. Maybe I could ask if anyone had seen that Jacobs kid. Maybe I should do that tomorrow. Maybe I should stop talking to myself.

I turned out the lights above my cot.

Log-in: JessReynoldi18851
Date/Time: 20 Oct 2201/2043hrs
Subject: first tests

I so really needed alone time after my first round of tests. I feel mentally exhausted and sick to my stomach. No amount of midnight cramming and days of studying could have made today any easier. The subjects are advanced, I know that. But the tests are so precise. I had to read the questions and read them again to make sure there were no tricks or that I was missing part of the answer. Hopefully I did well. We were told to expect results first thing in the morning, but I doubt I can sleep. I don't want to fail on any of these tests. I have put too much effort into my classes the past few weeks, especially as the classes really started progressing.

I have missed some social interaction. My time in the UV room was dually spent as I studied. Even the solarium found me with texts and assignments in hand. I even tried walking laps while I studied. I honestly don't know how these other cadets have so much time for the movies or even the genius chess matches and two sporting events this week. I have missed every chess match of my friends' since that first week or so in September, over a month ago.

Ian and Bryce popped in to check on me. So did James. Tori has only talked with me at meal times or on my data pod. It gets lonely.

ENTRY END

The knock on my door brought my head off my pillow with a start. "Coming," I called as I groaned and made my way to the door.

Cecile stood in my door frame. "Hi. Checking on you."

It was said so matter-of-fact that I just blinked in response, for several seconds. "Okay. Thanks."

She just looked at me, then up-and-down. "James said to make sure you are okay."

Again, "Okay. Thanks." When she didn't move, I added, "I'm fine. Just have been stressing my classes. I had all of my tests today..."

"We all did," she interrupted.

"...so I wanted some alone time," I continued. "Thanks for checking on me though."

Her stance told me she wasn't done talking to or with me.

"Anything else?" I couldn't help the tinge of tart I had used.

"Feeling better?"

Her question took me aback. After several blinks and a solid moment to look at the floor, I met her eyes. "Yep. I'm good."

"Sleeping okay? No more visits to the med shacks?"

I hated it when she referenced those. Despite my growing anger, I smiled lightly. "Sleeping well, thanks. Been doing so for a while. And no, no more *med shack* visits."

Still she eyed me up. "That's not what I heard. We're here to help, you know."

Again I thanked her.

With a brief nod, she left my doorway and I allowed my door to close.

"Not what you heard," I muttered. "Spying on me?"

I walked over to my portal and looked into the darkness around, waiting for me blue beacon of beauty. I didn't have long to wait, as I knew I wouldn't. With a smile, I watched it as it came and left my view, many times over. With deep breaths to still my nerves and quiet my mind, I decided I better make an appearance so I would never, *ever*, have another visit like that again.

After a quick look in the mirror, I pulled my brush through my hair, and left it down.

"Not what you heard, huh?"

Sighing, I grabbed my identification card and slid it into my pocket, and left the solitude of my quarters.

Tori hollered my name across the Commons as soon as I gave into view. That brought an unexpected smile to my face. She was with some cadet that I didn't recognize. I made a note to ask her about him later. As well as to ask what had happened to Adam. But for now, I had to brace for impact.

"Where have you been, Jess?" Her hug was strong. "You haven't even responded to my messages. You haven't seen any of the guys in their sport attire or anything! And boy! Have you been missing something!" She whistled low, with eyebrows high.

Tori's pitchy voice brings an annoyed quirk to my eyebrow, but I smile anyway. "Been studying. Don't you get lost in that time versus space and tests thing?"

"Nope." She tosses her hair. "Duh! Photographic memory. So tests are a breeze." The look she holds turned soft. "Oh, I'm sorry. You aren't like a lot of us that way."

That way. It had come about after that first chess match between Bryce and Ben that, that most of IDEA's cadets had photographic, or semi-photographic memory. Either that, or they were certified genius. I had wondered how people were able to recall the moves in order and with such clarity, and then it slipped. I was truly the oddity here. I was one of the two or three percent on IDEA who wasn't gifted that way. But I hoped I made up for it in tenacity and other skills.

"It's all good. How many common memory people can even make it to IDEA?" My comment still had come off bitter. "It just means I will always have to work harder than some of you do."

The guy at her side cleared his throat and made his excuse to leave. Tori batted her lashes at him, and said she's catch him later.

When he was out of earshot, I fire the first question. "Who's that?"

Tori smiles and looks around, prolonging her answering with her dramatic flair. "Andrew."

"What happened to Adam?"

"Don't know. He just stopped coming around. I think he's avoiding me," she hissed. Then she pouted. "I don't even know what I did."

"Maybe you didn't do anything," I offered, though I had my suspicions.

"Or maybe it's because he's like you, and had to study." After the words left her lips, she gulped. "I'm sorry. That sounded awful."

"I understand," I bit out.

"No, I just don't understand the amount of time one needs to study for the tests. I shouldn't be so…judgmental." She fluffed her hair. "Besides, he'll be back." She gave me a look. "I have something of his."

"Jess!" A feminine voice called, giving me the break from the excruciating conversation I was in. Ellie and Bryce were walking hand-in-hand in my direction. As they got closer, Ellie let go of Bryce's hand to give me a quick embrace. "Where have you been hiding?"

With a shrug, "I have been studying."

Bryce asked how I thought my tests had gone.

I answered. Asked how his went.

Seems everyone was feeling confident about the tests, except me.

Why did I bother showing my face?

"Hey, plebe."

"Hey, Genius," I called back to Ben. I had taken his name calling to a different level. If he thought of his nickname for me as a title, rank, but not really an insult, I have so called him in kind. "Do I even need to ask about your tests today?"

"Passed," Ben smiled before his eyes shifted.

"So modest," Bryce joked. "Jess is concerned that she didn't do so well."

"Bryce!" Ellie elbowed him, and grabbed my arm, successfully pulling me away from the guys, and gaping Tori. When we were a few tables away, she sat down and indicated that I take a seat. "Sorry, the guys will probably dicker and bicker for a few more minutes. Longer if we were to have stayed."

"Oh, I'm good," I said as a smile lit my face.

"Were the tests really hard for you," Ellie asked softly.

I tried to hold in my grunt, but it didn't work. "They weren't easy." After I saw her face, "At least for someone like me. What made it worse is that James sent Cecile to check on me."

"Oh, she rubs me the wrong way," Ellie hissed. "So superior because of who her daddy is. Please. Most of us have those daddies." Then she dropped her look, "Sorry."

"Don't be. I have had to work really hard to get here. I think I appreciate it more than she ever could." But I take a deep breath. "It's hard to believe you all can just hang out and socialize like you do."

Ellie nodded. "Some people have made comments over the years that they shouldn't allow common memory people access to IDEA." She made a face. "I don't know. I think their point was that it's so much harder on those cadets academically. Some people like to single out the ones they call the oddballs."

"Back home, a 'photo' was an oddball," I muttered. "Funny how much has changed."

Ellie touched my hand, "You...are not...an oddball. Goofball... maybe."

I laughed right along with her, glad for the change of conversation's tone. I noticed when her gaze went back to Bryce. "So? You and Bryce?"

"Oh," she scoffed. "Bryce and I are on an on-again, off-again relationship plan. He's always available, but not. Sometimes I just take him by the hand and lead him around." A smile lifted her face. "It's good for him. And me." She turned her head to the side. "I'm not sure it will go anywhere. But it's fun to play Besides we see each other in almost every class of the Encryption and Encoding for our Intelligence Program. It's like we're always together." She shrugged.

I smiled.

"What did you think about the chore test?" Ellie asked as she looked around. "Most find that the most challenging. 'Where will they see me fit in?'"

I admitted I wasn't sure where I should go because I felt a lot of the station's chore assignments would benefit me when I graduated.

"Besides," Ellie added, "the perk of having access to other areas and different people most of us will never meet?"

I nodded again. "And what did you get?"

"Kitchen detail, especially fitting after the complaints I put it. But welcome over tutoring."

The whole station's lights changed to red, and then the sound of the klaxon alarm filled the Commons.

"Attention, Cadets. Attention, Cadets. This is not a drill. I repeat, this is not a drill. Please return to your quarters immediately. Again. This is not a drill. Please return to your quarters immediately."

Log-in: JessReynoldi18851
Date/Time: 21 Oct 2201/0053hrs
Subject: not a drill

Well, I lived through my first lockdown.

I was so scared when I got to my room. My portal's shield was already in place. The eerie red glow that illuminated my room was just enough that I thought of vintage horror movies. So fitting that Halloween is around the corner, I guess.

Then I could hear the dull, and not-so-dull, thuds as IDEA was struck with debris or rocks. Some "thunks" were definitely louder, and I was very grateful to not be able to see what was hitting us. With the closer, more powerful thuds, the understanding that each cell can be isolated in case of hull breach replayed in my mind. I sent up a prayer that it not happen tonight.

After what seemed like an hour, it became scary silent. I could hear my heart pounding away within my breast. I hadn't even realized that I had been holding my breath. And I did not expect my jaw to hurt that much just from clenching my teeth.

ENTRY END

"Attention, Cadets. Attention, Cadets. Thank you for your cooperation. Thank you for your cooperation. Please report to the Commons and see your House Director for roll. Thank you."

That nerve-wracking red light changed back to its bluish white.

I let my breath gush out of me as the protective shield on my portal slid partially, then stopped. With a jump, I went to my window pane, and looked at the denting in the metal up close.

Some of the indents were rather large and obviously prevented the shield plate from completely retracting.

"Attention, Cadets. Attention, Cadets. Thank you for your cooperation. Thank you for your cooperation. Please report to the Commons and see your House Director for roll. Thank you."

I came out my shocked state and felt the thick glass. Its cool surface seemed unmarred by the recent barrage. I peered into the littered debris of rocks that must have struck IDEA. My mouth dropped at seeing the number and size of some asteroids quickly disappearing from my rotating view. Pausing once again to touch the glass, I thanked it for staying intact, before I went to report for roll call.

The halls were filled with cadets, some who looked like they had just woken up as they rubbed sleep from their eyes and wore casual lounge wear. *How can you sleep through that?* I noticed that the tenured cadets were moving quickly down the hall so I picked up my pace.

As we approached the Commons, the rest of Forshay House started dividing into academic years. We first years, we plebes, you could tell by the nervous looks on our faces, were guided by some of the upper classmen into our own line. Each of the four lines moved towards a line-respective table with three staff members and a mini-swipe machine like we used for scanning in order to get our meals.

A cadet in line in front of me asked a neighboring upper classman what was going on.

"We all have to check in. We scan our chip card. One of the staff is there to verify we're not in shock. Another is a maintenance guy who is there to see if there is any damage to report. The other is...I don't really know, probably just because three looks more menacing than two."

Chuckles erupted down the lines.

"Just kidding," the upper added. "It's another maintenance member. One listens to one cadet. The other listens to the next. Moves the lines along quicker."

Despite each line having five hundred cadets to get through, the lines did indeed move along. After only ten minutes I could hear the conversations in front of me. So when it was my turn, I let my maintenance person know that my shield didn't fully retract.

The man nodded and noted my quarter's number on the screen that they could see and assured me someone would be out to check it while I was in class tomorrow so I needn't worry about modesty or privacy. He thanks me and turned his attention to the next approaching cadet.

After I was done, I turned and looked at the lines and all those who still had to check in for both houses. Not recognizing any of the closest people I asked one of the uppers from my house if I could go back to my room. She told me I could, so I did.

Upon getting in my room I took a quick shower and crawled into bed.

A calming view of Earth passed by as I drifted off to sleep.

Visions of rocks pummeling our academy filled my dreams. They kept me tossing and turning on my little cot. The sounds of the metal being banged upon constantly startled me awake.

But when I opened my eyes, silence and stillness remained every time.

I gave up on sleeping when the dream that kept repeating was the body floating past my window like when I first arrived here.

With a growl of frustration, I peered into the blackness surrounding IDEA. Nothing hideous or grotesque greeted my view. No monstrous ice or rock chunks threatened. Nothing but the pin points of stars that slow-spin from sight, with the regular rotation of home in and out of view.

Log-in: JessReynoldi18851
Date/Time: 31 Oct 2201/2053hrs
Subject: Happy Halloween!

My first real holiday since arriving at IDEA? HALLOWEEN!

I had learned from the brochures that we could dress up some of the normal face paint, and gore make-up items from the Shoppette, but I didn't expect some of the guys to borrow some of the female cadets' uniforms. Too funny! Totally unexpected here, where IQs and family names rule.

And tonight, there's to be a dance! Apparently it's an even bigger ordeal than the brochures hinted at.

ENTRY END

The intercom screeched just before a voice crackled over it. "House Director Bradley call 201. House Director Bradley call

201."

"That's funny," Tori said as she played with the grilled chicken salad on her plate.

"What is," I asked.

She made a face and looked around the Commons. "Have you noticed that ever since the roll call from a week-and-a-half ago, Director Bradley has been called every couple of nights? It's always been after everyone has gone through the chow lines. Always at supper."

I replayed the past few days' meals. "You're right. I don't ever remember hearing it before that night."

"Because you didn't," Tori stated as she rolled her eyes. "I wonder if the Directors are supposed to carry radios or mini-comms for that kind of communication. Or send a message on their data pod or something. That seems like it would be a better choice, versus blaring it all over IDEA like that."

I had to agree with her logic. "I'm sure they must have a more...covert way to communicate." My eyes watched as Director Bradley crossed the Commons. "I wonder why they do it that way then. It's like they are broadcasting it on purpose."

After a quick glance around, I noticed other cadets looking about as well.

Costumes, if one can call them that, were visible at all of the tables. You couldn't help but smile at the guys who were trying their darnedest to keep their feminine make-up jobs intact. A few of them had long since given up on their beautification application.

After chow was cleared away, the tables were collapsed in an upright fashion and pushed away from the sculpture which was draped in fake cobwebs. The IDEA sculpture was to be the backdrop for those who wished to take part in the HOWL-a-weenie Dance, put together by some of the upper classmen of each house. Holographic images of scary scenes and a moon were being played. Already little tables were being set up for the appetizers, complete with fantastic and gory nametags.

I wasn't really fooled though, as it looked like the same nametags and items that were used for lunch and dinner. BLOODY FINGERS for the little sausages in barbeque sauce that were served with lunch. WITCH'S BREW for that Hispanic soup of hominy, chicken, and tomatillo sauce. BRAIN BREAD which was more like cinnamon rolls clumped together and glazed so that when you pulled the pieces apart your fingers were covered in sticky goodness. ANTI-VAMPIRE PASTA which had so much garlic you didn't need the little toast slices they offered with it, and the hallways still smelled yummy (if you like garlic) because of it. And of course the beverage bar had templates for the fruit punch and milk saying BLOOD and ZOMBIE FLUID. All rather cute and yet, it made me miss home and the things my mother used to make for different work potlucks which I got to sample.

A terrified scream caused me to jump and turn. I relaxed as I saw one of the male upper classmen from Bradley's House burst into laughter as a female from his House slugged him. His pals patted him on the back for his gruesome costume and makeup job while he continued to get a verbal reprimand from his scare victim. I didn't blame her for being upset with him, his costume was hideous, just like out of horror films.

"You jumped like *ten feet* in the air," Tori giggled as she gave me a slight push.

I pushed her back. "I was startled. You trying to tell me you didn't jump?"

"Nah," she flipped her hair over a shoulder. "That kind of stuff never really got to me. My brothers were all into the old gore and mangled zombie movies that were all the rage back a couple hundred. They have hundreds of the collector's editions, I swear."

"Well, I didn't ever get into those," I said as I picked up my tray. "I was more into the exploration science fiction stuff from then. Too bad movies didn't continue. I wonder what kinds of things they would have been making today."

Tori harrumphed as she followed me. "Who really needs them anymore anyway? Everyone, well, everyone except you, became so desensitized because of the violence and gore. People stopped going. Why make them when everything was a repeat of what someone already had done?"

I could only nod at her logic while I set my tray and eating utensils in the appropriate locations.

"So, I'm going to glam up for the dance. See you in about an hour?"

Again, I nodded and watched Tori flounce away, flirting via fingertip waves as she passed the same group of guys. Seeing that I had to shake my head all the way to my quarters.

The dance was definitely in full swing by the time Tori and I showed up again, way past the hour Tori had said we'd go. She wanted to make sure her fake angel wings would stay in place while dancing, and that required a lot more securing and refastening. So when we finally "arrived" several hundred students sat around watching the fantastic computerized light show and listening to the music that reverberated. Various students in varying rates of decay emerged, some pretending to be zombies, walked with limps or dragged a leg as they walked. It was starting to freak me out, how realistic and into it they were.

And seeing the elaborate bloody makeup of some of the cadets, I was reminded yet again of the sightless body I still swear floated by my portal when I first arrived here.

"Hey," and a firm grasp of my shoulder.

With a start I turned and saw someone with blood leaking from his eyes. "Oh my God!"

I burst from my seat. It wasn't until I was halfway across the Commons that I pieced that it was James. But with my outburst and hasty departure from the party, I had no intent on returning. Instead, when I got to my room I locked the door. Seeing Earth pass through the pane of my portal, I peered out into the void beyond.

I don't know when I started crying or why, but after a bit I realized that I was completely shaking. Gulping deep breaths I sunk to the cool floor.

A knock at my door and I jumped to my feet. But my mouth stayed shut.

My data pod chirped to life. And again after about a minute.

Another knock, and someone called my name via the door-to-room intercom. It sounded like Ben, and he asked if I was okay.

But I didn't move from my spot in my room, not for a long time, and long after he left.

I pressed the button to close the shield over my portal, and watched it cover my view of home…and nightmares.

I went into my medicine drawer and pulled out my few remaining sleep aids from when I first arrived on IDEA. Tonight I needed a little sleep without horrible visions. "Please."

Log-in: JessReynoldi18851
Date/Time: 1 Nov 2201/1904hrs
Subject: Avoidance

This morning when I woke up I decided that with my recent Halloween breakdown, I would avoid everyone like they had the plague, and focus fully on my studies. I had just kept all conversation on class and lectures. That was easy when I had slept through breakfast. Lunch was a little tougher though.

However, the feminine companions I have kept of late were only slightly interested in my extremely rapid departure and more about all the gossip of the dance. My fears about having to replay the terror and upset I had felt seeing James' eyes...

God...just remembering those horrible, grotesque...lifeless eyes. I keep seeing that body floating by my window...with his eyes...just all bloody and gruesome like that.

ENTRY END

"Hey, plebe."

Swallowing the lump in my throat I turned and faced Ben. "Hi, Genius." His weird shifty eyes looked over my features, causing me to hold my breath. When I could force my vocal cords to function, "What?"

"You okay? You took off...and...I followed you." Ben's voice seemed   distant,   or   choked.

"I know." I cleared my throat. "I heard you at my comm."

He squinted that weird way of his. "What did James do?"

"Do?" My face must have reflected my inner turmoil. "I'm not sure I understand."

"Did he hurt you, plebe? Did he...do...say something... inappropriate?" The look on Ben's face spoke volumes of upset and concern.

My heart softened just a fraction knowing someone on IDEA did care for me, even as creepy as Ben was. "No. I," I stammered trying to find the proper verbiage to convey, something he'd believe and that I would too. "I was startled by his makeup job. Then, I was embarrassed for my behavior." *Both very true.*

Ben let his eyes do that shifty thing he does when he thinks things through. "That was right after Grant and his cohorts startled Miriam?"

At first I had no idea who or what Ben was talking about, then remembered the incident just before James placed his hand on my shoulder. "I don't know their names, but if it's the scream that woke the Commons...yes. I wasn't prepared to see...see that I guess."

Ben sat down in an awkward movement while he processed whatever was going through his mind. Then he turned towards me. "Had you never seen such costuming?"

I couldn't fight the smile that came. "I have indeed *seen such costuming*, Ben. I just...I..."

I don't know what caused me to come clean in that moment, but I did with a blurting...

"I was freaked out because it looked like the body I swore I saw outside my portal when I first arrived here."
Ben just blinked at me.

I knew it had come out louder than I really should have allowed.

"I know it was probably just my nerves," I added, still a little louder than I probably should have been. But blurting it out like I had...I felt a teensy bit better.

And Ben just stared at me.

That was more disconcerting than his shifty eye thing.

Okay, maybe I don't feel better. I cleared my throat, then looked down. "I don't have space illness. I have taken lots of the tests." Then I peek up at stoic Ben. "I...I...swear I saw... something."

Ben looked down at the table before him, and brought his hands up on it. He splayed his fingers wide and tense as he continued his...*meditation*? For several long, silent minutes he stayed like that while I wondered if I should say anything else, but just bit my tongue instead.

"Hey you two."

My eyes went to the face of the speaker while I sucked in a gasp. "Hi James."

Ben jerked to his feet and mumbled an apology and stalked away.

I watched him go wondering if he thought I was crazy...if I was going to be locked up in solitary for observation.

"Oh! Did I interrupt something?" James stood over me but looked the way Ben had departed.

"Ben was just checking on me after...after how I left the dance last night." My neck felt tight and my mouth dry in remembrance. But I looked at James anyway.

He looked dashing and sexy, like usual. Not like the gore he sported the night before. No lingering red splotches of makeup anywhere. Just casual and take-my-breath away James. Probably should get past that, but who cares. *It's a harmless, far-off crush.*

"Yeah, well, I came over to apologize for startling you like that last night. I know I looked horrendous and forgot about that when I tried to get your attention." He rubbed the back of his neck. "Tori told me you weren't really into the whole zombie apocalypse rage that some of us play to on one day a year...to let loose. That's what I was doing. I wasn't trying to freak you out."

I smiled at his nervous mannerisms while he waited to be pardoned. After a few...long...drawn-out seconds I supplied, "I accept your apology."

He nodded and tilted his head in a mock bow and walked away.

Tori commandeered her seat next to me at that point. She proceeded to fill me in on who danced with whom, and who got bloody fingers in different orifices for photo ops and giggles. She just went on and on, and on. Food was gone and she just kept right on rambling away.

After what seemed like an hour of her gossip and reenactment of what she thought the highlights were, I pleaded off with a migraine. Despite her pouty face, she allowed me to retire for the night.

As I passed where Ben usually ate his meals, I noticed he was sitting, hands splayed like before. His face grim and every muscle tense. I called out, "Night, Genius."

Ben's eyes met mine and held them.

The intensity of the...anger, if that's right, I think it is... brought me up short. I just stood there, probably with my mouth agape, until he broke eye contact and hastily got up. I watched him leave the Commons, and noticed how he slowed down by House Director Bradley's still vacate seat.

But he didn't turn and look back at me.

He didn't see how many eyes of the onlookers watched me just stand there, agog.

He didn't hear the whispers that started.

"Cadet?"

I tensed and turned. "Sir?"

Before me Director Forshay stood with military poise and ease. "Lost Cadet Reynoldi?" "No." My voice sounded weak, even to my ears.

"Have a spat with Cadet Williams?"

My jaw dropped, then snapped shut. "No, sir."

Forshay just peered at me, eyebrow raised in argument. "Cadet Williams looked upset when he was sitting with you until your normal group of ladies joined you."

Normal group of ladies? Like they are such a thing. I swallowed carefully while finding the right words. "He was just checking on me. He seemed to think someone...offended me last night."

"Did someone?"

"No, sir.

"Did you *enjoy* the festivities, Cadet?"

House Director Bradley entered and scanned the Commons as he did. His stride slowed just briefly as his gaze landed on mine, and went to Forshay. Then he resumed his seat. Once there, his eyes found mine before settling on his data pod before him.

I hesitated before answering Forshay's question. "I left early. I wasn't up for it. If you excuse me."

Another early night safely stowed in my quarters with the portal's shield preventing any outer views. But my studying wasn't very good. Conversations played over in my mind, as well as Bradley's entrance.

Is it just me, or does he seek me out?

Log-in: JessReynoldi18851
Date/Time: 18 Nov 2201/2111hrs
Subject: Fishy business

I have tried to stay aloof and focus on my studies. But I find my mind wanders, and my appetite falters.

Food doesn't taste the same now. I feel like even what had been delicious fish entrées taste...odd, fishy, if you excuse the expression. Gone are the exquisite flavors and garnishments and relishes. The fish tastes like poorly prepared fish. The older cadets dismiss it as normalcy returning to the cuisine.

I know that the meals are supposed to supplement our dietary needs, and that the fatty fish served here on IDEA helps supply our necessary Omegas...but I long for more chicken. I know we can't have chicken every day as they take longer to grow and harvest. But what I wouldn't give for a full-out char grilled steak, medium well.

Sigh. Four more years and that steak is mine!

ENTRY END

    "I swear," Ellie began this evening's meal, "even the tartar sauce is rancid."

Looking at the creamy substance on my tray, I pushed the chunks of relish around with my fork. "It does get old after a bit."

"Don't worry. We're due for a cycle of guinea pig soon," Adam said as he stuffed some of the baked fish into his wide open trap. "Those lil guys will be a welcome break from fish at most of the meals."

At the mention of eating guinea pig again, I offered a pout. I still preferred them to be pets not cuisine. I have to admit that I didn't know what it was I was having at first. I thought it was *conejo*, as Adam joked with Ellie, or rabbit. Found out from Hanson and Adams afterwards what it really was. I had felt horrible despite appreciating something other than fish. *And it was pretty tasty, darn it.*

"Why don't the cooks make the food the way they did when we first got here?" Tori just had to whine what we were all thinking.

Adam offered her his pouty smile back. "I guess it sucks having to make awesome food for every meal. I'm sure someone here doesn't complain when it's this bland."

At that we all looked around the Commons to see who wasn't making a face.

No surprise, Hanson and his group from Bradley House were just digging in. My stomach did a flop just watching them pack away the food on their trays.

"Gross," Tori said as she brought her napkin over her tray. "That does it. I'm officially done."

Ellie mimicked Tori. "Yeah, if it's going to taste this bad, let the fish stay swimming. I'd do a salad instead."

I kept scanning the cafeteria, not ready to call it quits. Others were frowning and dunking their fish in the tartar sauce before eating it. In my opinion the fish wasn't horrible. It was just...more fish, without all the flair and fancy sauces. Just fish, not well prepared.

It made me think of the day when I had been watching them all feeding on whatever made them all freak out. I mentioned something about that now.

Adam frowned. "A feeding frenzy? That doesn't sound right." When he was asked why not Adam added, "Most of the feeders are in the walls so you wouldn't be able to see them feeding. I did a tour with one of the maintenance guys who showed some of us were the feeding stations are for the *pescados*...er, fish."

"Stop showing off, Babe. No one cares you know some Spanish here," Tori said as she swirled her strawberry juice around in her glass.

"But I saw them all worked up and going at something. I wasn't the only one. Another cadet saw it too. She even remarked that she had never seen them do anything like that before," I added.

I had Adam's full interest. "Show me where."

So, after dinner, we all went.

"When was this feeding frenzy?" Adam was peering into the tank ahead of us while I hung at the back of the group.

I quick pulled out my data pod. "Hold on. I wrote it down in my journal."

Ellie looked as Tori laughed and said, "She put it in your journal? That's just sad."

Ignoring their remarks, I said, "September ninth."

Adam's reflection on the glass showed that he had made a face. Then his face went rather...odd. And he bolted saying something about getting someone.

Everyone crowded around the tank then.

That's when I saw it nestled by the rocks. It looked like a human skull on its side.

Log-in: JessReynoldi18851
Date/Time: 29 Nov 2201/2202hrs
Subject: Investigation

So odd to know that someone died here on IDEA.

They made the announcement today. A member of the staff who maintained the fish tanks had been missing. Originally those that monitored attendance thought she had taken a shuttle back to earth and was AWOL. However this new development proved she wasn't absent without leave. It was believed that she fell into the tank and that her body was pushed along by the artificial current of the tank system, eventually parts separating from the whole. Some of the machines that maintained the eco structure were being blamed for her dismemberment.

But what was worse was the second broadcast played around dinner time. A young male cadet from Bradley House was missing and presumed lost. This declaration came after days of questionings and amidst several hush-hush meetings with the House Directors and who-knows-who-else. Even sporting events were postponed for what some were jokingly calling the "Spanish Inquisition". But I wasn't laughing.

Every cadet was questioned. Some of them, like me, many times.

Nobody felt like talking about their experience in the chair, not really. Especially me.

My last questioning happened this morning, before my Explorations lab. *I will swear until my dying day, that the putrid mess that did not make the trash receptacle was entirely their fault.*

ENTRY END

Once again I was summoned to a small room near the Commons. I gave my quick knock, like I had done a few other times now. When Director Forshay opened the door I could see the same four faces already positioned at the table. I glanced at the empty chair at the table, and he spoke simultaneously. "Please Cadet Reynoldi, have a seat." When I did as instructed he resumed his own. I smiled briefly when he looked first at me and then to one data pods that held the files before him.

Director Bradley just kept his eyes on my face while I shifted uncomfortably in the metal chair.

I couldn't help but note the other people in the room all had matching folders on the screens before them. Each person had identical files like those from my previous two interrogations.

I knew one file they had was for the lady they believed had drowned in the fish tank when we first arrived. From the limited knowledge I gleaned from limited whispered conversations that have been whispered, the woman had been an IDEA alumna. Her degree was for hydro-engineering with specialized emphasis in zero gravity maintenance. She had been an exemplary student and a mentor for some present students. Upon her graduation she had already applied, been interviewed, and accepted for a secondary hydro-engineer position on IDEA. That had only been about two years ago.

The other folder each staff member had was for the student who has been declared as missing. He was a member of Bradley House. Somehow I wasn't surprised to hear that. What I was surprised to learn today was that he and I apparently had been in the same transport to IDEA. In fact, he was only a few seats behind me after take-off.

Director Bradley brandished his data pod and a generic holographic academy photo of a male cadet came to life right before my eyes. My first time seeing who was missing. His soft blue eyes shone with genuine pride as he smiled for the photograph. His dark blonde hair was nicely maintained and I couldn't help but think he was definitely too good looking to go missing or be killed. Don't ugly people go missing? Do they? Or beautiful females like in those lame B movies? How could he just disappear?

Just like that, those two whole seconds to see his hologram, then the image of the body floating lifelessly by my portal made me gasp. My hand instantly covered my mouth while I tried to comprehend what I saw. *No.*

"Cadet Reynoldi?"

Swallowing the bile that had climbed into my throat, I turned to face Director Bradley, my hand still over my mouth. My eyes felt like they were bugging out of my skull. I had to look away from their blank stares. I wanted to throw up, and the nasty tang that ricocheted in my mouth wasn't helping. Every time I tried to open my mouth, I closed it afraid of what might spew forth. I don't know at what point it started, but I realized that my head was shaking to indicate a very strong negative.

"Cadet?"

This time it was a course instructor I turned to see. His stern look made me glance away. Then my gaze danced all over the small room, anywhere but on the computer-enhanced floating picture before me.

"Cadet Reynoldi!"

It was said with so much force I couldn't help but look at my director. And as I did, I felt tears well and then roll. But I couldn't pull my hands from their protective placement for fear of blubbering or making a mess.

Director Forshay's forcefully pointed at the three-dimensional likeness floating between all of us and I felt compelled to take another peek at it.

Confirmation with the mental replay again.

Wastebasket. Dear God, wastebasket! Turning about in desperation, my eyes found one behind me at the door. I bolted for it.

Hands reached for me and pulled my arms just as I released the contents in my mouth.

With extreme gruffness and callousness I was hauled backwards, still seeking the wastebasket beyond my reach. In that second while I was yanked backward, I still retched. While they pulled away with curse words, I was left shaking and mortified. Not only by the mess around me, but by the way I had been man-handled. I gathered they thought I was making a break for it.

"Sit down, Cadet!"

Keeping a hand across my lips, I met Director Bradley's hard and accusing stare. After swallowing the nastiness in my mouth, I choked out, "I swear to God, I didn't know."

"What didn't you know?"

Director Bradley's voice bit and I couldn't help but recoil. "I didn't know who he was or what he looked like. I didn't...I didn't believe...." I couldn't continue. My hand resumed its previous placement across my face.

My astrophysics instructor cleared his throat. "Cadet Reynoldi, could you...could you elaborate on that for us? What didn't you believe?" Then he covered his own mouth.

Director Bradley leaned back in his chair, hard like stone. "Yes. Please, elaborate."

"I didn't know what he looked like. I didn't think it was real. I know you have said before that he was on the same transport ship as me. But I never saw him that I can remember." Against my urge to purge, I continued. "How long has he been missing?"

"You tell us," said Director Bradley still deeply recessed in his posture.

A soft knock at the door earned a barked command to enter. A member of the medic staff opened it with a data file chip in hand. He stopped at the mess and stench and checked his foot placement. "You asked for this, Director Bradley?" Then he covered his mouth and nose.

With controlled movements Director Bradley got out of his seat and crossed to the door, missing anything on the floor. "Thank you. Please get Phil to clean this up right away. And bring in an air freshener or something right away. And leave the door open, for God's sake!"

After a quick head-bob, the medic left, mostly closing the door behind him.

One of the other instructors about gagged and asked to move the questioning to an adjoining room. He was denied. But Forshay went and opened the door, and waved it in an effort to air out the room.

Giving the small microfile in his hand a finger-flick that

created a "thop" sound, Director Bradley made his way back to his chair. He snapped the data chip into his reader before him and pulled the chair forward with an irritating grating noise. "Let's see. When we spoke the last, what, two times, you neglected to mention your recent visits to the medic station." His eyes sought mine. "Why?"

I made a silent plea for help from my director. His eyebrow was quirked and I just looked from his face to that of my instructor, and back to Director Bradley. "Recent? It was when I first arrived. Besides, I didn't think it relevant."

Director Bradley's face went from calm to outrage in point-one seconds. "You asked, repeatedly mind you, to be checked for space illness. And you don't see any relevancy in it?" He crossed his arms in a way that begged me to argue or call him a liar.

Again, I swallowed the yucky lingering taste in my mouth while I tried to find the right words. "I-"

A sharp rap sounded and the door opened the rest of the way. I recognized Phil as the maintenance man who helped clean up the blood splotches down the hall back in September. If he recognized me, he gave no indication. He just went about his business. I couldn't stand to watch how casually he worked.

The room sat in silence, except for Phil's spraying, and the sound of a mop being wrung. After about ten minutes, and the wrinkle-snap of a plastic bag being opened, Phil was done. And the door closed.

It did smell a lot better.

I wished I felt better though.

"You were saying?" Director Bradley prompted.

I couldn't look at them, none of them for fear of them seeing my shame or their accusation. "I went because my first night here I couldn't sleep and was restless. Everyone was preaching to watch out for signs, and I wanted to be sure. And then...then..."

"What, Cadet Reynoldi?"

Despite hearing my director's familiar voice, I didn't look his way. "I was getting more sleep. They gave me a sedative to help. But I had to keep taking them when, well, when I freaked myself out." I clenched and released my fists under the table. "One night during my first week I thought I saw a person outside my portal."

"Maintenance?" Director Forshay asked.

I shook my head. After taking a steadying breath I added, "A body."

"And you didn't report it?" Director Bradley asked in turn.

"No."

"Why?"

"Because I only saw it for a few seconds." I turned my attention from person to person in the room. "I wasn't sure. And I didn't know if I had space illness or not yet. And then in lecture you said it would be basically impossible to lose someone here."

All four other occupants stared at me as if deciding whether or not to believe me, seeking a lie in my demeanor.

Then, with a deep breath and gulp, I chanced another look at the smiling holographic image. "He was dead. He was outside IDEA and looked dead, all bloody." Tears started again down my cheeks. "I thought I was fighting space illness. That it wasn't real." And sobs racked my body. "I thought it wasn't real." After several long seconds looking at his picture, I brought my head down.

Their silence echoed until I could no longer hear my crying, just my heart thumping within my chest. Even my breathing was soft, almost non-existent.

I don't know how long we all remained in there because, for me, time was definitely all funked up. All I know is after a bit more, someone cleared his throat. When I looked up, the cadet's smiling image was gone.

"You say this happened your first week on IDEA?" Director Bradley was on his data pod.

"Yes."

"Rest assured. This cadet wasn't reported as missing until we had the lockdown for the asteroid shower we experienced in October," Director Bradley said.

"But that cannot be," I stammered.

"It's true. We have activity throughout IDEA, including assignments being turned in on his data pod up until that night."

"No, it can't be right," I argued.

But Director Bradley continued to talk, saying how he was putting me in for a psychiatric evaluation later this morning to rule out space illness or post-traumatic stress disorder. He assured me that he would give me ample time to clean up in my quarters before joining my regular classes. He must have seen my head still shaking no because he asked, "What's the problem now, Cadet?"

"You're wrong," I blurted. I could feel all four of them looking at me as I held Director Bradley's hard stare. "You're wrong, sir."

He licked his teeth in irritation. "Is that so, Cadet?" At my nod, he asked, "How am I wrong?"

"He couldn't have been doing homework and going through IDEA." I could see the suspicion my comment was raising. "I don't know how all of that is possible. And I am pretty sure I don't have space illness."

"You're not making sense, Cadet," my physics instructor said.

"I'm trying to tell you that someone must have had his chip card or data pod or something," I said.

"Why?"

With him saying it so coldly, I looked Director Bradley's way. "Because the body I swear I saw was that cadet you just showed me. And he was already dead when he drifted by my portal."

Again, stares and silence greeted my declaration.

Director Forshay cleared his throat. "How certain are you, Cadet Reynoldi?"

I met my director's eyes. "I'd almost bet my life it was him."

Several moments passed before my physics instructor spoke. "It is possible, Directors, that whoever is responsible for this young man's disappearance kept the cadet's chip card and data pod. We could run some-"

"Enough," Director Bradley blurted. "Let's release her so she can get cleaned up and make some of her classes. Forshay? Do you want to take care of permissions and excuses, or do you want me to?"

And then more hush-hush talking as the enormity of what I started hit me. Someone had hid this cadet's disappearance so completely it had fooled the house directors and investigators. Someone was also doing this cadet's assignments and had access to his personal assigned data pod. Panic filled me as the question wasn't "Why?"

It was "Who?"

Log-in: JessReynoldi18851
Date/Time: 2 Dec 2201/2157hrs
Subject: Isolation

We are all not quarantined, but I am wanting some isolation. I want to focus on my studies and do what I need to do for my academic health. It's smarter to get lost in my homework. Believe me, I have tried to buckle down and direct my attention appropriately. But I can only take so much of the NEO philosophy and asteroid mining versus lunar mining. Non-terrestrial material acquisition and space tourism even have lost some of their appeal due to my current state of mind.

Though I have loved learning about the space inhabitation techniques and expansion studies this evening, it makes me think about how that applied to the construction of IDEA. That leads mind wanderings to the recent deaths and how someone had covered it up.

How?

ENTRY END

With a sound of disgust, I sat down my data pod and work the kinks out of my neck. My eyes are drawn to my quarter's door as I wonder how someone successfully hid the death of a fellow cadet for so long, yet again, for what seems like the thousandth time today.

With a quick movement, I brought about my security card, my name card which I was told to carry with me everywhere I went. After just a second I cross over to my door and wave it like I have done probably a hundred times a week for access to various doors and for my meals. My door activated like it had the same amount of time from about three feet away, with a quick swoosh. After a few seconds, it closed, like it had done I needed it to. Again, I waved my card, and when it opened, I crossed the threshold to stand in the hall.

People were milling around the halls, talking in hushed tones. I didn't recognize anyone from my normal crowd so I focused on what I was playing at: trying to figure out how someone made it like the cadet had been in his room every night. Without another glance at anyone walking through this late at night, I stand outside my door and check the waving radius. Again it was about three feet. And with several in and out trial walkings I determined, that yes, a card must be within the three foot radius.

Whoopie.

After a final swipe to enter my quarters I stop dead center of my doorway and wait. The door doesn't close. It doesn't move at all.

Sensors.

I turned and peered into the crevices of the where the door opened into, checking the pocket seams and gaskets as best as I could. My fingers traced the thick metal of the door from top to bottom and back up again. Then I pushed them as far as I could into the sleeve of the sliding door, trying to find catches or mechanisms my eyes didn't see. The groove along the floor also received the same perusal. The receiving pocket, the part of the wall nearest the card reading mechanism in my quarters, provided me a small magnetic catch along the floor gaskets. All of my searching for a super sensor, and it was a small magnet with a red dot lens, about an inch in total length wedged in a manufactured crevice, which tripped the door's sensor.

"Cadet?"

I turned to face the voice behind me in the hall. The same maintenance guy from yesterday stood there. "Yes?"

"My readings showed an error with your door, multiple openings." He looked at me with suspicious eyes. "Everything okay here?"

I smiled, and nodded. "Yes. I was reading on the space habitations modules and became curious on how different deep space debris assaults affected various expeditions in the past fifty years. I was checking what measures are in place if there was a hull breach."

The maintenance man, poor Phil once again, pursed his lips like he was trying to figure out truth from trouble making. "A sensor on the bottom of the door trips if someone is still within the door frame to prevent accidental closure. A few years ago some student tried to manipulate sensors to-." Phil clears his throat and shakes off whatever he was about to say. "So, there isn't a problem here?

I mustered my most innocent smile, "Not that I am aware of. I was just conducting a simple experiment based on my studies, like I said."

"So you aren't trying to get to the pond?"

Blank. I couldn't have hid my numbness and confusion any more at that if I tried. "The what?"

Phil just eyed me. "No games, Cadet. With all the recent, abnormal, incidents, stay in your room at night. Don't try to trick the sensors." He straightened to his full height in a semblance of irritation and authority, "We see it all here."

My mouth spoke before I realized I thought it, "Then how did no one know about the cadet passing? How did that not get caught?"

Phil looked me over good and proper. "You were the one who vomited in the interrogation, am I right?"

With my mouth agape, "I don't see how that makes any difference."

"Thought so. Just know that heightened security measures are in place, so trying to trick the sensors with chunks of metal won't work anymore. Just go to bed, Cadet." With that Phil's data pod sensor lit up and he shook his head and went hustling down the hall.

But my curiosity was more than piqued as I watched Phil shuffle down the hall. I was blazing with more intense questions and the longing for answers burning chased that. So what did I do?

I followed Phil, of course.

I'm not dumb, so I made sure I was a ways behind Phil as he negotiate the halls and turns. I slowed at every one, and I was glad I did so as I heard him reprimand a cadet about the metal plate in the door. I peeked around the corner to see if I recognized the poor soul getting the third degree. My jaw dropped when I saw it was Tori being admonished in the hallway. I was more shocked to see her swim suit barely covered by a robe.

"But, honestly, I was just going to go to the UV room," Tori said as she placed a hand on her hip.

"Uh-huh, and where's your chip card?"

Tori reached into her pocket and came up with nothing.

Phil maneuvered past her and gave her door a slight push and it opened. Tori watched him go in only as far to leave his backside in the doorway. Then he was out of Tori's quarters and waved her little identity card in her face. "It was adhered to the wall, like the uppers no doubt taught you. Or maybe your brothers." He thrust the chip card in her direction. "Take it. Go to your room and stay there. No pond for you tonight, missy."

Tori snatched her card in a huff and gained access to her

room. The door slid closed quietly despite her loud sighs.

Phil tinkered with his data reader and lingered outside her door for several minutes, as if waiting for something. Then his unit lit up and vibrated in his hand, and he shook his head and took off for what I could only guess must be another violator.

Phil had to leave. But I didn't. My curiosity was amped even more than before.

I waited until my neck hurt from spying around the corner. I stood straight and worked the knots out. The snap and pop felt good, but sounded horrible. I twisted and cranked my neck from side to side to work out the lasting stiffness. I was still doing so when Tori bulldozed into me down as she came around the corner.

"Oh! I'm sorry. I didn't…Jess?"

With a quick jerking movement I stood from my sprawled position. "Hi. Wow. You're sure in a hurry." I dusted off my backside.

"Oh, yeah. Well some of us are going to…get together." Tori made a funny face while she thought about whether or not to invite me. "Want to come?"

I bit my lip while I weighed what I knew, what I wanted to know, and the regret if I missed this opportunity. All in all, I knew I needed to. I wanted answers. For the first time in my life, I felt peer pressure and wanted to belong, even if it was doing something wrong. But it was to do something right. Wasn't it? I smiled and shrugged. "I guess."

Tori squinted and took a good look at my comfy clothes. "You might want to change. Let's stop by your room so you can put on your swim suit."

"My what?"

Tori just rolled her eyes and grabbed my hand as she looked over her shoulder, "Come on. Let's just get to your room."

Log-in: JessReynoldi18851
Date/Time: 3 Dec 2201/0221hrs
Subject: The pond

I thought I knew everything there was to know about IDEA. I had seen diagrams and schematics. I had watched infomercials on it back on Earth. Apparently I was more than a lot mistaken on what I thought I knew. There is no mention anywhere about the coolest part of IDEA.

The pond. And I'm not sure I'm able to aptly describe it, but I will try.

ENTRY END

Tori had me change into a swim suit and grab a chamois for later. I put my comfy clothes on back over the top so I wouldn't be strutting around IDEA around midnight in only that. I'm not sure anyone would want to see that. I know I don't.

Then came the moment that I had been wondering about,

how Phil had opened Tori's door and how the card had ceased to be an issue. Tori had gone into my upright closet unit and wiggled a piece of metal from the back corner. When I watched her and asked what she was doing, she had told me that there were metal shims, spacers, throughout IDEA. She continued and said that some of the upper classmen had been shown this over the years and used this trick to sneak around.

My heart had done a doom thumping. My brain burned with what felt like a zillion questions: Who showed her? What House was he from? Or was it a she? How had they discovered the trick? And many more bounced around my skull.

The only one that came out was the one about how someone had figured this trick out.

Tori had smiled and said, "We're all engineers or scientists here, for the most part. Honestly, Jess. People get bored. Some decide to pass on what they have learned. They are, in essence, no different than the House Directors. Sharing knowledge to better the students of IDEA." She laughed at her joke while I watched in silence. Then she turned towards me and said both of her brothers had taught her prior to her arrival.

Tori went to my desk and carefully applied pressure to the thin metal scrap until it took an indented shape. With a pleased smile, Tori went to the door and motioned for me to open it. I waved my chip card and she quickly inserted the piece of metal in the bottom corner where the magnet I located would make contact. Then she quickly backed into my room and allowed the door to close. She motioned for me to do the door thing again, so I obliged. Tori checked her handiwork. She stood up and smiled. "Good enough. We don't want to alert anyone. Jess, put your card in the notch between plates, like here." She motioned to a place about three feet from the door. "It helps to keep it close in case the magnet doesn't hold the connection. It's close enough to trick the door into opening if you give it a gentle push."

I nodded as the understanding of what I had seen earlier came with her tutorial. And, with a huge rush of adrenaline and guilt, I placed my chip card in the crevice where Tori had pointed. And let go.

It stayed put.

Tori led me through the door to stand in the hallway, and gave it a gentle pull until the motor activated and closed the door.

My fate sealed, I followed Tori down a bunch of halls towards the maintenance section of IDEA. I recognized the door leading to the hydration rooms for the vegetation that produced the station's breathable oxygen. Tori pulled on the handle and went right through the doorway, as if it wasn't locked.

At my confused look, Tori pointed to the metal sheath covering the catch in the wall to prevent a click. And she didn't slow down after ensuring the door looked closed behind us. She put her head down against the bright lights offering the necessary ultra violet rays and synthetic sunlight to cultivate and maintain the millions of mosses and ivies and grasses that lined the walls. She had to turn sideways to make her way down the passage that was suspended between the vegetation on either side of us.
I did the same.

As we maneuvered around the walls, I couldn't help but take a good look at the true height of the massive oxygen-producing walls. They were about a hundred meters up and another hundred plus meters down from where I was standing on the suspension bridge. I could see a couple additional levels of passages above and below me. It seemed that the lights were suspended from beneath the walkway and running vertically along the wall support struts. It was both beautiful and very dizzying to take in.

After walking through several sweet and smelly sections, we

turned towards the center of IDEA again. I knew this because the water misting before was barely falling. The deeper we went into the flora, the lighter I felt. I breathed in the intoxicating, heady fragrances given off by the varying vegetation. I also noted how the watery nutrient mixture was fed via tubing to the miniature pots that protruded off the surface of the tall walls, and no mist lingered in the air as it had when we first entered this section of IDEA. In fact, with the lessening gravity, plants didn't droop from their own weight. They were more just sprawling and reaching through the air.

It made me uncomfortable, like the plants were reaching out to touch me, to stop me. I brought my arms as tight to myself as I could as I let Tori lead us through this encroaching growth. It became more and more unruly. I was becoming more and more uncertain of my decision to follow this female clad in a robe.

On and on we went, with softer and softer footfalls with the lessening gravity.

I was beginning to think that she was just seeing how long it would take for me to break, like she was trying to set a trap on me. But I know she ran into me in the hall, not the other way. I basically trapped her, not the other way around, and am now guilty by association.

I am an accomplice to some secret crime of trespassing. "Won't we get in trouble if we're caught?"

She turned to me and smiled, her hair still floating behind her in a weird way from her abrupt jerk. "Who's going to catch us? They don't have any other monitoring system here except for the chip cards because they thought all the cadets would never deviate from the rules and structure. Silly." She smiled at her own comment. "David definitely tested that." And she laughed at some story I must have missed.

I smiled back, heart pounding in my throat. But I couldn't

take my eyes from her weird halo of strands until she tamed them with a hand and turned again.

Tori pulled back an enormous floating flowering spider plant and pointed to a small door. When she let go of the plant, it stayed in the air where she left it with nothing to pull it back into position.

"Welcome to the pond." And she opened the door.

A long brightly lit hallway greeted my eyes for the long track as I followed Tori's form.

"They said it was triple protected and reinforced in case of asteroids or space debris," she called over her shoulder as she made her way down. "It's a super huge secret that only a handful of the upper classmen share with a few newbs every year so we know about it."

And I wasn't told about it.

"James and Hanson told me about it. Cecile wasn't pleased, but who cares? Besides, I already knew." Tori continued forward while she talked, her voice echoing where our footsteps would have. "I was surprised to see Ben here too. So you may see some you know. There are quite a few I haven't met. No one should say anything, because this is all hush hush. We can get in big trouble by being here."

"Then why are we here?" I couldn't stop the quiver that crept into my voice. "I don't want to get in trouble. I can't afford to be expelled."

Tori giggled, "So worried about academics. They were right. You are afraid to live a little. No wonder Ian didn't share this with you."

That stung.

A lot.

The silence allowed her last sentence to echo and

reverberate within my skull as I continued behind her, allowing more distance between us while I sulked. But my feet were only following the motion, and I needed to propel myself forward like Tori was, using my hands along the guide rails.

And then Tori side stepped at the end of the brilliant fluorescent lit tunnel. She turned the hatch and opened the door, blocking my view as she did. Then she took our chamois and pressed them against the side of the wall. With a flourish she indicated for me to look.

At last I was allowed to see what this secret was.

A huge, just massive, hovering bubble of water floated in the space before me. When I say floated, I do mean it was suspended by nothing. It physically was a blob that had...was that a person?

I blinked and looked carefully as something moved through the blob.

It was. A person had pushed off the outer wall of the room and propelled himself into the water, and through. When he was out he put up his arms to brace for impact and stopping at the other wall.

My jaw dropped at the sight.

"Welcome to the pond, plebe."

I turned against the lack of gravity to find Ben's face not far from mine, but upside down. I blinked again and looked at him in surprise. Without a word I looked back at the scene before me. "How?"

Ben hovered next to me, not on the ledge which I gripped to maintain an upright position. "Near zero gravity makes all this possible. Old Newton's laws of motion are truly tested here." He gently pushed off the wall by my head and turned himself so he was more parallel with me. "That better? Sometimes it's distracting and...I...well, welcome to the pond, plebe."

With my eyes again taking in all before me, I offered,

"Thanks, Ben." But then the sauciness grabbed my tongue. "How come no one told me about this place?"

"Because we didn't know you. You wouldn't open up. And your self-isolation. And mostly, because we didn't know if you could keep a secret."

The look in his eyes told me he was serious, that I was talked about concerning the pond. And I couldn't blame them. I really couldn't. I had been distant after seeing the body outside my window. Being afraid of suffering from space illness, I had basically alienated myself.

I suck at social skills.

I watched as a few cadets went in tandem into the floating pool. With a self-condemning nod I faced him, "I understand. I am a liability."

Ben did his darned shifty eye thing. "Hopefully *was* a liability. We can't afford to lose our *distraction.*"

And then he pushed off.

For the first time I realized that he was shirtless. And dang, he looked good in his trunks.

I have been alone way too long if I think Ben looks hot. Or not long enough.

I shook my head for the thought as I took in the other couple of dozen occupants. I was scanning the vast expanse of the room when I noticed Ian Hanson and one of the others from the male bonding episode. They were doing push offs and propelling themselves like darts into the water, all the while doing flips and turns like bullets. It was fascinating to watch. Water splashed out from their exit, and kept going out, not returning to the water's surface like I was used to.

Around the space many random and loose circles of floating water were being corralled by some laughing cadets and pushed back into the center to join back with the whole. Others were captured and launched as playful cannon fodder at a comrade's face or backside. I couldn't help but smile after witnessing the cool tricks and play.

After several minutes, I finally let go of my death grip on the wall.

When Ben came back and motioned for me to join him, I found myself pushing off towards him.

With close to an hour of water time, Tori found me and suggested we leave. She said we had to leave the pond at the same time, but not at the same as the others, to lessen the chances of being caught. She led us to the right tunnel, 3-F, and I could feel the gravity slowly taking ahold of me again. We passed through the door and Tori took the time to reposition the offshoots accordingly to mask the door. She led us through the maze back to the door I first recognized.

Before she opened it, she peeked out, and then turned to me. "Did you have fun?" At my nod she smiled. "Good. So you'll keep our secret?"

Again I nodded.

Tori peered out the small window into the hallway, ensuring it was clear, before she led me back to my quarters and gave my door a gentle push. When it opened she bent down and picked up the shaped metal. "Keep it hidden. Night."

As she walked away, I quickly passed through my doorway before the door closed with me on the wrong side.

With a smile on my face I walked over to my portal and watched for the familiar blue orb of home to pass.

Log-in: JessReynoldi18851
Date/Time: 7 Dec 2201/2357hrs
Subject: Findings versus fluttery feelings

I'm not sure my limited experience with those of the opposite sex, boys, or young man, rather, is enough to help me discern my... feelings. I do know that last night, or this morning (by the time I am done with this entry), had been a lot of fun. I want to go again.

I have poured over current schematics and found nothing that gives away the pond's position. I started going through archived information and found some files altered or blocked. I understand what they were trying to keep people from seeing. What I don't understand is why?

ENTRY END

When I finished my meal, I went to stare at the huge sculpture in the Commons. My thoughts were focused on where the actual pond was in relation to the sculpture. I had been looking at the various parts that have been built looking for how that place existed without everyone here knowing about it.

"Careful, Reynoldi. You're intent exploration of The Donut

could been deemed as dangerous. Can't have you giving us away." Cadet Ian Hanson passed by me without stopping. He tossed a quick look over his shoulder which prompted me to move away from the massive piece.

I collected my data pod and tray and went to the windows to dispose of my uneaten food. After being frowned at for scraping the limited bits into the bin, I dropped my silverware into the next tray. Without any sass, I retrieved my data pod and turned to make my way to my room. When I reached the hallway leading to my quarters, I found Hanson waiting for me. "Oh, hi."

He leaned across me, arm over our heads, his voice low, "You can't give it away. You can't spoil our fun."

I stammered, trying to find appropriate wording. "I'm not trying to."

"People might have asked what you were doing, scrutinizing The Donut like you were. What were you going to say?"

"That I was admiring how detailed the piece was," I countered with some sense of finality. "I have looked at the sculpture many times by the way. No one has challenged me yet."

"Yet," Hanson hissed by my ear.

Shivers went through me. I know it could have been, should have been, fear. But it made me want to turn my face towards his.

"Problem, plebe?" Ben's voice came out clear and strong.

I had never been so grateful for someone to interrupt a conversation in my whole life, at least that I can remember. When my first attempt at a word came up a squeak, I cleared my throat. "I'm good."

Hanson smiled down at me. "You squeaked. Adorable." Then he backed off me, winked, and patted Ben on the shoulder as he walked by.

Ben came and stood a respectable distance from me. "You okay?" Though his words were for me, his eyes followed Ian Hanson's smooth departure. When Ben finally looked back at me, his eyes were doing that funny twitch thing I had become so accustomed to. "Well?"

"Oh, yeah. I'm good." I tried to ease the tension I still felt in my throat.

Ben didn't seem convinced. "What was he saying to you?"

I rolled my eyes. "I was apparently spending too much time looking at the sculpture in the Commons and he thought it might compromise..." I lowered my voice, "...the pond."

Ben snorted. It took me aback hearing him make such a sound. He grabbed my free hand and hauled me back into the Commons. He practically marched me right up to the huge upright piece. "Look."

I just blinked at him.

"Not at me. Go ahead and look. Ask questions. Take pictures. I'll play bodyguard." With that, Ben crossed his arms and looked across the expanse of the Commons in a posture that basically screamed a challenge for anyone to come close.

I couldn't help but chuckle at his antics, which got me a raised eyebrow. After that I went back to my perusal of the engineering model, and taking Ben's advice, took pictures with my data pod as I did so. I noted several small windows that pointed inward to where I suspected the pond's structure to be. After tapping Ben's shoulder, "What rooms are these?"

He turned and gave a quick peek before taking a seat next to me. "Mechanical. The windows are for lighting only, in case of power failure."

It made sense, so I continued looking, squatting way low to see the bottom portion of the sculpture as it rested in the clear form holding it. The structure was, indeed, very detailed. Many layers of tiny windows lay in straight rows, spaced precisely apart. A total of eight rows of windows signaled the same number of living floors.

I knew four of the layers housed Plebes through Firsties, academically by year. "So why do you guys all hang out on the first-years' level?"

Ben didn't even turn around to answer my question. "Because most of the required rooms are on this level. UV room. Commons. Shoppette. Access to our chore duties. Access to other places."

I assumed that included the pond so I change topics. "So who uses the other four floors?"

"Take pictures, and I'll show you later."

I did as Ben instructed, all the way around as best as I could. I even resorted to standing on a chair to get more pictures from near the top. When Ben raised an eyebrow and then shook his head, I challenged, "What?" I got down and put the chair back where it belonged.

"We have inbound," said a barely audible Ben.

I turned to see what he was talking about and Director Forshay was crossing the Commons, definitely heading our way. In a soft voice of my own I said, "I have nothing to hide."

"Hello, Cadets. You're working mighty studiously over this sculpture, Reynoldi. What's going on?" Director Forshay stood, hands on his hips, taking in the structure while he waited for me to speak.

"I was doing some thinking on the engineering and design on IDEA. I was pulling up some of my old notes from lecture from when I first arrived. It got me thinking."

"Oh? About what?"

"How did that cadet end up outside of IDEA?"

That was not what I had meant to say. But it is what I said.

Forshay narrowed his eyes and said, "It was an accident that is still under investigation."

Now that my investigative slip was out, I looked back at the big model, and plodded on. "So where are we now?"

To his credit, Ben didn't say anything, nor did he allow his jaw to drop. He didn't respond at all like he did the first time I mentioned the sight of the body, actually.

My House Director just reached next to me and pointed to an expanse area, using both hands. "We are here. The Commons is two levels high and reinforced all around. It can be sealed off by doors on this level, which is why this is the only level with access to the Commons. Part of a design for an emergency, seal-offs, asteroids or whatnot." He moved his hands along to indicate other points. "The main hatches where all of you cadets arrive are there and there, respective to the house you're assigned to. Helps sort you faster and get the cadets where they need to go."

"What about the maintenance staff? How do they get out there to do their maintenance and switch out the oxygen tanks?" My scientific, explorative mind had kicked in and questions formed quickly, and rolled off my tongue just as fast.

His look became stiff. "As you can see, there are no outer doors for anyone to just step out and go for a stroll." He indicated another section on the sculpture. "Loading dock for supplies is here. There are maintenance doors within the loading dock. It's how the maintenance team gets in and out of IDEA. Even cadets can use the dock if they are assigned to External Maintenance. All of their maintenance gear is stored in compartments in the dock. The dock is also heavily reinforced due to the materials within and the necessity of the dock for supplies every six months." He lowered his hands. "And to answer your earlier question as to how the first year ended up outside IDEA, it is believed that if you are correct about the timing, that he somehow was trapped in the loading dock section prior to the last ship departing so when the bay doors opened, he was...expelled into the vacuum."

Ben chuckled at the word, but I didn't really find it funny. I tossed him a look but he wasn't paying attention. Another question came to mind. "Director, if he was expelled here, how did I see him pass my window?"

Director Forshay peered at Ben first, then the model and pointed. "This is my side of IDEA. This is the central floor. Your room is probably...here."

I looked where he showed. My guess was that it was, and that made me a little uneasy seeing how fast he was able to pick out my room out of the two thousand cadets who lived here. But then again, all cadets had an outside view and being I was a first year, maybe I shouldn't over think it. Back to the task at hand. "So? If he was in the dock here, and IDEA makes about a turn a minute...."

Ben spouted off correct speed and velocity while I still waited for my question to be answered. Then he looked at what I was trying to point out. "She's onto something here, Director. The loading bay doors open here, and a person inside would be siphoned out at such a force that the suggested trajectory doesn't match with what she says happened."

My house director frowned as he looked at The Donut in earnest. "Understood. A loose discharged item would continue straight out." Then he pointed to linear tracks along the outer hull that intersected and formed a grid for tethering and movement to cover all of IDEA. "Could it be that the cadet struggled to find purchase on the side of IDEA using the same guide railing our maintenance team uses? When he expired, lost his purchase? His form could have then tumbled past Cadet Reynoldi's-"

"He wasn't tumbling. He was just floating. Already dead,

bloody. Just there and gone."

Forshay gave me an odd look. "Okay. No tumbling is consistent with my hypothesis that he was trying to grapple for the guide rail. But enough of this. I'm going to run some analyses with Director Bradley." He turned away, then back again. "Nice work, Cadet." Then he walked away.

Ben grabbed my free hand again and I followed right along. We bustled past many slower moving cadets as we headed wherever Ben was taking me. He led me up a flight of stairs and down several long halls. The throng of people in our way lessened, so did our pace. Up another flight of stairs and more halls. As we went along, I realized that he still had my hand in his.

That darned image of Ben, shirtless, flitted into my mind. I pulled my hand so fast out of his, Ben turned and stopped.

"What? You okay?"

"I'm good." It came out as a squeak. "I'm fine." I motioned around to the empty hall. "Where are you taking me?"

Ben cocked his head. "A quiet place so I can answer some of your questions without interruption. I think you'll like it." He put his hand out again. "You aren't allergic to bees, right?"

That darned feeling of danged if I do and danged if I don't came over me for the second time in less than twenty-four hours. With a sigh of resignation, I let him lead me on.

We continued until I noticed the gravity was lessening. He went to a door and looked to ensure no one was around. Seeing we were alone, he gave it a little push. It moved almost silently inside itself like all the pocket doors on the ship did. It closed behind us the same way. A series of bright lights were on the wall at our back. Row upon row of shelved flowers were in front of us. Beautiful butterflies moved freely from bloom to blossom. Every so often I saw a bee crawling in, out and across a flower.

He let go of my hand, so I placed it over my heart.

The one holding my data pod came up and took a picture. And another.

"Pollination room." Ben grabbed my picture-taking hand and led me down between some shelving plumb full of foliage. "I'm one of the caretakers for this room. I can come and go, but I don't want others knowing about it and contaminating it. IDEA is home to some of the last bee species in existence. They hope to continue breeding them and reintroducing them other places." He turned a corner and let go of my hand. He pointed to a small table with some stools in lesser light. "Work space. Easier on the eyes. Butterflies don't like it as much though so you won't get good shots of them here. Besides, now I can answer some of the questions you were asking."

And we talked.

We were there for hours.

I asked him everything I could think of about the construction of IDEA, which doors led to the pond, the support structure for the pond, et cetera. Then I asked if anyone ever cleaned the water, and Ben assured me that every week, same day and time, one of the maintenance personnel cycled the "emergency life support water" to filter it, and certify that it was safe. Ben had a lot to share. He even added what he knew of why the pond was off limits.

"Apparently the first year of operation, years before cadets were allowed to come, an engineer was recording a scientist playing in the zero gravity pool. After the third push off, the scientist got cocky and really catapulted himself through. He had devised a sling-shot mechanism of sorts, and well, there wasn't anything to stop him from striking the other side. As reinforced as the pond is, he broke his neck. He was the first casualty on IDEA, but most don't know about it."

"So how do you?"

Ben smiled while his eyes did that weird thing they did. "I know a guy."

I could not help but give him a slight punch while I rolled my eyes. "Boys!"

When I felt like my reserve of questions had been exhausted, Ben asked one of his own. "Can you tell me what you saw that night? How was the...the body positioned?"

After a moment to collect my thoughts, I shared with Ben all that I had shared with the people at my interrogation. When I was done, I let him know he was the only other one I had told that to.

Ben nodded. After several seconds where only the sound of bees filled the silence, Ben abruptly stood. "I can take you back to your room now."

I blinked at the sudden change. "Okay." It was just like before.

He put out his hand and I gave mine.

In silence we left the pollination room, traversed the halls, and went downstairs. In a mish-mash of people I found my hand no longer in his. At my door some twenty minutes or so later, he thanked me for a wonderful night. Then he turned on his heel and headed towards his house side without a backward glance.

That I was looking for one made me do a forehead smack.

What was wrong with me?

Log-in: JessReynoldi18851
Date/Time: 17 Dec 2201/2202hrs

Subject: Need to study

So after all the interactions which have been causing me various levels of distraction, I have once again isolated myself in my room. I even have stayed away from the athletic arenas except when necessary for class. The guys have invited me to play wall-ball. I declined.

Tori has twice invited me to go to the pond. I went once, the first time she asked. However I found myself looking for Ben, James, and Ian Hanson. Not good. I don't need any complications in my life right now.

See Dad? I'm listening. I'm focusing. I'm ALONE in my room, doing homework, yet again. I'm not hallucinating. I'm just going to pass this exam tomorrow morning with flair. And I'm not getting in any trouble.

I received a transmission on my data pod to report to Director Forshay's office.

ENTRY END

Talk about sweating bullets. It was the one of the longest walks in my life as I kept running scenarios as to why I was being called. Did he have the results from the scenarios already?

I pressed the call button outside Director Forshay's office and waited. I clenched and released my hand as I maintained a poised façade for when he opened the door.

It opened silently and there he stood. His slightly creased crow's feet offered me small hope that he was in a good mood. "Evening, Reynoldi. Come in. The rest are already inside."

My stomach fell to the floor knowing others were summoned and that I was the last. Eyes cast downward I followed him as he led the way deeper into his roomy quarters. As I passed his latrine I saw the door was open, and it was larger than my whole quarters. Another turn and he stepped aside.

"Have a seat, Reynoldi," Forshay indicated a last open chair as he sat behind his big desk. He tapped on his data pod and a hologram appeared behind him, listing cadets. He kept tapping away so I chanced a quick glance around the room.

About a dozen chairs had been brought into this office in his quarters and I took the last unoccupied one. Some probably would have been correct in calling it his living room as there were other bits of furniture to sit on. Four students occupied the comfy davenport against the wall, and two others sat on matching arm chairs flanking the small table stands. On the sofa was James, who was squeezed in next to a smiling Cecile. I frowned realizing I had forgotten that she even existed until tonight. I recognized a couple of faces from when I first arrived; the ones I thought were stuffy and not worth me remembering their names.

"Cadets," Director Forshay's clear tone echoed in the space. "Congratulations. You all represent the current top rank of each of the ten academia, and of each year here, within my House. Uppers, especially you Firsties, for some of you this is a new achievement. Bill," he pointed to a stern-looking black cadet, "all four years and still top dog. Congratulations." Then he indicated the rest of us, "For all of you. Letters will be sent home at the end of the semester with a certificate of accomplishment for your family and friends to share in your academic success."

My jaw must have hit the floor somewhere along the way. I felt like closing my mouth was an arduous endeavor. *Me?* I looked around again and then back to the carpet in front of my chair. *I can't be top cadet for Military Exploration and Expansion.*

"Some of you surprised me. With past family history here at IDEA or other distinguished universities, some of you didn't. Others still had a rough go of it from the word 'Welcome.' Others, Jeanne, suffered terrible loss and still triumphed."

I couldn't help but dart a look in the director's line of sight to witness a sad but determined female about four chairs to my right and one row back. Her nod was slow and deliberate.

"So, finals are coming up, and this meeting is a reminder of what is at stake." He tapped his data pod and the hologram changed. Forshay came to stand in front of it, using his hand to point out what he felt most important. "Academic Elite status for employment. Recruiting ranks. Certificates and recognition for resumes. Extra tuition break."

Was I almost drooling over a tuition break? I knew I was not from money like most here, that I relied mostly on my grandfather's career and my father's position. But we definitely did not have solid financial means. I could still hear my dad telling me to focus and push for number one, that it would help me and them. Yeah, help them pay the remainder of my tuition until I can pay them back.

"Specialized duties and access to security rooms will be coming soon for you," Forshay continued. "And my personal favorite...drum roll, please." A couple of the upper classmen slapped their thighs until they had a rhythm. "Bragging rights with peers."

The room erupted in small whoops and cheers from various attendees. I didn't call out. But I did finally allow myself a smile.

"So, in showing my confidence in each of your abilities to continue dominating your fellow classmates," Forshay paused while some chuckles came forth, "I have invited you to my quarters for a little down time. A little soiree of success, if you will." He tapped on his data pod and the hologram disappeared and the lights came up. "Use this time to meet your counterparts and find out tips of the trade, or to just confirm that you are the best of the best. As some of you know, each semester top final rank of each academia is honored in a combined House ceremony. Consider this a precursor of what to expect. A light refreshment is now available." He pointed on the nearby wall where hor dourves were stacked by a beverage cart. "Just, please, do not spill on the furniture or carpets."

A few more titters of laughter floated through the cadets around me.

I didn't move. I didn't dare. I wasn't supposed to be here. Tori was Miss Photographic Memory. Shouldn't she be here instead of me? Or maybe someone else was also in Military Exploration and Expansion that I met, but didn't ask. It couldn't be me, could it?

"Well, well. Guess familiar smells helped you sleep after all. Now look at you," came Cecile's snide voice at my back.

I stood, gaining more composure, plastered a smile on my face and turned. "Yes. I guess it did help me settle in a bit."

"Jess!" James' came to stand next to me. "Congratulations! Good job! Closet studying at all hours really paid off, huh?"

I just shrugged and agreed.

Cecile frowned, "Didn't know you were ranked so high. What was your course of study again?" After she heard, she nodded and looked away. "Oh! Bill! Good job, hon!" And she was gone.

I heard my name and turned to see Kimberly Hess. "Oh my gosh, Kimberly! Hi!"

She wasn't really smiling though. "Congratulations."

"You too!" I tried to infect her with some of my feigned enthusiasm.

She waved her hand, "Oh stop it. Don't pretend. We haven't really spoken since that first week or so." Kimberly looked around the room. "I don't really know any of these people. I just kinda stuck to myself and my studies after..."

That piqued my interest, "After?"

"Well after they found out two people died." She covered herself and almost frowned. "I...I didn't want anything else to happen. I didn't want to think about it." But she didn't meet my eyes. "Excuse me. Must mingle and not draw attention to myself."

And she crossed over to the next cluster of cadets.

I was left wondering what had happened to staunch the bubbling personality that I wanted to hate so much.

"Reynoldi?"

Director Forshay was at my left elbow. I faced him with a soft smile. "Yes, sir?"

"Not getting something to eat?

I shook my head. "Maybe in a minute."

He smiled and turned to walk away.

"Director?" I couldn't help but call it out. "Are you sure it's correct? I'm top of the course ranking?"

For half a second, he squinted at me. "Of course. Numbers don't lie, Cadet. Enjoy it, and study so you don't slip."

After about an hour of socializing with my peers, I thanked Forshay and headed back to my quarters. Once there I pulled up my courses and past grades. Everything looked to be correct, including the one quiz where I had four wrong for misreading the instructions. I scrolled back to check my percentages. Military History was just under ninety-five percent due to the botched quiz and two lackluster assignments. Physics and Zero Gravity was sitting at a solid perfect score, with only one wrong on an assignment that was tossed out after I first arrived at IDEA. People Management was at a decent ninety-eight percent, but grading was based on instructor feedback on each cadet, I could see how perhaps I was higher than other cadets in the same course. My mathematics and finance classes were also resting in the upper nineties. So looking at all of my grades to date, it was entirely possible that I was top of my class.

I let out a whoot, whoot in the solitary confines of my room.

My data pod chimed with a notification. It was from Tori, wondering if I wanted to go to the pond for some R and R before finals. I politely turned her down, but added that a play date after finals might be more rewarding. She sent me a few more lines about needing to live a little.

Forshay's voice echoed in my head. "Academic Elite… Recruiting rank…Extra tuition break."

"Thanks anyway, Tori," I said as I typed back. "Going to sit this one out, too. Really need to study."

She gave up and told me she'd enjoy all the attending male escorts by herself then.

If she was trying to make me jealous, it almost worked.

Extra tuition break.

My dad would kill me if I didn't save the family the extra five thousand keel per semester.

The keel was the modern equivalent to the old dollars or lire or euros from over two hundred years ago. The idea that governments formed one united currency seventy years ago to save dozens of countries from bankruptcy and financial ruin at the mercy of others had taken up a couple of lectures in my finance class. Amazing that religion and money caused countries to spend what they didn't have to fight for what wasn't theirs.

And five thousand keel times every semester potentially would be five years' worth of my father's salary, not including interest. My grandfather had given me the initial deposit of forty keel from his savings after Grandma died, saying the money was going to a good cause. It was a combination of graduation, many future missed birthdays and Christmas presents, and IDEA graduation all rolled up in one. He only hoped that he would live long enough to see me graduate.

Extra tuition break.

That was something I could deeply appreciate. A dip in the pond tonight? Not so much.

My data pod chimed again, breaking my thoughts. But I didn't want to be bothered by Tori's taunts any more. I shook my head and set my device down on my bed as I got ready to run my few laps and then get my fifteen minutes in the UV room this week.

No one else was running that late, nor in the UV room, so I allowed myself an extra five minutes in each. I figured it had to help me feel good before exams, right?

When I got back to my room, the light indicating a message was still flashing. Muttering to myself about making Tori wait, I decided to take a shower.

All five minutes of my bathing I wondered who was at the pond: Ben, or James, or Ian, or all three. I started wondering what it would be like to not have to worry about the money like Tori. Quick showers make even faster conversations with yourself.

Going to my bed, I snatched up my blinking data pod. I was determined to sass off and tell her tomorrow was off too. Instead, a beautiful drawing of a butterfly among blossoms greeted my eyes. A message was attached. "Will told me. Congrats, plebe. Study hard."

No name.

But I knew.

I smiled, then looked back at the picture. I ran my fingers over the colorful image. Thinking it was a trick, or graphic art being used, I enlarged the butterfly. I could see the strokes and soft sublines before the more prominent lines were laid down, especially around the proboscis. I had to know, so I said as I typed. "Did you make this?"

The answer came back in an instant. "Yes."

Who knew Ben could draw?

And he had been waiting for a response for about fifty minutes.

Log-in: JessReynoldi18851
Date/Time: 24 Dec 2201/2011hrs
Subject: First Christmas Eve on IDEA

I'm missing my family for Christmas. I wish I could hear the timber Grandpa's voice as he sings Silent Night and changes the words like his grandfather had done. I wish for a meal of everyone reaching for their food at the same time at my aunt's place. I miss the smells filling the air as the meal is prepared, then demolished. I miss their faces. I long for a hug. I want to hear everyone's voices and stories since I have been gone. I wish I could share with them all that I have accomplished. All that I have learned so far.

I know a missive was already prepared, and with it a recent picture of me in my class As. Top of Class, Semester 1A, Cadet Jessica Reynoldi! Hoo-rah! 5 keel credit! Dad, I hope I made you proud. Tori and Kim did my makeup and hair for the photos, Mom. I think it makes me look different. Definitely proud, but I also believe more mature.

I miss you. Love you all.

Now to have some holiday cheer, or to try and find some.

MERRY CHRISTMAS!

ENTRY END

I had mentioned to Tori how I saw Kimberly Hess, and how her distant behavior affected me. Now it felt like Kim and Tori are best buds. And apparently they both loved to sing, so at the table dinner you could hear the two of them singing softly. At the end of the meal, when others started louder caroling, they did too.

Again, I felt like the outcast, but I smiled at their merriment.

Tori winked at me and asked if I was having a good time. Seems Tori is all about a good time and making sure she's important to everybody.

When she said that, I interrupted their singing long enough to ask her about her grades and she pretty much told me passing with an A is all she needed to do to make her family happy. She knew how much I had been worried about it and working so hard, so she let herself slip to a low ninety-three to ninety-five average in every class depending on what I had shared. I told her that I didn't believe her for one second, that I had earned my grades. She just laughed when I said that, and said next quarter she might not make it so easy for me. Then she was back to singing, and a male tenor complemented hers from across the Commons.

Again, I smiled despite missing Grandpa. Shoot, I missed everyone back home. I knew I needed to continue to do well or I would be answering to Tori, as well as my family.

Guess I hadn't noticed that I had been voicing my financial concerns so much during my first semester. Nor had I really paid any attention to anyone else. Well that was going to change. I had said that I was going to leave something behind for others to remember me, to note my worthiness. I haven't yet decided what that will be, but I know doing something for others is on my list.

So with Kim and Tori already on their way for Kim's induction to the pond night as her Christmas gift, I decided to surprise Ben. I hadn't really seen him since the Pollination Room night. I had seen him from across the Commons a couple of times. James asked me if I was looking for someone, and I actually blushed. Ellie burst out laughing which disrupted those who were still singing.

But this was Christmas Eve. And I wanted to ask Ben why he kept shutting down. I wanted to know what he was thinking. I wanted to ask if that was the same cadet as he had been asking about all those months ago was the same one they announced as missing a few months ago. I remember some questions about IDEA that I didn't ask. I wanted to ask him questions about the track where the woman's skull had been found.

Who was I kidding? I just wanted to see Genius. I wanted to wish him Merry Christmas, or offend him by assuming he was a Christian by doing so. I wanted to share stories like we did in the Pollination Room. I wanted to see if he would try to hold my hand again or not.

So, when everyone was busy sneaking off for the pond or for mistletoe, I went to my room to freshen up, as Tori would call it. When I felt like I was both physically and mentally ready, I sent Ben a message.

And I waited.

And waited.

He waited almost an hour for me. I could wait too.

Two hours later I still hadn't heard from him. I wondered if Ben was in his secret hideaway of flowers, bees, and butterflies. I decided to try and find it on my own. I brought my data pod in case he sent me a message while I was en route.

After negotiating IDEA to the halls and the right stairs, I went up. I went along some more passageways until I found another flight of stairs. All of it seemed to look right, but being I was in a place that was basically a replication of another section, over and over again, I wasn't sure. So I decided to pull up the schematics of IDEA on my device to be sure of where I was, and where I was thinking I was going.

A muffled blood curdling bellow and scream came from the side hallway I had just passed.

My heart stopped. I was afraid to blink. The image of the bloody body floating by my portal replayed again. I swallowed against the fear.

A plea and another siffled scream.

Am I a chicken?

I lowered my data pod and started heading in that direction, one tentative step at a time, looking all around me as I went. I made my steps fall soft, ready to run at the first sign of a door opening.

Another plea, and again. A scream. Followed by laughter.

I froze.

Was it a movie room?

I took another step towards the direction of the pleas. And another. The lone door on my right seemed the likely one to check. With a timid hand, I slowly tried the handle. It didn't move. It was locked. I placed my ear to the door.

"Oh please! No." It was hushed, but it was definitely from the other side of the door.

I stepped back, trying to figure out what I should do. A glance down both halls showed no one to help me. Seeing no call button, I went to knock on the door and looked down. I paused just before I rapped.

Blood. I knelt down to be sure. Still wet and shiny. I stood up and looked at the door in horror.

A million thoughts went through my head. Was someone injured? Was this an exercise for a class? Or was someone being tortured?

I glanced down at the red splotches. Taking out my data pod I took a picture. Then I pressed my ear to the door again, but could only make out muffled sounds.

I listened for about two minutes while I warred with myself about what would happen if someone opened the door. What if I was just blowing this out of proportion? What if it was one person versus a bunch of people? What if my worst imaginings were really happening on the other side of the door? What if I became next if I did knock? I panicked and backed away.

When I did, I noticed that I had stepped in some other spots of blood that I hadn't noticed earlier, and I was tracking. Quickly I took off my shoes and hustled back the way I had come, down the halls, shoes in hand. I made it all the way to the main level and I all but ran into the nearest latrine and secured the stall. I turned my shoes over in my hand and saw blood was indeed on the bottom. I quickly rested the underside barely in the water of the toilet and watched the water bleed red into pink. Grabbing some toilet paper I blotted the remaining moisture and tossed the evidence into the bowl. I looked at the proof of what I had just witnessed, and flushed.

After the fresh clear water settled, I sat on the seat, shoes in hand. Dazed, I took out my data pod and looked at the picture of the blood spots. Then the realization of what I just did made me sick.

I ran. I was a coward. I erased the evidence. Literally, I had just flushed it down the toilet. I was a horrible human being. I needed to try and fix this. But how? I brought my hand to my face. I didn't want to face another series of interrogations. Not again.

I sent a quick message to Ben. He'd know what to do. My data pod chimed in my lap. It was Ben. His message said that he was busy and would catch me later.

My erratic mind raced still in its panic mode. Ben? Busy? Had Ben been in that room? Was he one of the spectators? Or was he the one being tortured? Was someone using his device like they had the other cadet's?

"Are you avoiding me or something?" Again, I found I spoke while I typed it out, and then hit send.

"No. Just busy."

I waited, all the while I thought about all the things Ben could be doing right then. Dying was one of them. "You okay?"

"Yes, Jessica. I'm fine."

My heart stopped. Ben never called me Jessica. He had

never used my name. He always had called me "plebe." In fact, no one here called me Jessica. But my messages would show that they are from a Jessica Reynoldi. I swallowed the growing lump in my throat and typed out silently, "Oh. Okay. Just wanted to wish you a Merry Christmas. Night."

I didn't want just anyone to hear that I thought something was fishy. I wanted someone else to check on it. I wanted someone else to prove me wrong, and show me everything was just fine.

But I needed to report my concern about that room in Bradley House. I wondered who I could go to. Tori might be done at the pond, so I sent her a quick message.

Her response was only a few minutes behind, but they seemed to take forever. "Hey, Jess! You missed a fun time. Small group. Most of the guys from Bradley House weren't there, but James gave us all a kiss under Missy's toe saying it was close enough to mistletoe."

I smiled at the image before I asked if we could get together.

"Uhm, not a good idea. That maintenance guy, Phil, and his counterpart are definitely prowling tonight. Catch me tomorrow? Oh, and Merry Christmas!"

I agreed to and told her to have a good night. When I knew she wasn't going to respond, I tried James. But I received nothing in turn. So, like we were taught when we first arrived, I brought out the chain of command tree and messaged the person above James. Getting no immediate response, I decided not to go above the two of them, and waited.

Then I remember what Director Forshay had said about under an emergency how to alarm the whole station. I didn't want to do that, but maybe a quick message to Director Bradley would work. I kept it short saying that while strolling I had heard something very concerning and found some blood on the floor and that maybe someone would want to check it out. Then I sent it.

When I looked back at the message I sent, I realized it didn't really sound calm at all. It wouldn't appear to be coming from some cool, calm, and concerned cadet at all. It was a rambling mess at best. So, I tried again. I apologized for the lateness in the hour, as well as the previous message. In the missive I told him that I had gone to the Bradley House looking for some classmates (not entirely a falsehood), and heard some crying and screaming, and found some blood on the floor. I told him that I didn't know if it was a movie night, part of a lab, or if someone had had an accident, but I felt compelled to report it. I told him that I didn't know what else to do or who to report a concern to. Then I hit send.

I hung my head and exited my stall. I slipped on my now clean shoes and looked at my reflection in the mirror above the sink. I washed my hands and checked my reflection again. And very casually I headed back to my room.

When I was safely in my room and my comfy wear, I sat on my bed and checked my device for messages. Then I watched Earth pass by twelve times. Before the thirteenth cycle, I closed the shield on my portal. I sat wondering if I should anticipate a reply, and not quite sure I could to sleep.

After about ten minutes, the call button to my quarters sounded.

I didn't know who to expect, but it definitely wasn't Director Forshay at my quarters. He looked like he hadn't even changed yet, or maybe it was a clean uniform he wore, or maybe he always wore the same thing in case of emergency. "You messaged Director Bradley. Where did you find this blood, Reynoldi?"

My jaw dropped while I blinked at his form in my doorway. "I...I..."

He scowled. "Is this a prank, cadet?"

I shook my head. "No, sir. I did find some blood in a hall when I was in Bradley House. I was hoping to catch up to some of my friends-"

"Heading to the pond?"

I frowned. "What? The solarium? No." I mentally applauded my quick wit. "I said I was in Bradley House. I was up two levels from this one and walking down a long hallway I thought I had been in before with a classmate." I looked him square in the eye and said firmly. "I heard what sounded like a scream, and...when I got to the door, it was locked. I panicked when I realized I was standing in blood." I dropped my look, my voice dropping as my gaze did. "I was afraid in case it was something bad, someone doing bad things. I didn't want to...fall victim myself."

Forshay squinted his eyes. "Show me."

Log-in: JessReynoldi18851
Date/Time: 25 Dec 2201/0056hrs
Subject: Worst start to Christmas EVER

Why? Why did I open my mouth? Why did I try to make things right? Heck, why did I go try and find Ben when he clearly didn't want to respond to my messages.

At least I didn't blow the cover of the pond

Worst freaking start to Christmas Day that I can ever recall.

I want a DO OVER button.

ENTRY END

So, in just my comfy pajama-wear, I had to go with Director Forshay across the Commons. I kept my gaze down as we walked in silence. For some reason, I felt like the naughty child about to be disciplined. I didn't like that at all.

Director Bradley met us at the edge of the Commons, but he was in more casual attire than my house director. His clothing may have said "comfy" but his cold look said, "Don't touch me." As we approached he offered a stiff, "Evening."

Both directors started talking between themselves. Forshay said I was looking for friends, but not going to the solarium. Bradley said he had sent for Phil, then gave me a raised eyebrow. We only had to wait a few uncomfortable seconds before I saw Phil shuffle into sight.

Phil looked like he usually did when I saw him, bland. He walked over to me, one hand out, the other with his data reader. "Chip card, cadet."

I made a face. "I beg your pardon?"

His fingers moved. "Chip card. It's going to show us where you've been."

I handed over my card and watched him wave it over his device and released a calming breath.

An instant later a detailed listing of entries and meals

appeared. Phil hit a couple of buttons and moved his finger across the screen. "Yep. She was on Level 3E Bradley House about 2048 hours until a quick restroom pit stop on the same floor about 2104 hours. Then she went directly to her quarters. No other deviation from her quarters to or from her room." He looked at me. "What room were you trying to go to, Cadet Reynoldi?"

"Where were you going on this side of IDEA, cadet?" Director Bradley asked over the top of Phil's, trumping for control.

"I was hoping to run into Cadet Ben Williams. I haven't seen a lot of him lately and I wanted to wish him a Merry Christmas," I said softly. "He had taken me for a walk down that hall before. At least I think it was that hall."

Director Bradley took Phil's data pod. "Phil, didn't you put Cadet Reynoldi on watch for a door activation and possible curfew violation?"

Hearing that, my head jerked. "What? When? Why?"

Phil paid me no mind, but pointed to notes on his device for Director Bradley. "Cadet stated she was doing some integrity and hull breach reading and was checking how the doors sealed off. I found no other evidence of tampering in the few rounds I have made."

Bradley nodded and asked if Phil had actually checked my door for tampering.

Phil indicated that he had indeed checked my door on four separate occassions.

I raised my hand and got everyone's attention. "I'm sorry. What's going on? I reported blood and potential screaming. Why are we discussing my door?" I lowered my hand.

Bradley's eyes narrowed. "We're verifying your character and accountability, cadet. Especially since you didn't report a body drifting by your window in a timely fashion."

Wow.

I lifted my hand again. "I reported my concern this time, sir."
I stood taller, daring him to mock me.

He raised an eyebrow and checked the data in front of him.
"So, at approximately 2100 hours you heard something, found
blood, and are got around to reporting it at," he checked the
current time, "about 2115 hours." He looked at me while he gave
the data pod back to Phil. "Why didn't you report it when and
where you found it?"

I wasn't sure if it was a real question or if he was attacking
me. "I was trying to figure out what to do." I glanced between
the three men. "I don't know Bradley House very well to be
honest. I didn't know if I was hearing a movie, or if someone was
in a lab. Then when I was listening at the door, I realized that
there was blood. I freaked out." Seeing their faces remain blank I
added, "I tried to ask for advice, but the cadets I tried to contact
didn't really want to talk. I tried James, Cadet Bennett, and then
the cadet above him. I didn't receive a response from either of
them. I waited before I contacted Director Bradley."

Forshay made a face. Then he asked if I had told James and
whatever-his-name-was what I found and suspected.

I told them that I had not. But I told the three of them that I
tried to get ahold of Ben and that I thought someone else had his
device. When Forshay asked me why I felt that way, I told them
that Ben used my full first name, and that no one did that here. I
also said that Ben had never called me anything but "plebe."

Director Bradley said that Ben was supposed to be mentoring
tonight. He indicated we should all follow him to assess whether
Ben was doing what he was assigned to, where he was supposed
to. "He's to be there until 0100 hours when Cadet Karen Jamison
relieves him."

We walked down the hall to the stairs I had gone up before.

"Aren't we going to see if someone needs help first?" I pointed to the stairs. "I went up these. Maybe there's some blood so you know I'm not making this up."

Bradley made another face and consented to check out my concern. He led the way up and at the top of the second flight of stairs, he asked Phil which way to turn.

While Phil tried to bring back the information from scanning my chip card, I motioned to the direction, and Bradley waved me ahead. We passed the latrine that I had used in the removal of evidence from my shoes. And as I got closer to the hall, I slowed down. The floor had been recently mopped and was still damp in spots.

I stopped as the realization of the wet floor hit me. "Someone cleaned it all up."

Bradley turned to Phil. "When is maintenance done on this level?"

Phil checked with his device. "Due for cyclic cleaning at 0300 hours." He scowled. "This isn't right. Someone must have accessed the custodial supplies closet." A few more taps and finger swipes. "None here. But a closet on Forshay's side was accessed twice. No card access. Just the door is opened. Once about an hour and a half ago. The other about twenty minutes ago."

"What? Where?" Forshay peered at the device. "That's near Reynoldi's room. I didn't see anyone when I passed to collect her."

Bradley walked ahead of us and indicated a hall. When he pointed, I nodded. Then at the door I had stood at before, he asked, "Cadet, was this the door where you heard the sounds?"

At my nod, he checked the door. It opened freely, so he went inside.

The automatic lights spilled into the hallway all but calling me to investigate.

So I did.

Everything had a strong aroma of cleanser, as if someone didn't want any lingering scents to draw attention. The counter top surfaces were still slightly moist. Even some of the walls had been washed down. I went to the trash can to check, and yep, the bag was new.

I was right. Something had been wrong.

And I had been a coward.

I could hear the directors trying to determine a course of action. A drill to have all cadets accounted for was thought to be the best option. That led Bradley into wanting to check to see if Ben was where he was supposed to be. And I was to follow. I didn't have it in me to do anything but. Numbness surrounded me, and I wasn't really focusing on what was happening.

Lights out. Door closed. Procession down the hallway to the stairwell. Down three flights of steps and down more halls. A door stood ajar with light pooling into the corridor. Bradley marched right in. Phil stood at the door. I peeked past him with Forshay standing behind me.

There sat Ben with his back to the door. Beside him there were three cadets each on their data devices. A hologram of a remote civilian outpost floated above all of them. It was clear that the holographic image was what they were working on. "So, that is how the condensers pull and siphon at this location where there were no other options," Ben's voice echoed in the small room.

"Cadet Williams?" Bradley said with some authority causing everyone to startle. "How goes mentoring?"

"Long, sir. But I think they have their questions answered." Then Ben saw the rest of us in the doorway. His face pinched and his eyes shifted, especially when he saw me.

"Good. Cadets," he addressed the three others, "Mentoring is suspended temporarily. We need to ask everyone some questions. Please present your chip cards."

As Phil scanned each cadets' security card, everyone was asked what time they started. Was Cadet Williams present the whole time? Did any cadets leave the room? Okay, besides to use the latrine? How long did it take? Did anyone hear anything suspicious? And then Ben was asked if he had his device on him. He brought it out of his lap and waved it. Chip cards were returned. Everyone was released, except Ben.

That earned me another funky look from Ben before he swiveled to face forward again as Director Bradley took one of the seats opposite him that one of the cadets had previously used.

"Williams, did you have your data pod all night?" Bradley began the questioning.

"Yes, Director Bradley," Ben answered.

"Did you receive a message from Cadet Reynoldi earlier this evening?" Bradley asked.

"Yes, quite a few actually." Ben didn't even look my way, but his tone was terse.

My jaw dropped, then I clamped it shut.

"Did anyone else use your data pod tonight?"

"Yes, everyone held it while I tried explaining the processes and then to verify answers when the cadets quizzed each other."

"Did you personally send Cadet Reynoldi messages this evening?"

Ben shot me a look before turning back to Bradley. "Sir, I'm not sure I understand what is going on. I told Cadet Reynoldi that I was busy. And I was. I have been here."

"I understand. Apparently Cadet Reynoldi had some concerns arise this evening and one of the messages she received from you that alarmed her."

Ben sat up rim rod straight. "I beg your pardon."

Bradley couldn't keep the crinkle out of the corner of his eyes as he said, "Apparently a message came and she thought you might be in trouble, or hurt, or that someone was using your data pod."

Ben looked at the device in his hand and tapped away at it. "I sent every one of these messages, sir. I didn't send anything indicating I was under duress. Nor did I send her anything inappropriate."

Bradley motioned for the unit and Ben handed it over. Bradley read our messages and worked his lip hard. "Okay. Thank you, Williams. Sorry to have interrupted your mentoring group. I know you like helping them."

Ben nodded but didn't turn around.

Forshay told Phil that he'd take me back to my room.

I kept waiting for Ben to turn around so I could see his reaction. I held my breath, anxious for a glimpse.

But he didn't.

Forshay led the way all the way across Commons. He paused at the custodial door that was only about thirty meters from my room. He worked his lip when he spotted a few drops of water by the door. But he didn't check the handle. He continued on. As we neared my door he told me we were going to his office to talk.

I didn't want to argue. I was processing everything. Ben was okay. He was part of a mentoring group. He was safe. But someone had been bleeding. Someone had cleaned up the blood. The whole room had been given a go-over, walls and all. Someone potentially used a janitorial closet in Forshay House to clean it all up. Why? What did it mean?

At Forshay's office I didn't even notice him open the door, my thoughts were so distracted. I recognized the small office that he had led me past only a week before. This time he offered me a seat while he sat in his large leather chair. I sat down on the seat and tried not to draw any more attention to myself by moving.

Director Forshay cleared his throat. "Let me begin this with, I appreciate your attention to detail. I also appreciate your concern for fellow cadets, especially due to the unfortunate loss of one. But do not, *ever*," and he bit out the word, "go to Director Bradley with a concern. You are my cadet. You are supposed to come to me."

I swallowed at the tone. "Yes, sir. I'm sorry, sir. I didn't want to bother you when it was in Bradley's section of IDEA. I didn't know what to do." I could feel my voice cracking and tears threatened. "I wasn't trying to disrespect you, sir."

Forshay leaned way back in his chair, looking at me.

The silence continued for about two minutes. But I didn't dare make a peep after that. No flippin' way.

Forshay pressed a button on his desk, and the faux wood cabinet doors behind his desk opened to reveal a beautiful bronze replica of IDEA suspended at an angle, unlike the perpendicular Donut in the Commons. Three small lights illuminated the small sculpture that was about two foot in diameter. It offered brilliant highlights to the encased piece. It was far more ornate and fantastic to behold that what the student had created.

"I have two thousand cadets to supervise, Cadet Reynoldi. Director Bradley has two thousand cadets, or just under, I guess now. My point is that if my cadets go to him, then his can come to me. Now we each have four thousand. And he and I are different. We work differently. You were placed in this house based on certain aptitude and personality scores. You tested into my house, if you will." He looked at me for comprehension.

"I understand, sir," I said trying to look at him and not the bronze glowing behind him like some mystic halo.

He leaned back again. "Good." He drummed his finger tips

on his desk. "Very good. Also, while we investigate what happened tonight, please don't discuss it with anyone else. We don't want stories going around. Understood?" When he saw my nod, he stood. "Glad we had this chat."

I rose as well. "Permission to return to my quarters?"

"Granted."

I hustled back to my room all the while reprimanding myself for trying to do good, and still screwing up. When I was safe inside my space, I let out a huge sigh. I saw the light on my data pod indicating a message, and hurried to snatch it up.

I smiled seeing the message was from Ben. Then I read it and stopped smiling. "What is wrong with you? I told you I was busy. What made you think I was in trouble? And then you brought both directors in to check on me? Didn't like the getting the third degree. Not even a little bit. Bye."

Seriously?

I had to reread it.

And again.

Oh my gosh! Tried to do the right thing, all the way around, and I screwed up all of it. That's it. I quit. Stick to the dang academics and forget everything and everyone else. Screw doing right. Screw the male species. And screw Christmas. Bah-freakin'-humbug!

Log-in: JessReynoldi18851
Date/Time: 25 Dec 2201/1856hrs
Subject: STILL Worst Christmas EVER

That's it! Focusing on next semester. People can just stand back and let me be. I'm not owing anyone anything. Tori is going to make it tougher? Let's just see about that!

And the next guy who corners me to talk is going to get punched. So help me!

Merry FREAKING Christmas!

There. Venting over. Lunch was tasty. It reminded me of the cuisine when we first arrived. Turkey and ham was on the menu, which was a happy surprise. Rows of pies and bars and cookies filled the line, and I put three kinds of desserts on my tray.

I kept my head down and ate while others talked around me, appreciating a day off from class. Apparently movies were going to be shown after lunch and going into the evening. It sounded like everyone was going to hang out.

Sans me.

ENTRY END

James stopped me by grabbing ahold of my arm as I was heading back to my quarters. "Hey, aren't you going to watch some old Christmas classics with us?"

I kept my head down and told him that I didn't feel like it. When he persisted, I told him that I was missing home and hoping to just call it an early night. He kept trying and it really started to irritate me.

He offered to spend some time in my quarters, so I wouldn't be alone. I thanked him, but firmly said no. "I hadn't been able to get much sleep the night before, so I would not be much good as company. I don't want to ruin anyone's evening." Then I wished him a Merry Christmas and eased by him.

When I got to my quarters, darned Ian Hanson was leaning against my door. "What happened last night?"

My mind raced a million miles a second. What did he know? Who told him? I wasn't supposed to mention anything per Director Forshay. And I wasn't going to botch that up. "I'm not sure I know what you mean." I indicated for him to move, and he only shifted a little. I gave him a loud sigh and eye roll. "Please."

"Heard you had both directors in tow following you around until almost midnight. Heard your little tea party interrupted some studying." He put an arm across my doorway in an effort to keep the conversation alive.

I blinked in response and pointed to his arm. "Please move it." When he didn't, I sighed again. "I was concerned when I thought someone had taken Ben's data pod and sent me an odd message. I sent a message to Director Bradley, who must have sent a message to Director Forshay. Now everyone is pissy and I just want to go to my room." I forced a smile. "Happy? Informed? Can I go to my room now?"

He leaned over me, and this time there were no butterflies. "What kind of message?"

I looked him in the eye. "One that made me concerned. Are we done here?"

He tilted his head. "You and Ben, huh?" He made a face while he processed the idea. "Nope. Don't like it."

"I could care less what you like."

Ian smiled. "That, by default, implies that you care what I like."

Frowning, I bit out, "Not anymore. And besides, there's no Ben and me." I tried to straighten myself up as I realized I had angled my own head. "We're just friends."

"Plebe?" Ben's voice wasn't far away.

I turned to see Ben's shifty eyes on me, assessing the situation. It was probably safe to assume by his close proximity that he had heard what I had just told Ian. "*Now* I'm plebe again?" I waved my hands in frustration. I shoved at Ian's rock-hard chest. "Oh, leave me alone."

But I needed to shove harder because Ian didn't move at all the first time. "Seriously, Ian, leave me alone."

Hanson backed up two steps, hands spread in a gesture of innocence, and with a grin as big as his ego. "Yes, ma'am."

"And you," I turned to where Ben had been. But he was gone. "Ugh!" I threw up my hands in annoyance as I faced my door and brought out my card. "Boys!"

Ian's voice purred in my right ear, "I'm a man."

I spun and shoved. "You're not helping right now." I waved my card and slipped into my quarters. I turned to make sure I was in my room alone.

All the while the door closed, Ian waved his fingertips at me like Tori did. I couldn't help but offer a little saucy smile of my own as the door slid home. I didn't know if it was because he was trying to be cute and failing, or if I was glad the door was closing. I hit the lock mechanism on the door and sagged to the floor. Once there, I exhaled loudly and rubbed my face.

Knowing there was no way to get a message from home, I

started scrolling through future assignment requirements. Then I read snippets from outdated news articles from home. Feeling no peace at all, I decided to change into my comfy clothes and go for a stroll, or maybe a jog on the track, far from the Commons and various rooms designated for different holiday films. I wanted to go someplace peaceful, or where I could vent. Right now my room wasn't that.

I hit the unlock button on my door and waved my card. Seeing no stalker outside my room, I snuck the back way to the solarium with my data pod in hand. Once there I went and pressed my free hand against the glass of the aquarium in the corner. The calm nature of the fish moving to and fro brought me an immediate sense of relaxation. I moved back and sat on the bench where I would have the best view, and watched.

I thought of the first time I saw this place. And of that day when the fish did their frenzy. And then the discovery of the skull. How had such a beautiful place become a place of doom and gloom? It didn't make any sense. A lot of things weren't making sense.

Thinking back, I thought of my initial feelings of enthusiasm and pride at being accepted here at IDEA. It was like being on some euphoric cloud after all the testing and interviews. I recalled the first time I put on the pant suit version of my uniform. How much I have grown since my arrival. I also remembered seeing the body float by, and how I dealt with that. All that came from that. And I thought about everything I now knew about IDEA.

This space station-turned-campus was designed to support life against all odds.

Somehow, I was supposed to learn from this. Maybe this was another lesson to be learned during my time here. Maybe this is what it was really like in the field for exploration and civilization start-ups. My grandma used to say that nothing happened without a reason.

I closed my eyes and let the heady scent of the nearby flora ease my anxieties. What am I here for? What am I supposed to learn?

The sound of the klaxon interrupted my meditation. When I opened my eyes, the red glow made the water in the fish tank look like blood.

"Attention, Cadets. Attention, Cadets. This is not a drill. I repeat, this is not a drill. Please return to your quarters immediately. Again. This is not a drill. Please return to your quarters immediately."

I jumped to my feet and hustled towards my room. Fear of another asteroid shower mingled with the remembrance of the directors' discussion as to how to find out what happened earlier. At that point, I didn't care which it was. I wanted to be safe and sound within my room, no matter what hit.

When the all clear was given without any thunks and bangs, I reported like every other cadet was supposed to. I silently waited in lines that spoke in confused tones about what had just happened, and whether the movies were going to continue. At my check-in, I reported no issues, and overheard cadets assuring each other that the movies would restart when the lines dissipated.

Upon completion of check-in, I headed straight to my room and prayed that whoever had lost blood earlier was recovered safely. But it made me wonder why it took them so long to do the drill.

Perhaps it was to do their own inquiries.

I hit lock on my door when I was inside. I watched Earth pass several times. Then someone checked my door. Or at least I think they did, as I heard pressure against the door.

Good ol' Phil and that pond.

I turned my view back to my portal and every time I saw it, I wished someone, no everyone, back home a Merry Christmas.

Log-in: JessReynoldi18851
Date/Time: 31 Dec 2201/2026hrs
Subject: End of the year goal...find purpose

I have done a lot of reflecting on the past five months. And what I keep hearing is: Everything happens for a reason.

I am here for a purpose. Then, that being said, I love being here, except for the scary and bizarre things that I keep coming across. And I believe that something is preparing me for a bigger obstacle in the years ahead of me. Be it here at IDEA, or if I gain placement at an outpost.

So, as this year ends, I will strive to make friends with as many as I can (and keep the ones I have), and figure out what pieces of the puzzle I have been given. I also vow to be stronger, both academically and emotionally. It shouldn't be too hard, as before here, I was the whistle blower and the strong for the weak.

It just makes me wonder what changed in me. Guess it doesn't matter, because I am coming back...with a mission.

ENTRY END

As I strolled the halls yet again, I found myself in the halls of Bradley House, pushing past the negative and trying to figure stuff out in my head. Down one of the less travelled halls, I came across James, Ian, and some of that group of guys doing their line and chant thing again. I tried to make out the low chanted words. But all I heard was something about time and someone they had to meet, and they broke apart, grins from ear to ear, patting each other on the back. I saw a new male face in their midst, and the guy seemed pretty proud to belong.

Boys sure are weird.

Trudging along through the halls I realized that deep down, I must have been feeling pretty sorry for myself before. I didn't have any confidence in my academic abilities, or in the face of potential danger. That's not who I wanted to be known, or remembered as by my peers. I wanted to leave a legacy of doing the right thing. Of displaying excellence. That is what I had said time and time again when I was interviewed for acceptance to IDEA, as well as for all the scholarships I tried to acquire to ease the financial burden.

There's never been a better time to regain control of my destiny.

"Cadet Reynoldi," I heard Director Bradley's voice call from behind me.

I turned and forced a smile. "Hello, Director."

"A moment of your time, Cadet?"

A quick nod and I followed him down the hall to a nearby room. He checked the hallway before he closed the door. He indicated for me to take a seat while he brought out his data pod and typed away. "There's an investigation brought about by your vigilance."

The smile left my face and I looked down. Part of me already knew. It had to have been something bad. I could hear each thump of my heart while I replayed that night. I couldn't think of anything to say, but felt I should say something. Without glancing up, I said, "Oh. That's not good." *That didn't come out sounding concerned or educated.* A million thoughts seemed to careen in my skull, so I shook it trying to get them out. "Maybe if I had knocked on the door, the cadet would be okay, there'd be no investigation."

A quick rap, and Phil entered with another member of the staff. Bradley's gaze took me in before he sat in a chair by me. The four of us sat in that uncomfortable silence for what I thought was an eternity. All I could hear was Director Forshay's last lecturing of my contacting Director Bradley. I felt my arm pits go wet with sweat. Despite my best efforts to remain still, I felt myself pull away, and he noticed. He flinched.

Director Bradley cleared his throat. "Cadet Reynoldi," he began, "I want to thank you for you diligence in reporting what you saw and heard. In reflection, with what you had already experienced here, and how some of us, myself included, treated you in your first series of interrogations, it is easy to comprehend why you didn't investigate by knocking on the door. Had you, we might very well be dealing with more than we currently are." He cleared his throat again. "I came to let you know that I probably didn't handle the situation well. You were looking out for your fellow cadets and friends. I looked at someone trying to break protocol. You sought answers, and found ridicule." He paused and tried to hold my gaze, but I broke it. "Cadet Reynoldi, I apologize. I understand that my brusque interrogation had interrupted a friendship with Cadet Williams..."

I sliced a look at him before I focused on the table before me, "His loss."

He continued as if I hadn't interrupted. "I had interviewed all the cadets Williams was mentoring a second time the morning after the reported incident. Turns out one male cadet did type a message to you, and deleted it on Ben's side, before giving the device back to Williams. The same cadet had to explain that to Williams, who didn't keep his normal calm, to put it lightly."

The words all just ran down my back like water off a duck's feathers. They were just words, sounds echoing off the walls. "So who is missing?" I asked.

Director Bradley pursed his lips. "No one said anyone is missing," his gaze found mine. "Apparently another of my male cadets, but not Cadet Williams, obviously, had not reported to the drill roll call. The investigation is still ongoing, but I thought you should know you may have been correct to be alarmed. And for that I am sorry."

I shook my head. "So, why tell me? Why now?" I wasn't able to keep the snippy tone out of my voice. I sensed the heads turning in the room, so I looked between the people.

The staff member identified himself as John, and a part of the Hatchery and Incubation section of IDEA. "It was thought by the directors, that with your careful eye and recent academic success, perhaps you would like to have Hatchery Room as part of your duties."

It was a privilege and resume builder to be selected for a chore, if you will. Only about fifty cadets an academic cycle were permitted to work in what were termed as real-world capacities on IDEA. The idea of baby birds and the "peep, peep, peep" made me smile despite myself. But I didn't want to be locked in if I didn't like it. I told John that, and he assured me that it could be on a trial basis. When I asked when I would have to start, I was told I could be given an orientation immediately, as I was done with classes for the day. I acknowledged that I didn't have any plans, so I would be happy to check out what assisting in the section would entail.

Both Director Bradley and John looked at Phil, who asked for my chip card. He swiped it, and hits some keys on his device and handed it back. "Access granted until you don't want to, or they don't want you." He kind of laughed at his wit.

Then the realization that I hadn't included Director Forshay in this made me ask how he would feel about it. Director Bradley assures me that everyone was in agreement. I just took back my card and nodded.

John indicated the door and smiled broadly, "Shall we?"

I walked with John as he talked about the Hatchery section being a separate area from Incubation. He said that I would be welcome to aid in the transfer of poultry chicks from one area to the other, following safety and hygiene protocols. He led the way to the maintenance doors I remember seeing when James first gave us a tour. John waved his card and pushed, and the door opened. We went down a few halls past the rows of huge cages where the chickens could roam. I kept looking over at the multiple tiered cages that housed dozens of hens. I didn't see any roosters like I remember from books or studies on agriculture while back on Earth.

When I asked John about it, he said that the roosters weren't put with these hens. The hens where I indicated were for egg laying purposes, and a rooster for fertilization wasn't necessary. He did tell me that there were many other racks of caged hens and roosters together for cycling of livestock, especially for the meat birds. I hadn't known there was a difference before, but John said it was imperative to know the differences, especially for someone like me, who might go to a remote civilization outpost. Apparently a lot of people messed it up and were trying to get meat birds to lay more eggs and were eating what they thought were sickly birds. "Egg layers don't need as much meat on their bones, and lay for anywhere from six to nine years, tops. Meat birds are bred to put on as much muscle as they can in a short timeframe, and should be harvested every few months, or they break bones from their own body weight."

Already I found a way to make my real-world assignment after IDEA more productive. It made me smile, and that sense of purpose feeling swelled within me.

"How many meat birds does IDEA have?" I asked John.

John tilted his head side to side while he thought of an answer. "Well, they are on the back side, on the inner-most section of the Coop. There are about five thousand egg laying hens. All rooster eventually end up meat birds, but most eggs can be heated, or so they predict, to make more females versus males. As for true meat birds, there are about twelve thousand butchered every month on IDEA, except for December with the seven hundred turkeys raised for the holiday dinners. The young chicks are brought up when you arrived and ready just in time for the meal. They eat a lot more and are harder to maintain as they are a foraging bird. They like to roam around, and sometimes the hens can be as aggressive as toms. Makes for bad fights if they get too old and big. We tried doing frozen turkeys or hams, but the freezer burn taste was horrible. Besides, it gives cadets like you an opportunity to learn hands-on."

Again I nodded as we trod along. We came to another door and John presented his card again before the door opened. Inside were contamination suits that hung on hangers along one wall. John indicated that I was to put one on. He did the same. Then he gave me a pair of slip-on covers for my boots and a cap to hold my hair. I put it all on, and John checked me over to make sure I did everything right. He pointed out that this was the only way into the Hatchery and Incubation area. We went through another door and John showed me how to wash and sanitize my hands. Then through another door.

As soon as the door cracked the heat from the incubators made me blink in surprise. John showed me how in this section, about four hundred eggs on rotating beds, that were layered floor to ceiling, which slowly turned the eggs and kept them warm. Then we went to a section were chicks were struggling to free themselves from their shells. In next section I saw new chicks standing on their own toes as they staggered around, making the sound I had only heard about. I couldn't hold back my grin.

John turned to me. "Show time." With that he grabbed a big tray with three inch edges, and a long strap, and handed it to me. He took another and demonstrated how to wear the strap around my neck to free my hands to grab chicks. He reached right in and started gently lifting two or three chicks in each hand and placing them on the tray.

I tried to copy him, but only mastered one chick in each hand at a go. The soft little bodies didn't even have all their feathers, with bald spots especially on their abdomens. I was afraid I was going to squeeze them too much, but John was just busy quietly catching chicks and gently setting them in his tray, that I tried to move with more confidence.

After his tray was full, and mine wasn't even close, John indicated for me to follow. We passed through another room that was almost deafening with all the peep, peep, peeping. John led me to a twenty foot square cage with foot high walls, and five heat lamps, a long automated feeder tray and three automatic waterers. With practiced precision he placed the new chicks in their new home and helped me do the same. It was how he did it that intrigued me. He took every chick and put its beak in the feed and the water before he moved on to the next. When I asked what he was doing, he said he was training them, like a hen would, by showing them where to find food and water, and how to get it.

John also taught me how to code the cages for date of hatching so the system could cycle food and water and eventual transfer to other pens. It was interesting how much of IDEA was automated for this, and what wasn't.

All in all, I spent about three hours learning my task. But it hadn't seemed like that much time had passed. Thinking back on it, was this a distraction? And if so, for me? Or Bradley? And why wasn't Forshay involved today?

Though the thoughts ricocheted in my head, I remembered my chore test taken a few months earlier. And that I had first been excited to hear the peep, peep. But now, I was more looking forward to sleep, sleep.

Log-in: JessReynoldi18851
Date/Time: 13 Jan 2202/1847hrs
Subject: Match

I have steered clear of others while perfecting my chick chore, as Bryce calls it. The name has grown on me, so I will allow it (as if I have any other choice).

I have worked on my fitness as a way to work through my bad days. The track isn't my foe, but I definitely prefer running it alone.

I was sent a few messages about this chess match. Part of me didn't want to go. Part of me didn't want to see Ben. I understand what he saw and guessed when he had come across Ian at my door a few weeks back, that he wanted to talk to me about what had happened, and apparently what Director Bradley had shared with me. I just didn't want to deal with it. I felt like he didn't know me at all, nor I him.

And I have school to focus on. Besides, I have seen like, what five of them now? Wall-ball seems like more fun (especially when Tori drags you along for her eye-candy buffet) versus watching someone move a chess piece. That was mean. I just don't want to go. Enough said.

ENTRY END

I sat my tray on the table with a ready smile on my face, and data pod in my hand. Today was casual night, so I could have dinner with some of my friends. Bryce, Ellie, Adams, and Ian sat across from Tori, Kimberly, and myself.

"There she is! Miss Chick Master herself," Bryce said loud enough to draw notice from almost everyone in the Commons, and a scowl from me. "And how is the chick chore?"

Ellie slugged him playfully. "Stop." Then she turned to me. "And how is the cripple one?"

I brought out my data pod and showed the group a picture of a chick with a twisted leg. At the females cooing, I added, "John said it's an egg layer so it may have a chance. I have to wait a few more days to see if it's a female." I turned the image towards me. "If it is, I'm calling her Hope."

"Shouldn't give your food names," Ian said as he sipped his juice.

Adams chuckled and Ellie elbowed him.

"I like it when it snuggles against my neck," I said as I showed her a picture John took of the little peep in such a position.

Ian shook his head, "Playing with your food."

"Egg layers don't make the food chain here until they're older, Ian. I won't even be here for that. Heck," I added as I set my device down to eat the spaghetti before me, "if I get sponsored right away, maybe John will let me take it to my first assignment."

The guys chuckled while the gals all thought that would be very cool.

The banter continued as the focus of attention went from cadet to cadet. Ellie and Bryce talked about some cool communication and intelligence stuff in their lingo. Adams piped up about something he was working on. When it got to Bryce, it somehow landed back on me with this comment, "Sure, the match is still on. He might stop moping if someone came tonight though."

Being not up for the challenge, pretended not to hear.

Ellie clicked her tongue. "Is he still not talking?"

Still pretending not to be listening.

"He didn't even want to play," Bryce said as he threw me a look.

Still not taking the bait.

Ellie and Tori shared concerned looks, but Kim is the one who asked, "Why not? I thought he loved chess."

James took that moment to interrupt our lively chat when he stood behind me. "Bryce, still on for tonight?"

Bryce nodded and cast me a look before looking around the room. "Ask him. Last I hear we were starting at 1900."

I thought my spaghetti wasn't turned enough, and focused my attention there.

"Awesome! I heard rumors that he didn't want to play?" James threw it out there like we all should know what was going on in Cadet Ben Williams' mind.

Ian chuckled. "He walked in on Jess and I having a conversation a while back. Guess he didn't like what he heard."

My look went straight to Ian's. Was he right? Was that what this was all about? "Our conversation? Which one was that? The one where I told you to bugger off?"

Everyone chuckled or snickered except Ian. He lifted his eye brows while he looked back at me. Then his cocky smile returned. "Yeah. The one where you said there was no Ben and you."

Tori sucked in her breath. "Jess, you didn't!"

James whistled low behind me. "Wow. Ouch, Jess. What did Ben do to deserve that?"

I calmly set my eating utensils down, very slow and deliberate like. My gaze went to Ian's, and his eyebrows raised again. "Someone tried to get a little close and wasn't taking 'No' for an answer. Then this same said guy says he doesn't like the idea of Ben and me. I didn't know that Ben was right there." Somehow, all of that was said very calm, and very quiet, and no one interrupted.

Everyone looked at Ian, so I was out of the spotlight. While they drilled the man who was loving the attention, I peek to where Ben usually sat. He wasn't there, again. Which meant I was back to focusing on my spaghetti.

After a bit Bryce asked if I was going to come the match, again.

Tori grabbed my elbow in a rough way. "She wouldn't miss it."

I rolled my eyes. "Oh yes, she would."

Tori gave me a very determined look. "Five keel says she wouldn't miss it."

Dang it! I bit my lip before I said something I would regret.

"Oooh!" Adams cooed. "Which side to root for? Team Tori? She's a vicious competitor. Or Team Jess, who broke a man with one sentence." He sucked in his breath. "Dang. Tough one."

I sighed loudly, hoping to end the conversation. When the barbs were still hitting where it was raw, I smiled and collected my tray and stood. "Have fun. I have some studying to do...five keel's worth."

Tori smirked and said, "I'll be by to get you by quarter 'til!"

"Don't waste your time," I hissed under my breath.

What was with my so-called friends anyway? I understood that they didn't know everything that I knew, but seriously? Tori was all but telling them I would be there or I wouldn't get the five keel next semester on my own. I needed to prove her wrong. She may have a photographic memory, but I had attention to detail, determination, and willpower. And those things better count for something, dang it.

Before I left the Commons, I did one last scan of the room. I saw Ben sitting next to a female cadet, and I felt surprise, hostility, and loss all at one. As if he sensed me watching him, he chose that moment to look right at me. Bitter, I turned and walked down the hall towards my quarters.

Once there, I threw my data pod on my bed and leaned against the wall of my room. How had my day gone from a chick loving on me to my friends are dissing me in a matter of about thirty minutes?

I growled in frustration and stripped out of my class As. I took my hair out of the hair clips I had used knowing I was going to be going to the Hatchery before dinner. With a heavy sigh I looked at my reflection. My hair fell in curly waves about my shoulders as I really looked at how everything about me had changed.

Shoot. I remember my first time in my uniform thinking how awesome it was, to now, where I couldn't wait to shower, change into some comfy casuals, and maybe read. How different my life and my views of IDEA have become.

After a quick shower, I toweled off. A glance at the time showed that it was about quarter to seven. I didn't expect Tori to swing by, and yet I did. Fearing and preparing for the worst, I put on my better comfy clothes over my swim suit. I was prepared to use the excuse that I was planning on getting some UV time so I couldn't make it. And I didn't want to be in my room if someone came to collect me.

Then the time was ten minutes to the hour.

Then five.

All gussied up in my lounge wear, and with no place to really go, I grabbed my key card and headed towards my bed to retrieve my device. It had slid under my pillow, but I managed to find it. I didn't bother to check my data pod until I got to the UV room so I would be able to study there. I knew I would pretty much have the room to myself with the both a gymnastics meet and the chess match going on.

Once there I took off my layers and laid on a chaise lounge farthest from the windows and the door. I put my ear buds in and selected my music for the next few minutes. I balled up my sweatshirt and used it as a neck roll and closed my eyes.

The sound of the door opening was accompanied by Bryce's loud, "There you are!"

I quickly scrambled to cover myself as I blinked against the light. I cowered just a second when he stood over me, the look in his face was pure upset.

"He threw the match. He threw the match because you weren't there!" The accusation in Bryce's voice definitely echoed his words. "Now pull yourself out of your little pity party and come with me, or I will tell Ian where to find you." And with his parting threat, Bryce was already striding to the door.

I checked the time. I had been in the room only ten minutes.

"Now, Jess. Or do I get Ian?" Bryce had his data pod out and was typing away.

I scrambled to pull my clothes over my modest swim suit and grabbed my chip card and data pod. "I wasn't having a pity party, Bryce." I flipped my hair over my shoulder as I followed him to the door.

But the look on his face wasn't a happy one. "You didn't respond to any of us."

I frowned, trying to catch his meaning. "Huh?"

"We sent you messages. Lots of messages. And you didn't respond."

I looked at my data pod. It was on mute, and message light was definitely blinking away. "Oh, crap. Sorry." I took it out of mute and gasped. "I'm sorry. I had to put my device on mute in the Hatchery. I forgot to turn the sound back on."

Bryce did a face palm. "Seriously?"

I assured him it was an honest mistake. I walked beside him so he wouldn't tell Ian I was in my swim suit, while I checked messages. "So, what's the big deal?"

Bryce faced me as he led me closer to the Commons. "Tori lost her five keel."

"No. She just meant that she would make it tougher for me to make top in our academic courses, because she knows what five keel means to me and my family. I really was going to study." I come across two messages from Tori, and showed him, "See?"

He read as he strode down the hall to the Commons. "Whatever. I told him he couldn't throw a match. He said it didn't matter anyway."

"Do they?" I blinked at the look Bryce shot me. "I mean, do they really matter? Aren't the matches just for fun?"

Bryce exhaled, a quick irritated sound, "It's only fun if everyone is playing." His sing-song tone indicated he didn't thing I was funny. "Two moves. I should have seen it coming. Two moves."

Was it true? Had Ben really thrown the game? And because of me?

The sounds of the Commons greeted my ears and brought me up short. "Is everyone still in there?"

Bryce nodded.

"I'm not going in there." I felt like I needed to dig my heels in. Grab the walls on either side of me and brace myself.

He cocked his head. "Why?"

"Uh, how about because everyone will see me come in, for starters. I look like crap for seconds." I was trying to come up with another reason, but Bryce gave me a solid look over, so I waved my hands to emphasize my point. "See?"

He shook his head. "Jess, you do not look like crap."

There she is!" I heard Tori's outraged call way before I

spotted her huffing her way towards us. "What is the matter with you? You cost me five keel!"

I blinked. "What are you talking about? Tuition credit?"

Tori stopped and looked thunder struck. "Oh m'gad. You were thinking that was the five keel?" At my nod, she made a face I have never seen Tori make before. "I was placing a bet that my girl was going to be there. I didn't actually think that I would have to collect you. I sent you messages about going to regret it. Didn't you read them?"

Bryce shook his head. "She just got them."

Tori spun on her heel and headed back to the Commons, muttering as she went.

"You found her," came Ian's sultry voice from behind us.

I dropped my shoulders and turned to face him. "I wasn't hiding. I was in the UV room."

"I told you I could check there," Ian admonished Bryce.

Bryce scowled, "We wanted her to get to the Commons, Ian."

I pushed by the guys and braced myself to walk into who-knew-what in the Commons. As soon as I entered, I saw the hologram above the table and I verified what Bryce told me. It had been two moves. Ben let himself lose. But why?

The room started to fall into a hush when people saw me. Talk about uncomfortable. A few parted until I had a better view of the center of the Commons, and the lone person at the table. I looked at the projected image of the board and I saw Ben, just sitting there, not really seeing. Whispers kept circulating through the room, and I knew the chatter was about me.

I glanced back up at the screen and saw Ben, poor Ben, just staring at the board, his data pod on his lap like normal when he was busy or thinking.

An idea hit me. I brought out my data pod and started whispering as I typed. "Can't take back that move." I hit send and looked up at the screen and the lone figure at the chess board. I turned when I felt someone at my elbow and acknowledged Bryce and Ian.

Ben slowly glanced at his lap and brought out his device.

My device ting-ed, no longer in silent mode. "Yours or mine?"

I worked my lip while I thought about how to best answer him. "Both," I said as I typed.

"I'm going up there," Bryce said. He started his way through the throng of people.

My device chimed again. "Ian?"

My brow creased. "What about Ian?"

"Me?" Ian tried to peer over my shoulder to read my message.

Crap. I forgot I talk when I type. "Ssh! He just said your name. Nothing else."

"We're over here!" Ian called and waved one arm, while he tried to put the other one around me.

"Stop it!" I gave Ian a firm shove that got him nowhere. "Stop."

For a second I didn't know how to take the look on Ian's face. There were a multitude of emotions that went from surprise to anger to hurt to shock, then blank. It was the blank stare that made me hold my breath while I kept my free hand in front of me. It scared me.

My device chimed and I took a couple steps back before I read the message. It was from Tori. "Never mind. You didn't cost me five keel. That was priceless."

My gaze went back to Ian's. His look was still bland, so I asked, "We good?"

He blinked. "Yeah. We're good." His voice was hollow and made me shudder.

"Are you coming to watch this match, or what?" Bryce bellowed across the Commons, causing waves of laughter.

A quick peek at the monitor showed that the board had been reset for another game. Then I felt Ian's arm at my back, "Shall we?" Swallowing past the lump in my throat, I allowed him to guide me to an open seat. Once there, he moved off a few seats with some of the guys I recognized from the whole male bonding experience. One said something to Ian, who shrugged. Then they all looked my way a few long seconds before leaving the match.

Now that I felt like I could breathe, I looked around the room. I caught both Director Forshay and Director Bradley's eyes, though they were on different ends of the Commons. It felt odd, so much attention on me. It should have been on the young men playing chess instead.

So, since I was coerced into attending, I focused on the match.

It was good. Another Endgame.

Log-in: JessReynoldi18851
Date/Time: 14 Feb Jan 2202/2127hrs
Subject: First Valentine's on IDEA

I have never been a hopeless romantic, nor as the old saying went, "twitter pated." But it was a nice day, with sweet gestures, even though I hadn't really sought any attention. It was nice to have a wall-ball match to distract the hormones of those on IDEA and Valentine's Day.

Don't know what else to say. It was an uneventful day. But... there was a little thing, a sweet thing, which made it special.

Oh, and Hope is doing well. Her real feathers have started to come in. Working in the Hatchery has been a nice distraction. It's better than moping in my room, or just studying. I'm still doing well, and trying to give Tori a run for her keel, and I like having a pet chick. I know I shouldn't get attached, but she made it past what John called the danger zone, and she likes to sit on my shoulders when I visit her cage. Chick chore perks? Chick pecks.

ENTRY END

"You have a little something on your shoulder there," Bryce teased. Every few days he rehashed the lame joke, because I about a week ago I showed my friends the pictures of Hope standing on my shoulder while I was in the suit. There had been a little evidence of bird droppings, so he loved to give me a rough time ever since.

Ellie gave Bryce another lecture while I ignored him and proceeded to show the next picture. This time Hope was sitting in my cupped hands as if they made her nest.

These times in the Hatchery were helping me find purpose and more sense of belonging on IDEA. Twice I had helped chicks who were too weak to free themselves from their shells. It was always sad to realize when I hadn't gotten there in time, which happened about a couple dozen times. Ian had given me a rough time about saving the weak, to which I replied that showed I was humane and willing to give things a chance, not just allow a struggling infant to get snuffed out. He made a face.

Tori asked again if she could go check it out sometime.

"Sorry, Tori," I said with a frown. "You can't. John made it clear that there is restricted access there for sanitary reasons." I put away my data pod.

That always brought up how she had shown me a couple things with restricted access and sanitary issues, but she had trusted me.

I hated it when she tried to guilt trip me. "You had a choice in showing me the pond," I whispered. "You weren't granted special privileges. Your brothers told you. It's not the same thing."

Tori quirked an eyebrow. "You're right. I did have a choice. Apparently I made the wrong one."

"It's not the same, Tori," Ellie said as she backed me up. "You know it. Stop giving Jess a hard time."

I gave Ellie a grateful look and started eating my dinner.

James interrupted the table to see if he could steal Ian. Ian got up and followed James out of ear shot. The two heads were bent in discussion on something and they kept darting looks around the Commons before Ian clamped a hand on James' shoulder and nodded. Then James went one direction, and Ian came back to finish his meal.

Adams asked if everything was okay, and Ian just nodded.

Tori broke the silence at the table asking who was going to the dance later, or if they were going to watch the match.

I wasn't dumb. I knew Tori was going to make an appearance at the dance, but had plans to go to the pond. That was her real agenda: which guy will be there tonight? I listened as the table's occupants answered one way or the other, indicating "and maybe something later," so I knew who was going to play in the pool, so-to-speak. It sounded like fun, so I said that I was expected at the match, but didn't know if I would stay for all of it.

That got some lift of the brows from the guys. Adams asked if I was getting tanned enough to be in my suit after being under the heat lamps for the chicks, and everyone laughed, including me. Bryce indicated he could throw the match if it got me in the water. I told him he better not after all the crap that I was given for the last chess event when Ben lost on purpose. Ian asked if Ben had asked me out yet. I assured him that Ben hadn't. "Still on the market," was his response.

Boys. I just don't understand their interest, especially when none of the guys in my secondary school ever looked my way. It makes me a little uncomfortable.

So after dinner I went and changed out of my class As into my one-piece swim wear and layered my comfy clothes so no one would be able to tell. As a last measure, I let my hair down again, and checked my appearance. The long, soft waves really gave me a nice look, and I smiled at my reflection.

A chime on my data pod alerted me to the time, so I quickly hustled down to the Commons to have a look at the nice little dance going on for some of the romantically inclined cadets. Seeing the few hundred couples gently swaying like they did in school back on Earth made me tear up. What a softy I was after all. Maybe I did want someone's interest.

Casting one last glance and the more adept dancers doing tangos and who-knows-what –else, I again moved towards the room where I had had lecture about living on IDEA all those months ago. The stadium style seating was thought to be better for the venue tonight with the dance in the Commons.

I came in and looked for a seat next to someone I recognized. I finally found some classmates a few rows up, but not ones I usually hung out with. I saw a few empty seats near them and asked if I could use one by the aisle. They said it wasn't taken, so I settled in.

As the hologram above the players came to life, my data pod chimed again. I looked at the message from Bryce. "Are you here, or do we have to find you?"

I returned with, "I'm here. No need for a search party."

"Prove it."

How? I apologized to my classmates before I stood up and belted out, "I'm here!"

Ben and Bryce looked up and smiled. Bryce shouted back over the audience, "Goooood!"

The auditorium erupted in laughter while I took my seat.

After a two hour match, which I would bet Bryce lost on purpose, I headed towards my room to place my chip card. I wanted to go feel light and free and play in the floating puddle, especially when Ben and Bryce asked what I was doing later. I deserved to live a little, to relax, to appreciate all IDEA had to offer.

As I came around the corner, I stopped in my tracks. Phil was checking my door. After it didn't open he pulled out his data pod and I could only guess he was wondering where my card would say I was. So I started for my room again, head down as if I hadn't seen him. I blinked in pretend surprise when I came up to him. "Oh, hi. Excuse me." I waved my card and went into my room and let the door close behind me.

I sagged onto my bed, wondering why he was still checking my room. I went to use the latrine in my quarters and showered off, in preparation for a dip in the pond.

Then I braided my hair into a single plait that eased over my left shoulder. To kill time, I again checked my reflection. I checked to see how much time had passed since I entered my room, and my device chimed simultaneously. Placing a hand over my heart, I willed my heart to stop beating erratically. Tapping the screen, I read the words Tori sent telling me to stay in my room, that something was wrong.

I didn't want to attract any attention. And I knew we didn't know how much of our messages could be read by others, so I wished her a Happy Hearts Day. I didn't get a response.

But I did get a knock at my door. When I opened my door, there stood Ben, holding a small flower, probably from his time in the Pollination Room. "Hi, plebe."

Despite myself, I smiled. "Hi, Genius."

He shifted more than his eyes normally did. "Here." With that he thrust the bloom at me while he held the three inch stem.

Carefully, I took the delicate blue flower with five, full petals with a violet center and bright yellow stamen from his fingers. "What's this?"

He shrugged. "A blue scarlet pimpernel." His eyes did their shifty thing. "Usually they're a reddish color. Only a few are blue or white." Now his feet did a shifty thing. "I thought you'd like it."

"I do. Thank you." My mind reeled by all the things this could mean. "You won't get in trouble for giving me this, will you?"

Ben tilted his head. "I'm not sure. I don't think so."

That he would do something like this for me, knowing he could get into trouble, I shook my head.

"You don't like it?" His head angled the other way. Then he reached for the little blossom, "I can get rid of it."

"No!" I closed my hands protectively around it. "Don't you

dare! You gave this to me. Don't waste it. I just don't want you to get in trouble over it."

He pulled back his hands and stood a little off to the side. "So, you like it then?"

Giving Ben an honest smile, I nodded. "It's very pretty. Thank you."

He bobbed his head and opened his mouth, then closed it. He started again, "I...I..."

"You want to go for a walk to the solarium?" *I can't believe I just blurted that out. He must think me forward.*

"Okay," he said.

I grabbed my data pod and chip card and let my door close behind me.

We walked almost all the way to the solarium in silence. I don't know if he thought it was uncomfortable, but my mind was thinking about five dozen ways to start a conversation.

But he asked, "How is your chore duty thing?"

I glanced at him. "Oh. It's good. I'm in the Hatchery. I get to help with the chicks and their transfers to the cages." We walked several more minutes quietly. "I have a chick, like a pet. I named her Hope. Do you want to see a picture?"

He told me to wait until we reached the solarium. Once there we sat on a bench and I used my data pod to show him what I did, and pictures I had of Hope, and those John had taken of the bird and me. I shared with him everything I had learned about poultry care, especially on IDEA. He was quiet and paid attention, or at least pretended to, the whole time I talked about the kinds of chickens and how the whole cycle of each type of bird during its life here.

When I was done, I looked down at my little bloom and saw how it was already starting to wilt. I tucked it behind my ear. After I did, Ben made an odd face, and asked if he could take a picture of me. Giving him permission, he brought out his device and took close ups of the bloom amidst my hair, then my face with the flower. He looked at the pictures, then thanked me and started to put away his data pod. I asked to see, and he showed me.

I brought out my device and asked if I could get one of us together, and he smiled. Such an odd thing, Ben smiling, but I was able to take a permanent reminder of what it looks like. I saved it to my album journal to send home with some of my other memories when the time comes.

"I am sorry," he said which broke up the moment we were in.

"For?"

"You were concerned, and I was cynical. I was told the next day about the message one of my underlings," he said the words so easy, "had sent." He looked at me. "He used your name, and that is what tipped you off that it wasn't me." It wasn't a question. It was a statement. "You were right, and I acted rashly. When Director Bradley brought me aside the next morning, after talking with the others..."

I waved him off. "You didn't know until you were told. I get it. Whatever. That happened over a month ago."

"Almost two months ago." He looked at the fish tank before us. "I tried to apologize, but Cadet Hanson was at your door, and you seemed...uninterested in my presence."

I fought for words that I would not regret, and not wish I hadn't said. "I was irritated because first James had stopped me, then Ian was getting pushy. I was still on edge from the night before. I didn't get a lot of sleep."

Ben pursed his lips. He was quiet for several seconds. "You said something that affected me." When I asked what it was, he said, "You said there was no me and you."

I looked at the floor in front of me. "I was angry with you.

More angry with Ian." I thought and added, "And I was tired. Exhausted, really."

"I heard him. I have heard him tell people he's going to get you," Ben said softly. "He usually gets what he wants."

I percolated on his words. "Ian's pushy and full of himself. Good looking? Sure. But also arrogant and pompous. It's a turn off." I waited for Ben to say something, anything. But I listened to silence.

"I can take you back to your room now," he said, after several minutes. He stood.

I checked the time on my data pod.

It was almost eleven.

But I had so many questions, and I didn't want to go back to my room just yet. "If you want to, but I'm okay. I'd rather stay a bit longer."

He sat and went very still. "Okay. What do you want to talk about now?"

The burning question. But I had one subject that still needed discussion.

"Was the cadet who you were looking for that first week the one that was determined as missing?"

He looked me in the eye. "Yes."

Next question. "If transports are supposed to be separated by House, why was he on my transport to IDEA?"

Ben tilted his head while his eyes did that thing they do. "Odd. Perhaps he changed seats with someone on a different transport. Seems logical."

"Huh." Next burning topic. "Why did you throw the chess match against Bryce?"

He turned away and stood. "I didn't want to play."

Oh. "So, why was I given grief because you didn't want to play?"

He faced me. "Because I didn't have a reason to play when you weren't there. Bryce made you come so I would play, because I would want to...to impress...you." He shrugged. "Before it was who was the better player. Now it's if you come and watch."

I thought again on that night while I took in his words. "Me?"

Ben made an odd face and turned away.

The awkward silence made me uneasy. "Okay." I stood. "I guess I'm ready. I'm getting tired."

Despite my protests, he walked me back to my room. Once there, he again thanked me for a wonderful time. I, in turn, told him I appreciated the flower and his conversation.

This time, while I watched the door close, he turned and met my eye. "Happy Valentine's Day, Jess."

He said my name.

I smiled as the door secured.

Guys are interested in me? And I want them to be? No, no, no! I'm supposed to be focusing on academics!

Forehead smack.

Log-in: JessReynoldi18851
Date/Time: 15 Mar 2202/2233hrs
Subject: Ides of March

After a fantastic round of mid-terms, I have to say, I'd better be holding my own against Tori. I have been studying a lot and keeping personal progress and finance comments to a minimum. I know it makes me sound immature, but I have so much to prove.

I have asked to go to the pond, but everyone is still closed lipped about when we're going to go again. I even asked James and Ben, but it seems like it's not happening. At least, not with me. Part of me thinks this is payback for something, like no Chick Time or something. I did try the door Tori took me through those couple of times, but it was secure, not jimmied like when we went.

So, instead, I have been spending more time with my chick. Some may consider that childish, but back on Earth, my parents would even have loved this opportunity. I know I shouldn't think of her that way, but it's so cool the way she recognizes me and hobbles over when I get to her cage. I still sneak pictures and videos of her, even though some of my group don't care to see. I'm sure a lot of them couldn't care less, but I love it. It's part of my time here, and I want to record everything I can. I'm glad the journals were suggested when we first arrived.

ENTRY END

Hope pecked at my data pod and I couldn't hold in the chuckles. She turned her head first one way, then another, as she regarded the device again. Hope sat quietly peeping at my ear for fifteen minutes or so. I wanted another memento of our time together, so I did an up-close recording of her contended sounds, but this was great too.

Seeing the time on my unit, I put Hope back with the rest of the chicks. When she wobbled off towards the feeder, I went to the room where I returned my suit for cleaning and sanitation. Since they could be salvaged for more wearing, I removed my booties and hair cap and tossed them in the bin as well. Using the cleanser, I scrubbed my hands up past my elbows, and under my nails for longer than the required two minutes that John stressed. Then I used a couple of the sanitation wipes for my data pod. I really didn't want to chance contamination because of neglect.

Checking to make sure I had done everything correctly again, I exited and almost knocked James over as I did so. I had apologized immediately.

"No problem," he said with a quick smile as he held the door open. "Heading to chow?"

When I said I was, he said he was waiting for Cecile. So I headed off towards the Commons. After I went through the food line, I saw Cecile already seated at a table with some of her friends. I turned back to see if James had seen her, but he was just getting in line, so I guessed he had seen her.

My eyes scanned the Commons for Ben. Seeing his gaze already on me, I offered a smile and timid wave. Ben was lacking his normal shifty eye movement so I was again given a glimpse of Ben's grin. He tapped the empty spot next to him, which meant one of the many cadets he tutored wasn't bothering him with questions like was the norm. So, tray in hand, I sat next to him. "Hey, Genius. How was your day?"

I liked our simple conversations, whenever we could get them. Sometimes it was in the solarium, other times the Pollination Room. We even started walking around, he called it strolling, which cracked me up. But our talks were simple, and yet, informative.

Being with Ben was super casual, natural. For the first time ever, I thought about how guys must see me. Back on Earth, I didn't have a lot of friends. Being books and studying meant more than popularity, I wasn't on the dating auction block like most of the other young ladies I had grown up with academically. Mom and Dad had always assured me that I would be a treasure to the right guy. I admit, at seventeen, I had believed they lied to me.

Yet, here I was having feelings for this sweet guy with shifty eyes that he had when he was thinking. And unless I have been very much mistaken, Ben has similar feelings for me. Such unchartered territory for me, but...welcome.

After Valentine's, I started asking about his family and where he was from and now we're on to telling funny childhood memories, or sometimes, just talking about our reasons for coming here to IDEA.

Ben was studying advanced horticulture engineering with an emphasis in agriculture in new terrains, and with his father being prior military, IDEA had been his family's number one choice. He didn't mind where he went as long as he was going to be making a difference in a career doing what he liked to do, so attending IDEA made him happy. Upon his first few weeks, Ben had made a genetically altered vegetable that required less carbon dioxide to grow, using instead a mutation which utilized gases found in space: hydrogen and nitrogen. That deed had earned him all-access, rights and privileges in the Pollination Room. He had worked on cures against blight and other afflictions of vegetation in foreign environments. His list of accomplishments astonished me.

He always listened to what my ambitions were and why I

wanted to help colonize remote areas and help maintain some semblance of humanity and control while doing so. He occasionally would ask for more specifics, and never seemed to judge.

"Mind if I interrupt?" asked a voice from across the table. Adams set his tray down and took a seat. "Ian's in a mood, so I'm staying clear."

When I asked what the problem was, Adams just shook his head and said something always was bothering Ian, that the question was more like, what was irritating him more on which day. I tried to smile, but with Adams being so serious, we just let him eat in peace.

After dinner, I headed off to my quarters to work on my homework. Since I knew Ben had his study group later, I wanted to give him plenty of time to prepare for the work he did with those cadets.

As I came around the corner, I stopped short. James and Ian were in a heated discussion just outside my door. James noticed me first and looked away in that, "oh boy" kind of way.

Ian took the bait and turned. "There she is!" He started toward me with his arms spread open, smile equally as wide.

"Hi, Ian," I said as he approached. "What's with the gathering at my door?"

James gave us a funny look and then turned his attention to the floor.

Ian sidled up close to me, "We were just discussing some stuff while I waited for you."

I switched my gaze between them. "Oh. Well, what did you want?"

Ian dropped his arms and chuckled low, "Just to talk. I don't get to see you much lately, especially since you're always doing your chore or hanging out with Ben." He gave me an odd look. "I thought you said there was no you and Ben."

Shaking my head, I just stepped around his arms. "Ian, please. Don't tell me you're jealous. You can pretty much have your choice of girl here."

He nodded as he looked over my head, "Yeah, true. I'm about brains, not body, so...I choose you."

I blinked at the slight, no casual, insult as I assessed the look on his face. "Oh, you're serious." At his affirmation, I couldn't help but run a hand across my face. "Ian, I thought you were joking."

He seemed surprised. "I don't think I am the kidding type. At least not about this kind of thing."

I couldn't move. Couldn't think of anything to say. My mind was running a million miles a minute. I felt my lids blink and my mouth do the open-fish-mouth thing, but nothing else seemed to be working.

Big, bad Ian Hanson sighed. "He's asked you out, huh?"

I frowned. "No. He hasn't." *Come to think of it.*

The beam on Ian's face was intense. "Good." He asked if I would care to take a walk.

I didn't want to seem rude or misleading, so I let him know that I had planned on doing some studying. At his odd look, I added that we could go for a short walk.

James excused himself and walked away, which left Ian hovering next to me. He offered an arm like a true gentleman, and I felt obliged to take it.

Despite my mistrust of the situation, Ian behaved the whole hour we walked and talked. He even asked about Hope, using her name, and not giving me crap about playing with my food. He was pleasant. The entire time, just super casual and, yeah, like I said, pleasant. When we got back to my quarters, he brought my hand to his lips, and kissed it. He wished me a good night and left, smiling over his shoulder as he did.

What the crap! What just happened? Now I have two guys interested in me? That would have never happened back home. It was enough to throw me, make me feel like an immature Earth-bound classmate, with...feelings.

But didn't Tori get all...emotional...over guys? Maybe I was finally catching up, or...lost because of the interest.

Focus! Study hard, or Dad will kick your butt.

I entered my room and flopped on my little bed and watched as the familiar blue vision of home cycled in and out of my view.

My data pod chimed, so I brought it out to check it.

It was a message asking if I wanted to go to the pond.

Did I ever!

After a quick reply saying that I would meet up with Tori in her room, I opened the door and checked my hall. Seeing no one, I set my metal piece and watched my door close, leaving my chip card and data pod inside. Smile on my face and in my heart, I bee-bopped to Tori's door, and pressed the call button. After a few seconds, I hit it again, thinking that she may have been using the latrine.

And I waited.

But she never answered. So, two questions came to mind.

Do I continue on to the pond, in case she didn't get my message before she left? Or do I go back to my room and study like a good little cadet?

I turned down the hall, decision made.

Log-in: JessReynoldi18851
Date/Time: 16 Mar 2202/0002hrs
Subject: Trespassing

I am not sure what just happened.

When I got back to my room, the first thing I noticed was that my card had been moved. The next thing was that my data pod was not in the same place.

Someone had been in my room.

ENTRY END

Slowly, I opened my mini closet door and put the little metal piece where I had been storing it, which is not where Tori had put it. Seeing nothing missing or moved, I secured my door and checked under my cot. I also looked in the latrine. Nothing was moved or missing that I could tell.

I turned back to my chip card sitting in the groove, but at a different angle. Without touching it, I looked for anything else out of the ordinary. There weren't any obvious finger smudges that I could see.

Then I went back to my bed where I had left my data pod right out in the open. A screen was still open. It looked like someone had tried to access my journal entries. But I had a different password for that than I did for using my device.

Which meant someone either knew where my room was, or went through the trouble to find out.

And that this person seemed to think he or she knew the password on my device.

It also meant someone knew about the pond, and that I had gone there before.

As careful as I could, I used my bedding to touch the edges of my device to look for a finger print on the screen or any surface large enough for me to see. But I didn't see anything. Besides, how could I prove someone's?

Then I realized that I wouldn't be able to talk to anyone about this. I had to be more vigilant about how people behaved around me. I was going to pretend like this never happened and see what I could learn. I wasn't going to break any more rules. I was also changing my data pod password, and journal password, just in case.

I went through the entries and didn't see anything missing. Dates the entries were done and saved were the same, so I felt confident that the perpetrator didn't get past the second password. I saved my new passwords and looked back at the message sent earlier.

My mistake was assuming it had been from Tori. It didn't list any particular sender's information, as it had been sent blind, so I wouldn't know. And I guessed Tori.

Crap. That wasn't good.

I sent a message saying that I had gone to her room, but she hadn't answered. I told her I apologized for a late night call and told her that I would see her tomorrow.

I tried to back track on my outgoing message saying I'd go to Tori's room. I realized that I could still salvage my name. So, as was my norm, I said as I typed, "Sorry. Tori didn't answer so I didn't go to the solarium after all. Who is this, by the way?"

My dad's words of wisdom started replaying in my head, as if he was lecturing me right then and there.

Lesson one: Don't trust anyone...ever. Why hadn't I listened?

Lesson two: Keep your friends close, and your enemies closer. Which meant someone here considered me worth keeping an eye on. But who and why?

Lesson three: Document everything. I already was.

Lesson four: Let them swing first, then finish the fight. I was tough. I just needed to know who had swung. Let the hunted become the huntress.

Okay Dad, time to really make you proud.

Log-in: JessReynoldi18851
Date/Time: 1 April 2202/2154hrs
Subject: Not funny

So, who would have thought that the IDEA staff, including the House Directors, had a sense of humor?

Well, with everything that I have noticed and seen since being on IDEA, I'm not just letting this stuff slide.

Progress report, Dad? Grades are solid in the 98% and up.

Huntress is still pretending to be innocent and hunted so she can glean more intel.

Wow, even some of my verbiage is changing. I got here because of my smarts and how I had been able to carry myself throughout the interview process. I'm noticing a lot of things changing about me. No longer will I allow my naïveté to run amuck.

ENTRY END

The sound of the klaxon erupted and I jumped out of my cot while trying to wake up.

Actually, that was how everyone at IDEA woke up today. Then that female voice came over the intercom and announced that there was no breakfast, just an emergency which required everyone in the Commons immediately. I scampered into a comfy sweatshirt over my night shirt and grabbed my chip card. Other plebes still in the battle of waking up also ventured into the hall.

As we approached the Commons, the klaxon sounded again. That time the female voice announced "April Fools!" It took that voice repeating itself all three times for me to realize what was really going on. I wasn't the only one who took some time to figure it out, but I was definitely a quieter one. Some fellow cadets blurted colorful metaphors and obscenities. Others still needed to be convinced that nothing was wrong and that we could indeed return to our rooms.

Then, since I had been awoken two hours ahead of my normal time, I worked on homework until breakfast chow was served.

Everyone had cold cereals versus a warm breakfast, as we were told that the kitchen staff was on strike. Milk was put in the water containers and water was in the milk dispenser, so many of us young cadets had watery cereal. The upper tenured cadets just watched with mild amusement for the most part while we plebes negotiated through our first April Fool's Day here.

As breakfast was assigned seating, all of us first-timers just took our seats and kept our heads down for the most part. Some chuckled, while others lost their cool and let out an expletive...or seven. I couldn't help but smile when they lost their collective mannerisms and let their mouths run free.

After a similar bunch of supposed fun by the instructors and directors the first two class periods, an announcement was made about another cadet who had been missing, had now been found in a pond. Several people laughed at the message, and I could see they didn't know what I did. They didn't know about the pond, or if someone was, in fact, missing.

My calm façade had gone to stoic, then to almost pissed, as I pushed my way through the halls to get to my next class.

That announcement was in very poor taste. It was a deliberate taunt by the members of IDEA to alert those who knew of the pond's existence. It also made fun of the cadet I presumed was still missing from months ago, though no other public notification had been given. It was horrible to think that the message was right, and that the cadet had been found in the pond.

It explained a lot if the cadet had been found in the pond. No one wanted to talk about the last time they had all gone. No one wanted to go anymore, at least that I was told. Phil was still checking doors. Something definitely had been wrong. Was a cadet found there? And if so, when? Was he alive?

Who was I kidding? Ben said that the pond was cleaned every week, like clockwork. And they all had stopped wanting to go to the pond after my concern brought both house directors to Bradley House. The cadet wouldn't have been alive, or would he?

What if he was left in the pond for days until the group found him?

But why the heavy and obvious cleaning of the room and hall?

I was going to Bradley House again, soon.

I needed some answers.

A quick meal of sandwiches served as supper, and I pleaded off the proposed movie night so I could do some investigating-slash-homework.

A few people joked about the fun of the day as we walked towards my room. I looked around the Commons as I left with Tori and Kimberly.

James and Ian and a couple of the guys from the arm-swaying group were pushing each other off in the attention of Bradley House. James caught the eye of Director Forshay and nodded before disappearing from my view. I noticed Director Bradley watching from his normal seat across the way, and then he turned his direction back to the data pod in his hand. I looked for Cecile and found her with a gaggle of females making themselves comfortable for the upcoming film night. I noticed Ben was already leaving, and he just did a head bob in my general direction.

Tori and Kimberly were talking about a night of spa-lendor in Tori's room, and extended an invitation my way. Knowing it was an opportunity to find out what had happened that night, I agreed to come get my girl-groove on, as Tori called it.

After a quick change of clothes, I messaged Tori saying that I was on my way. When I got there, neither even mentioned anything about the pond or the odd announcement from earlier. I couldn't keep my mouth shut any longer, and asked what they thought about it.

The look the two shared spoke volumes. Something had happened.

"Come on!" I said as I thumped the bed with a small fist. "You had to have heard it? That was not funny. They mentioned the pond to all of the cadets, whether the other cadets know of it or not. And to say that someone was found there? Tacky."

Kimberly looked into her lap while she covered her face.

I looked at Tori. "What? What's going on?" I played so innocent.

Tori glanced at Kimberly. "We all agreed not to talk about it, but you weren't there...so I guess we should tell you why we don't want to go there anymore." She set her nail file down beside her so she could use her hands to talk. "So, we start walking down the hallway like we always do when we're going, and we see Phil checking the maintenance door that I have always used. It opened freely, so he checked the catch and removed the metal shim." She smoothed back her hair as she continued. "So, I told Kimberly that we were going to meet up with the guys from the other side and use some of their doors. But I couldn't find the guys. I went to one of the doors a couple levels up, and it was still shimmed so we could enter. But there was blood in splotches here and there."

I turned towards Kimberly for confirmation, and she nodded, her hand still over her mouth.

Tori continued, "But we didn't know what it meant. I thought someone must have had a bloody nose or something, you know?"

Instantly, I remembered having walked a hall and thinking someone had had a nosebleed. I remembered everything in a flash, including Phil coming when Marshall had got him to help clean it up. "Seems logical," I heard myself say in a soft voice.

"I know, right? But when we got to the end of the tunnel, there was...this...bloody like...skeleton...floating near the end. All of the muscles were...like missing. It was just...just...gross. At first, I thought it was some sort of hologram. Kimmer persuaded me otherwise." Tori dropped her hands as she looked down. "We hustled out of there and wiped the door so no one would find our fingerprints."

Kimberly brought her head up, hand fully over her mouth. She removed it briefly to whisper, "It was awful."

Tori nodded. "Someone had to have done that to him..."

"Or her," Kimberly interjected.

But Tori kept right on talking, "...and then drug his...his body in there."

"Like a warning," Kimberly added.

I blinked. I couldn't find anything appropriate to say. Though I doubt that it was possible, I asked if they thought it was a hoax.

Tori said that they thought it was possibly a hologram, but were afraid to asked people because of being somewhere they shouldn't be.

I figured that these two ladies were not ones who had done anything negative that I was piecing together. But I wondered if anyone had been sent a message like I had. So I asked them.

Tori and Kimberly both nodded.

Tori started talking first though. "I had, and then someone hit the call button on my door a few minutes later. I waited, sitting on my bed, afraid to move and answer. I waited and waited, uncertain as to who it could be. Then it chimed again twice." She shook her head, "I didn't know until your message later that it was you."

I frowned. "I only hit your call button two times. Not three."

Silence filled the room for several minutes while Tori picked up the nail file and turned it in her hand.

Kimberly said that she, too, had received a message from some undisclosed sender and had responded with a message saying she didn't know what he or she was talking about, and that she didn't want to be harassed, or she was going to talk to her house director.

I felt badly for Kimberly, especially after knowing how she had felt when we spoke in Director Forshay's quarters back in December, when we had all been congratulated on being top of our courses. She had wanted to keep her head down and said how she had not wanted be next. Then, when she and Tori had gone to the pond, Kimberly had seen what next could look like. I shuddered.

"What did you say?" Tori looked at me expectantly.

I cringed. "At first, I thought it was you inviting me."

Tori groaned.

I did too, but I continued. "I said I was going to your room." The look of horror on Tori's face kept me talking, "But when I got back from trying your room, I messaged back saying that I wasn't going to the solarium after all, since you weren't answering your door."

"Solarium?" Tori turned to look and shrug at Kimberly.

"That's what I have said any time Phil or the directors have talked about the pond. I play dumb."

Tori dropped her shoulders. "Well, maybe that'll help."

Kimberly nodded, "I'm going to start using that."

I bobbed my head. "Or, instead of putting ourselves at risk, we could just do things like other cadets. We could go to the UV room and the real solarium." At their looks, I added, "I love going there."

Tori rolled her eyes. "I know you love being the good little plebe, but I loved the pond." She made a pouty face. "I'm just afraid to go back." Then she asked for my hand so she could shape my nails.

I sat and watched her work. Then a thought sprang forth in my head and out of my mouth at the same time, "But how come the guys don't even talk about the pond?" Realizing that I had said it out loud, I glanced up. "Sorry. Just curious if they weren't with you, how come they don't want to go or mention it?"

It was Tori's turn to think. "Don't know. Hess and I agreed we weren't going to ever mention it again." She looked up from my hand, "But I guess you're safe enough to tell."

That I am, I admitted.

But that got me thinking, "So, wanna go to the real solarium and see how the other half lives?" I couldn't help but wink to add some flair to the words.

For some reason they just rolled their eyes. But after finishing our nail trims and make-overs, we headed out in our casual clothes towards the UV room. Once there, we laughed and joked...while Kimberly said we baked. Afterwards we strolled down the corridor towards the solarium. While we sat in the diminishing light to indicate twilight, we told stories from our pasts.

The sound of the klaxon broke our ladies' night.

But instead of more joking, sounds of objects hitting IDEA ended my first April Fool's here.

Log-in: JessReynoldi18851

Date/Time: 19 May 2202/2204hrs
Subject: Searching for Answers

I have a theory about a couple of things here. After the last external barrage of debris, someone on IDEA must have authorized the disposal of the remains of the cadet.

I believe that because on April 2nd, an announcement was made that a cadet's cell wasn't functioning. It was presumed, as the voice narrated on, that he had been safe inside. But when maintenance was checking, they had to go externally. We were told that there was sufficient damage to indicate that the cadet had been siphoned out of his room. He was IDEA's second reported cell loss accident.

I have asked to do a voluntary maintenance service walk. I think I have to, to see if my theories are correct. I haven't told any of the people who I usually have associated about my real reasons, because I don't know who sent me that message about the pond. I am trusting no one, except Tori and Kimberly, and maybe Ben. I dare not tell them what I had experienced that night months ago. But I want to see the hull and see IDEA from the tethered lines on her.

                                                    ENTRY END

The past few weeks' journal notes haven't had much to report I realized looking back.

I had put notes of my time with Ben, and with Ian. Both guys asked to spend time with me. It still takes some getting used to.

Ian might be the better looking of the two, but I was still left wondering why he was interested in me versus someone like Tori or Cecile. He always seemed to know when Ben was tutoring and mentoring, and chose to find time with me then. He wouldn't try anything other than to kiss my hand every time we hung out. And he only asked to date me once, last week. I hadn't really answered him, but challenged him by asking why he had waited so long. Let him think what he would while we talked about our pasts.

Turns out Ian was very much the military-mindset man. He wanted structure and a military presence at every outpost to prevent uprisings. He wasn't the smartest cadet, as he compared himself to Bryce and Ben, but he said he was the most determined.

I had found that rather humorous, considering what kind of elite campus we were attending. He didn't find it so funny. Again, that lack of joking thing.

My time with Ben was different than with Ian. Ben would try to teach me chess and other games. He would take me to the Pollination room every time the butterflies would be breaking free from their chrysalis so I could watch as they took to flight for the first time. He only mentioned one time that he had heard talk of my time with Ian circling around. I didn't deny it, saying Ian was more interested than I was. He asked me to be honest. I told him I was, and that I hadn't even answered Ian's question, and the look on poor Ben's face was as if he was sucking on lemons. But we talked about IDEA and his post graduate plans. That usually was a good distraction for him.

Another thing I had neglected to write in my journal about included were updates on Hope and her progress. She had been able to transition into the free range cage with the rest of her group. Though that had made me happy, I also knew that meant I was going to see less of her. John had told me that I could visit her with him, but on a very seldom basis, so that I wouldn't accidentally contaminate future chicks. Seemed so unfair, but I knew she'd lay eggs since she had lived long enough.

I had asked John about switching to the mature cages, and he told me that that area was mostly automated, so I wouldn't be needed there. And lately, he asked if I even wanted to keep in the Hatchery, because I seemed to have lost my excitement. I had agreed that it was different for me now, but that I had learned so much. Also, I told him that I wanted to see what other options that were out there to learn from while still on IDEA.

He had given me a list of other voluntary chores. Cadets could help in the kitchen, the waste recycling and management section, the seedlings, the harvesting of foods, external maintenance, internal maintenance, and as an instructor's aide.

My ears and mind had perked up with the idea of what was needed for external maintenance, but I didn't want to seem too eager. So, I asked what was involved with some of the tasks. With the referral documents he gave, I was able to research some of the duties and responsibilities of each chore. I had also charted which would help me discover more things about IDEA faster, and maybe help answer some of the questions that still plagued me.

So, I set up a meeting with Director Forshay to see if he could help me.

He sat in that big chair in front of that beautifully illuminated bronze sculpture. "External maintenance? And you think that could help you grow in your field?"

Like I had rehearsed, "Absolutely. With my focus on Military Exploration and Expansion, it seems that I should probably work in every capacity here, to be a better and stronger asset in the field. I believe that some time with external maintenance would help me if I am sent to a remote or circulating civilization." I was glad I had used both types of artificial homesteading terms. "Should an emergency happen, I may be required to work in a zero gravity situation. What better location to learn than this academy?"

Director Forshay regarded me while he tapped his index and middle finger on his large desk. After several seconds he sat straight in his chair, startling me. "I like it." He brought out his data pod. "I think you're correct. This is a perfect setting. Perhaps we should allow other cadets this opportunity as part of the curriculum."

I smiled while he was occupied on his device.

"Asking Director Bradley for his input," Forshay added. When he finished his message, he set his data pod down on his desk. "If I didn't have to have his support, should other cadets in your study want to do this, I wouldn't be forwarding it on." He looked at the model behind him. "Sometimes I wish I could just make a judicial decision and let it stand." For several seconds he just looked at the shiny model. "But, here we need to talk and work together." He turned and smiled at me. "In the meantime, I should be able to help work you into the maintenance cycles in the upcoming weeks."

"Thank you, sir."

"Did you want to stop in the Hatchery?" He brought up his data pod.

"I...I think I would still like some time there with the chicks."

Forshay nodded. "Keep the grades up, and done." He set the

device back down. "Anything else, Reynoldi?"

"No, sir." I stood. "Thank you for your time."

"Certainly. I'd rather keep my cadets happy and learning." He stood and walked with me to the door. "Phil will message you to coordinate your external runs."

My heart pounded. Always Phil. "Okay. Thank you, sir."

I stepped into the hallway and almost knocked James down as he went to hit the call button for Forshay's office. "I'm sorry, James. That's twice now I've almost plowed you over."

James just smiled and apologized for being in my way once again. Then he was called in by Forshay and the door shut behind him.

I headed towards my quarters. Ben was waiting at my door as I came around the corner. The smile that came to my face before he saw me brought me up short. I was genuinely happy to see him.

Then he turned, and seeing my grin, gave me a chance to see his again.

"Hi, Genius," I said as I walked the rest of the way over.

"Hi...Beautiful."

I paused.

He dropped his head.

"Ben? You called me Beautiful," I said in a hushed whisper.

He shrugged. "Well, you are."

"But I thought I was just a plebe."

His eyes did their shifty thing. "Well, I...I want to ask you if you want to be...to be my plebe." Then he exhaled so loudly, I had a feeling that I knew how hard saying that was for him.

But I didn't answer right away, because I was shocked and overcome. That was horrible of me. Horrible in so many ways.

Because poor Ben mumbled to forget it and started walking away, shoulders hunched. And he was moving quickly.

"Wait! Ben!"

"Jess!" came Ian's voice from behind me.

But I didn't turn around to see his approach. "Ben, wait!" And I was going after Ben, hearing Ian follow.

This wasn't going to be pretty. But I think it was going to be honest.

I turned with my hands in front of me ready to push Ian away if I had to. "Ian, stop. I'm going after Ben."

"But," he looked past me, "are you dumping me?"

I shook my head in surprise. "I'm not breaking up with you." I turned and saw Ben watching from down the hall. "Okay, stop. Both of you." I exhaled while I gave them each a profile view while I found the right words, or what I hoped were the right ones. Then I turned to Ian, "I never answered your question. You just assumed that I said yes. While I have enjoyed getting to know you, I don't think I'm the one for you. You're a nice guy, just...I'm not sure that I want anything more than your friendship. I'm sorry." I looked down, too chicken to see his reaction, while I exhaled again. "I'm sorry."

Then I turned towards Ben, who was shifty in both feet and eyes. But he wasn't looking at me. He was watching over my shoulder.

I turned back around.

Ian's face was red. His body was tense.

I took a step backward and put my hands up ready to deflect and defend.

He snarled, "Oh, give me a break. Like I would attack you in front of someone? I said I was interested. You knew that."

I took it for the accusation it was. "I did. And I gave you a chance, but tonight...just now, I felt something change in me. Please. I wasn't trying to lead anyone on." I swallowed the lump rising in my throat. "I wasn't trying to hurt you or mislead you."

Ian's eyes narrowed. "Well, you did." And he turned and huffed away, pushing some poor unsuspecting male cadet out of his way as he went.

I watched until he was long gone, and my breathing had returned to normal. Then I looked to see if Ben was still there.

He was.

I shrugged and dropped my shoulders. "I am sorry you had to see that."

Ben stayed where he was and lowered his gaze to the floor.

"And I am sorry that I didn't answer you right away. You surprised me." I took a hesitant step towards him. "I didn't expect that. I didn't expect you to call me beautiful. And I sure didn't expect the reaction I had felt when I came around the corner to see you at my door." There, that was my confession.

Ben took two steps towards me, then stopped as my data pod chimed.

I looked at the ceiling in frustration before I checked the message. I read it and responded, saying as I typed, "I will be there." Again I faced Ben. "Of all the horrible timing!" I exhaled loudly. "You should know that I love our time together, that I look forward to it. There!" I threw my arms up. "I said it."

Ben took a couple more steps in my direction.

My data pod chimed again, so I read the message. "Okay." Then I turned towards Ben again. "Suddenly I am so popular," I grumbled seeing he was only a few feet away.

"What is it?"

I shook my head. "I told Forshay that I wanted to do some training in some more of the various voluntary chores here. He just told me that I have to report tonight for a meeting and briefing on all the gear."

"Oh," Ben sounded like his normal self. "What chore are you doing instead of the Hatchery?"

"I'm still allowed to help with the chicks. I just wanted to learn some of the internal and external maintenance aspects of IDEA in case it comes in handy when I get placed."

Ben's eyes shifted. "Which are you doing tonight?"

I smiled. "I'm reporting for external maintenance orientation."

The panic on Ben's face was quickly replaced by his normal shifty look. "Ian's on external maintenance, plebe."

Crap.

And just like that, he's back to calling me "plebe."

Log-in: JessReynoldi18851
Date/Time: 8 June 2202/2311hrs
Subject: Close Call

Tonight, I am lucky to be safely back inside IDEA. And I have Ian to thank for it.

The hug I gave him was genuine.

The kiss on the cheek, friendly, but it made us both blush.

I just want to see Ben.

I'm so very lucky.

ENTRY END

I loved the eerie silence while being out on the external maintenance runs. The first few times I was shocked at the lack of sound, except for the direction given through the comms in the helmets we wore. Now that I knew what to do on the runs. It was fun to see how fast we could use our two-hook tethering systems and maneuver all over the hull of IDEA. I had quickly mastered the one hook secure, before securing a hook to the line we were going to. Sometimes the maintenance staff would set up races as part of a real-world scenario to see if we could do our jobs and still be safe, and with the goal of "saving lives" training.

Today I was paired with Ian and Jackson as externals on a routine oxygen tank swap training. Other times I had been with James, and some other people I don't really have any other interactions with, and only know by last names. I have done runs previous to today, so I knew how to disconnect the storage clamps and efficiently complete the whole tank switching. But today was a timed competition exercise, as if there was a system malfunction with current units. We were to coordinate with internal maintenance on the switching of "faulty" units for fresh, external ones, and return as fast as possible. But maintenance usually threw in a wrench here or there to make it more realistic. Today we had to release and secure specific tanks only. That usually meant tampering. However, the fastest internal team and external team would each earn points. Points were turned in at the Shoppette. But more than that, it was usually a good time complete with bragging rights.

So, at the start of the competition, our team had to wait in our rooms for a notification to suit up for the "emergency". We would be timed from the message to our safe arrival back in the dock with door secure and all tanks properly stowed.

As soon as my data pod chimed with the message, I was booking it down the hall, smile across my face as I hollered that I was part of a drill and to clear the hall. All my extra time running the track has helped me become faster for the drills, if nothing else. I made it to the dock second and was in my suit first this time, by seconds over Ian. Jackson was right behind us. Then we did our safety checks on each other's suits by standing in a circle and checking the person ahead of us. Then we turned around for our second check. Even though these types of suits were long outdated, they were perfect for academic purposes. The suits protected us from the extreme cold of being in space. They were cumbersome, but efficient.

Giving the all clear signal, we each grabbed both sets of our suit hooks in our hand so we could transfer into the loading dock ready room, and tether up. This usually only took less than a minutes to decompress and get us out into the next section. Once in the decompressed dock, we each took two of the tanks and secured them to each other's left side on the suit where there was a large loop for tethering them. We found it faster to tether them to someone else versus trying to find the hook on your own during these runs.

Within ten minutes of the message, we three cadets were in the vacuum of space tethered to IDEA, each by our own set of two hooks.

Immediately we each secured ourselves to one of the tracks leading to the oxygen storage areas and began pulling ourselves along the metal lines, hooking and unhooking and hooking as we went. I was happy to see Ian and Jackson closing in on their tank sections as I reached mine. I quickly undid the toggle clamp holding my two tanks in place. As fast as I could, I hooked the closest tank to my tether and began unscrewing of the units from its hold. Once it was free, I pulled it from its nesting and secured one of the "bad" tanks in its place, ensuring the training chain indicating that it was "bad" was visible. Then I secured the tension clamp back over the tank. Done, I pulled myself to the next tank.

"How's it going, Team?" came a voice via the helmet's comms.

Being Ian was the lead, I waited for his voice to answer. After a few seconds, "Swell. You guys rig these things for errors or what? Mine doesn't want to release."

As I released the clamp and looked over towards Ian. He was definitely struggling to free his first tank. "Ian, leave the spare tank and go for the next one. I'm complete on one. I'll get my second and be there to help you in a bit." I knew better than to look where the maintenance guys supervising us were, because it would cost us valuable time.

"Roger," he said and moved to the next tank.

Jackson chimed in that he was done with his first tank and would advance to his next tank.

"Copy," Ian said again.

I tethered and unscrewed my second tank and pulled it from its nesting. Then I replaced the training tank in its place, ensuring the tag was visible on it as well. I checked my tethers and tanks, still on my left, but this time "good", and said, "Complete. En route to your first tank."

"Copy," came Ian's voice.

Upon nearing Ian's first marked tank, I could reach the clamp easily enough as well as the tank tethered beside me. Knowing time was wasted with Ian struggling with the first, I tried to stretch my tethers without reattaching to save some valuable seconds. But as I looked at the clamp and from my angle, I could see that a spring was broken which would prevent its release. "Broken clamp. Going to force it."

"Careful. I'm almost done with my second," Ian said.

"Me too," came Jackson's voice. "Dang sabotage."

"Keep the chit chat down," Ian said.

But I was already turning onto my back so I could grab the tethering pipe and kick the broken clamp with my boot. I kicked. The clamp shifted. I kicked. And kicked again. It broke free. Physically, the clamp started floating away. "Crap. Ian?"

"Give me a second," he said.

So I repositioned myself to tether up to the tank and free it. I reached to unscrew it, but the angle was difficult. As I strained, I looked back and saw why. One of my tanks was caught along the tethering line. When I gave it a light tug to free it, I realized my error too late. My tug was the wrong move.

The top of the tank, usually and mostly protected by the rim, was angled just so that the valve stem wedged. The release of the stored gas inside happened at the same time as the stem broke. I was pulled, still holding the now free tank by my tethers, by the erratic jerking, expelling tank dancing crazily about. I released the free tank to protect my head and face with my arms. The pain that bounced across my side and arms told me that I had moved just in time. I felt the tumbling sensation of being knocked loose.

"Cadet!" A voice boomed through comms.

"Jess!" Jackson said. "I'm coming. Holy crap! Watch ou-"

And again I was hit, my head, my back, and I felt more disorientated, but kept my hurting arms by my head. I blinked and saw red spots floating before my eyes, and on the reflection of my face in my face shield, but the quick, jerky view was dizzying, so I closed my eyes. I felt the tank pulling me this way and that, and I felt like I was going to be ripped apart. I couldn't breathe when I felt my ribs take another blow.

But I kept my head protected.

That's was my last thought when pain hit my head again.

"I can't get to her!" Jackson shouted in comms.

Maintenance guys came to rush the scene, trying to decide what course of action they should take.

"Fuck this," Ian said and drove along the tether line as low as he could, back out and exposed, and his head and helmet facing the batter Jess. "I'm coming, Jess. Hold on."

But no one acknowledged.

Ian looked up and saw Jess' arms floating freely by her helmet. "Jess?" Ian ducked and felt the erratic tank bounce off the tethering pipe next to him. "When will that thing be empty? Damn!" The thunks and crashing sounds told him the runaway tank was still active.

One of the maintenance guys said something about it being another five to ten minutes, depending on actual fissure.

Ian reached Jess' tether and pulled her lower. Then he reached for her side and fumbled with the jerking tether. He opened the clamp and pulled it free from her suit. He felt the powerful tank bounce again into his back. "Ow! Damn!" Then he kept his head down and waited.

After several seconds, a voice Ian recognized as one of the maintenance staff asked, "Cadet?" Then several people's voices melded together in a blur of sound.

Ian looked up, and tried to shake the pinpoint vision from his sight.

Three maintenance guys were surrounding Jess's form just feet from him. He felt pressure at his shoulder and turned towards it. Another maintenance staff was there, looking him over. "Alright, Hanson?"

Ian pushed himself up and winced. "Been better. Dang." He sucked in a breath. "Not cool." He gave a thumb's up and waved the guy off as he blinked off the narrowing vision again.

Jackson showed up next to Ian. "Smart, man. I didn't think to get that low. I knew we had to lose the tank, but couldn't think as to how." He patted Ian's shoulder, "Guts of steel. Seriously."

Ian nodded as best as he could in the suit. He watched as one of the maintenance guys took the remaining attached tank from Jess's suit and tethered it to himself. "Is Jess okay?"

Jackson turned towards where the other two staff where securing Jess to themselves. "I think she got knocked out. Tank hit her hard twice. They were saying blood in the helmet. Didn't you hear that?"

Ian shook his head. "Musta missed that." And he went limp.

I woke in a bed in the infirmary section, in the back room of the larger medic station. To my right was Jackson sitting in a chair. To the right of him, Ian, also in a bed. They were talking about what happened, but I couldn't hear everything they were saying because they were being quiet.

I just stayed quiet and still while I tried to piece together everything that I remembered, and how I was where I was. My arms were in inflated air braces, and I had an IV in the back of one of my hands. I tried to turn my head and felt the stiffness of a brace prevent me. I saw my toes upright through the blanket and decided to test their mobility. When they wiggled, I exhaled loudly, glad I wasn't paralyzed.

Jackson turned my way and repositioned himself, "Hey! You live! How you feeling?"

Swallowing the dry cotton feeling in my mouth, I mumbled

that I felt like crap.

Ian leaned forward in his cot to look at me. "Dang, Jess. What happened?"

I blinked at his tone and against the pain I felt coming on strong. "My tank got caught." When he just stared at me, "When I kicked the clamp free, it must've become stuck. I didn't notice."

Jackson stood and leaned over me. "Get some rest. I'll go spread rumors and tell everyone how I saved both of you." He gave me a tentative hug. He whispered in my ear, "Go easy on him. He saved your life." Then he was walking out the door where a medic was standing guard.

The silence was loud.

"How did we end up here?" My voice was soft and yet echoed loud in the quiet of the room.

"I got to you and untethered that stupid tank." Ian said it so calm.

I tried to turn towards him, to see his face and reaction, to see how bad he was. But not being able to see him, I said, "The spring was broken on the clamp."

"Okay."

I heard some rustling of the bedding, and Ian came into my view and sat in the chair Jackson had occupied. I cleared my throat. "Was the tank still moving, when you untethered it?"

"I wouldn't have had to come in with a concussion if it wasn't," he said as he arranged his medical wear.

I couldn't judge him or his answer. So I retraced what I did remember in silence. "So...how long are we in here for?"

Ian turned towards me, then quickly away. "I can leave in a little, after they finish clearing me. You? I don't know. I'm sure they will want to keep you until morning."

I squirmed at my uncomfortable position and the growing pain. "Oh, okay." I thought for a moment in the lingering silence.

"So who won?"

"James' team. They had the run before ours. The maintenance guys said that James said he had trouble with the same clamp when securing the replacement tank. He also said, that we could have beaten their time until the tank fiasco." He looked at me and quickly turned away.

It got me thinking. "How bad is my face?"

Ian turned to look at me then straight ahead of himself. "Not bad, why."

"Well, because you won't look at me. Not for long anyway."

He stood up and sat on the edge of my cot and looked me in the eye. Then he sighed and looked me all over. "Every time I look at you I see that damn tank beating the shit out of you." He swallowed and looked at his hands. "It was not my idea of fun. Then you went limp when I was getting close. I thought you were dead. That's all." He looked me in the eye. "Besides, the crooked nose might grow on me."

My arms tried to move to check my face, but with the big air casts on, I couldn't do anything but flail in pain. When Ian laughed, I gave him a dirty look. "Shut up." But he kept laughing. "I thought you weren't big on jokes."

Ian shrugged.

The door opened and Director Bradley entered. He took one look at Ian sitting on my cot, and raised an eyebrow. He didn't say anything on that. What he did say was, "Great job out there, Hanson. Way to think fast. You probably saved Cadet Reynoldi's life tonight. You made us proud." And he put out a hand.

Ian took it and pumped it. "Thank you, sir."

"You're free to go. I signed you out with the medic station." He helped Ian to his feet. "Check in tomorrow morning and let them check you over again. Got it?"

"Yes sir." Ian stood and grabbed the bag of belongings off the end of his cot. "Going to change." And he went into the latrine against the wall.

Director Bradley looked down at me as he handed me my data pod and said that Director Forshay had retrieved it from my quarters. Then he added, "You are lucky to be alive, Reynoldi."

I thanked him.

His features twisted a moment as he thought. "Why are you tied to every mishap here, I wonder?"

I said that I have been wondering the same thing.

Then Ian came out, pants on, shirt off. He came right over to the side of the cot as he pulled the shirt over his head and jerked it down. "Okay?"

I put up my air casts and reached for him. He leaned over and I gave him the only kind of hug I could give and a quick peck on the cheek. "Yeah. Thanks to you." I smiled and blushed when Director Bradley cleared his throat.

Log-in: JessReynoldi18851
Date/Time: 1 July 2202/2152hrs
Subject: Break

Since I have been recuperating from my ordeal, I have been able to focus on classes from the confines of my room. It was nice of Director Forshay to suggest it while I mended. My meals were usually brought by Tori, who would fill me in on things I might need for a particular assignment or quiz. She also filled me in on the rumors going on about what had happened that night on the run.

ENTRY END

"Wait," I held up a hand, with an arm still supported by a cast. "You mean that people knew who had what tanks assigned? Oh, why does it even matter? Accidents happen."

Tori leaned in with a conspirator's movement, "But the maintenance staff said they never had seen anything like it. You flipped over to kick the broke clamp and all hell broke loose. At first they didn't know what had happened. They said you were being thrown around like a rag doll."

"I really wish you would stop telling me this part. I remember. I was there," I said as I pulled from her reach. "It doesn't matter. I keep telling you, accidents happen."

"Seriously? You don't think it odd that James had issues with that same clamp? He reported it and no one checked into it?"

"I guess I figured it was part of the scrimmage run. Sometimes they mess up something to see how well we react. I've told you. That's the nature of the training."

But she scooted over closer to me, making me feel uncomfortable. "I think someone tried to kill you. There are rumors going all over the place. We have even received messages from the house directors to 'cease all speculation and rumor spreading' concerning this accident."

"Good!" I stood to put some distance between us. "I find it hard to believe that anyone would be trying to hurt me, much less kill me. Why would they?" I stomped over to my data pod and stopped a blinking light letting me know of a new message. "Besides, that was Ian's tank. Not mine. He couldn't get it free, so I was going to try. I noticed the clamp spring was gone when I got to it. It's what I told the investigation and that's because it is true. If anything, someone was trying to kill Ian with that. But my tank was the one that got caught on a tethering pipe. No foul play. Just an accident. Why is it so hard to believe? Just stop."

Tori stared at me in surprise. Then she casually stood and collected her things. She left without another word.

I sagged onto my bed and worked the kinks out of my neck as best I could without the use of my hands.

After a few minutes, my data pod chimed with a message light. I picked it up and checked. It was from Tori, saying with everything I had seen, rumors were going around about me stumbling onto something, and someone needing to cover their bases. She said she thought I would be interested, not offended. She also said she wasn't bringing me my meals anymore, so she'd see me at dinner. And to brush my own dang hair. *Wow.*

I checked the other messages I had not checked while she had been in. Indeed, another message about stopping rumors had come from Director Forshay, and I deleted it on principle. One was from Ian, again checking on me, and blaming himself since he couldn't fix the clamp which made me do it, blah-dee-blah, blah blah. I responded to his message reminding him that it was an accident, and that my tank was the one that caused issues, not his, and thanked him, like I did every day, for helping rescue me. And then there were some more concerned messages, again from some people I didn't even know.

The idea that people were talking about me, some concerned for me, made me think about what Tori had implied. She was correct in that I had stumbled on or found things, but she didn't know about the room a few months back. Or did she? Or was I missing something being cooped up in my room the past few weeks while on the mend?

My device chimed in my hand and I jumped. This time it was from Ben. Like every day since the accident happened, he asked if I was okay, and if he could see me.

I looked at my reflection. The bruises and swelling had dissipated with every passing day. Today I hadn't yet taken a shower, because it was awkward and I couldn't brush my hair on my own yet. Luckily Tori had brushed it prior to her bringing up the accident.

I sent him a message back that I wanted to get out of my room anyway, and said I would met him in the solarium in an hour.

So saying, I struggled out of my clothes and took a shower, without getting my hair wet as best I could. Then I fought my way into some of my casual attire, knowing I couldn't manipulate myself into my class As. I brushed my teeth and checked the time. Almost an hour had past. I was going to be late. I sent a message telling him that it had taken me longer to get ready, but that I was on my way. With it sent, I grabbed my chip card and took the back halls to get there. Most of the people I encountered I didn't recognize, but all gave me sympathetic smiles and comments. I just thanked them and ambled down the necessary back halls on my way to the solarium.

I heard the male chanting before I came around the corner, so I stopped short, not wanting to have a conversation with Ian. The same guys, Jackson, Ian, and the others, again all swooping low and side-to-side, arms over the shoulders of the guy or guys next to him. They were so absorbed in their chanting they didn't see me, so I backed up and took a different hall, which made me even later getting to the solarium.

When I came around the last corner, I finally saw him.

Ben was sitting on the bench looking at his data pod. Just waiting. As I got closer, he turned, and seeing it was me, he stood. He started walking towards me and I felt a lump rise in my throat. I stopped, nervous, but he kept coming until he just wrapped his arms around me. I choked back a sob and smiled as he pulled away enough to look at me.

"Did I hurt you?" he asked as he let go.

"What? No," I said as I continued to smile.

"But you made a sound," he said.

"Boys," I said softly. "It was a good sound. You hugged me. It took me by surprise."

Ben took my hand and led me further into the solarium down the small path that weaved through the vegetation. He was so careful, asking if my arms hurt, and if he was hurting me. He was...tender and tentative. He told me how the last chess match had gone, since I had been in my room, hiding as he called it. Then he showed me pictures of some of the blooms and butterflies from the Pollination room. He even confirmed Tori's comments about someone must be out to get me.

I assured him that it had been an accident, told him everything that I remembered until I was knocked out by the broken tank attached at my waist. And he just listened, occasionally asking for clarification. I told him about waking up in the infirmary and Ian's guilt. I even told him how I thanked Ian for saving me, the simple kiss on the cheek and poor excuse for a hug."

"You kissed him?"

I took in his incredulous look. "A peck on the cheek. I was

feeling grateful for still being here."

Ben looked straight ahead, and it seemed like more of a pout.

I rolled my eyes. "Oh, for crying out loud! I didn't kiss him on the lips or anything." When I saw Ben nod his head, I continued, "So no more on that. Sorry." I thought of what other things we could safely talk about, and asked about classes, and how it is up here when the next group of cadets arrive. After listening on what to expect, I told him that he was going to have to come up with a new nickname for me once the current semester was over.

It only took him a moment to come back with, "Second year plebe?" Then he beamed that smile on his face.

I couldn't help but laugh at his wit and sense of humor. "That's special," I added while I wiped at a tear in my eye. "Oh my goodness. Too funny."

We strolled, hand-in-hand, around a few more times around the path making small talk.

Ben even brought up something about what I learned from being out on external maintenance. That had me thinking beyond what I told him, which is about that peaceful, indescribable feeling of being weightless when I was outside of IDEA, that I was glad to have learned what I did, and that it was completely different from working with the poultry.

I didn't tell him I hadn't seen any hull breaches when I was on my maintenance runs, but maybe I didn't see any because I wasn't working where they were. But I knew just my thinking that thought got a seed of suspicion growing, and I wanted to do more research. There were supposedly two cells sealed because of hull breach. But my external escapades never showed more than some denting and welded repairs to tethering pipes.

Maybe one more jaunt outside was in order before I was pulled from that detail. No one had mentioned it, but I was sure a few people were thinking I shouldn't go back to external.

"Hello?" Ben's voice said at my left.

I focused on his face, "Hmm?"

"You were lost in thought. Care to share?"

A dozen or so thoughts ran through my mind at the same time. Ben had been told about the floating body, but I had never told him about the blood and clean-up that was done that Christmas eve. I had a feeling knew more than most people, and I wasn't sure who knew what. I wanted to figure out what it was that I thought I knew, but to do that meant I had to have a Watson to my Sherlock Holmes. Decision made, I brought up a picture of the blood outside that door in the hall of Bradley House, and said, "I think something is going on here." I showed the picture. "Horrible things."

Ben looked at the picture and frowned. "Where was this?"

I swallowed, "Bradley House. I heard a scream and begging and laughing. Down one of the hallways off the one leading to the Pollination Room. It's what really freaked me out about the messages when you were busy Christmas Eve." Seeing a bench ahead, I steered towards it. "I had been on my way to find you, thinking you were in there with your bees and butterflies." I shuddered at the memory.

"You never said anything about this before," Ben said as we sat.

"I was told not to." Then I told him what I heard, in detail. How I took a picture of the blood. That I was afraid of what was happening in that room. That I had stepped in the blood and took off my shoes and hid in the latrine while I tried to get a grip. I even told him what I had heard about someone accessing a janitorial closet in Forshay House that night, and how the whole room and the hallway had been thoroughly scoured. I also said that it was probably why they had done a drill the next day. When he just looked at me, without his eyes doing their shifty thing, I asked if he knew why no one was going to the pond anymore.

He pursed his lips. "I was told a health hazard and that someone had given away our accessing it." Then he faced me. "Was there more to it?"

I relayed Tori and Kim's find, without giving their names, only saying someone had stumbled across blood in a tunnel leading to the pond. I didn't mention the skeletal remains Tori and Kim hinted at either. I guessed that the blood had been found during the cleaning cycle. I even told Ben of my theory of how the faculty or staff was trying to get a confession with the whole April first announcement. Then I asked him what he thought of the probability of the hoax being real, though I knew more than I let on.

"April first," he said. "I remember. I was wondering what kind of trick it was, but like you, thought only a select few would get it."

"And Ben, this isn't the first time I have found blood like this. That cadet from your house," I quickly accessed my journal, careful not to let Ben see my password, "Marshall, and I found some blood way back when I first arrived. I thought someone had had a nosebleed. That was my first interaction with," my heart dropped while I said his name, "Phil."

Log-in: JessReynoldi18851
Date/Time: 3 July 2202/2204hrs
Subject: Accusation

Ben and I have been meeting and working through scenarios of how things appear to be. I am confident in my belief that Phil is somehow involved in all of the odd things that have been happening. Phil has to be the culprit, and I want to explain my reasons to Director Forshay. Phil has an all seeing device and can access any room. He patrols through the halls after us cadets. He was there that first trace of blood. He knew of the metal plates in the doors. He found the metal shim in the door that Tori told me about. He could access janitorial closets.

I think back to the day when Director Bradley asked how come I was always where mishaps, and I feel the answer is...purpose. I am meant to blow Phil's cover. I am meant to save the next cadet or cadets from whatever fate I narrowly escaped.

I had a meeting with Director Forshay this evening after Ben advised me to keep his name out of it, especially since Forshay had told me not to talk with anyone about what I came across.

ENTRY END

I took a deep breath and hit the call button at Director Forshay's quarters. Exhaling, I went over everything I had rehearsed. I had practiced various versions with Ben, to be ready to keep on point and prove my case. Phil was the perpetrator.

When the door opened and James bowed his head and

stepped out, I smiled briefly his way before I met Director Forshay's look.

"Reynoldi?" Forshay stepped back to allow me access. "What can I do for you?"

Once the door was secure behind me I told him that I have been doing some thinking and going back through my journal and have found some things that I thought he should know. After he brought me to his office and sat at his desk, I started with the beginning, the body past my portal and the blood in the hall and how Phil had helped clean it up. I went on about my theory of Phil having access to all of the rooms and people's devices via chip cards. I was able to go through my whole rehearsed speech without any interruption. Once I was done, I just remained standing at his desk, and waited. Since Forshay wasn't looking at me, I looked at the bronze sculpture glistening behind him.

Forshay tapped his fingers on the desk while he gazed off to the side. Occasionally his fingers would stop moving, then they'd start again. Then he took a deep breath and addressed me. "That's a serious allegation, Reynoldi." When he saw me open my mouth, he put up a hand to stop me. "I understand all of your reasons.. I will order an investigation immediately. But during the investigation, I need you to not discuss any of these issues with anyone." That said, he stood and came around his desk. "Thank you for seeing me and bringing your concern." Then he ushered me back down to the door and told me to rest easy and have a good night.

I sighed and allowed a smile to spread across my face knowing Phil was going to be stopped.

Log-in: JessReynoldi18851
Date/Time: 8 July 2202/2131hrs
Subject: Bradley

I received a message to meet Director Bradley in his office after dinner. I mentioned it to Ben, who seemed concerned. He offered to wait outside Bradley's quarters, and I accepted.

I wasn't prepared for what happened.

ENTRY END

I hit the call button on Director Bradley's office. Turning towards Ben, I was relieved to see him nod and lean up against the hall wall, a sign he wasn't going anywhere.

Director Bradley opened the door. He didn't smile at me, but he acknowledged Ben with a casual, "Cadet Williams." Then he ushered me in and closed the door behind us. He indicated for me to follow him, and I was feeling relieved that I had a witness to my potential demise.

Bradley took me to his office, which despite it being set up in the same fashion as Forhsay's, I was surprised to see. The desk had three framed photos of people I assumed were family. A group picture that had Bradley, a middle-aged woman, and three teens, a son and two daughters, took me aback. Another photo showed all the same people, though aged, and sans Bradley. The encased sculpture of IDEA wasn't lit and highlighted like it was in Forshay's. Literary works filled gaps on the shelves and the door to another was open, showcasing a degree with a female's name. He turned and followed my gaze. "My daughter, Victoria." He smiled, and I realized he was a different person when he did so. "Made Harvard and graduated two years ago." He snorted a little through his proud dad look, "And she sent me proof of her success, there. Honors."

I nodded seeing the summa cum laude decal prominently displayed. "You must be very proud, sir." My throat tightened.

Bradley nodded and indicated I should take a seat. "I have heard, and have been asked to comment on, the allegations you have made against Phil Macke."

It took me just a moment to realize that it was the first time that I had heard Phil's last name. But, I didn't fold, if that was what Bradley was after. I just sat, quietly awaiting insight as to why he had called me to his office.

As if on cue, "I bet you're wondering why I asked to see you, Cadet Reynoldi." He didn't pause to give me a chance to answer. Instead, he plodded right on. "I have been assigned to IDEA for a total of seven years. My son," he points to the young man in the picture, "attended here for his four years. He graduated four years ago." Bradley sat in a chair next to me, not in the manly, very ornate leather one, like I have seen Forshay do. "He was a decent student...studied, surprisingly, the same thing you are. But, we didn't have Forshay as his instructor. Todd," he waved to the picture again for clarification, "didn't want to be in my house, for many reasons."

Bradley leaned back in the chair next to me, "I read the complaint. Would you please tell me in your own words why you think Phil is behind all the...oddities you noted." With that said, Bradley kept a very open posture and looked me in the eye, like an equal.

After taking a deep breath, I started with my trying to justify how someone could have access to all the areas and with the data pod issues. I felt encouraged when Bradley looked down while I talked, listening, and he even asked questions to make sure he understood my perspective. It was the first time I have spoken with Director Bradley that I actually felt good about. He listened and treated me with none of the contempt he had shown me previous.

When I was done answering all of his questions on Phil, he thanked me and started to walk me out. I paused, and then scrambled to follow him. "That's it?"

He nodded and smiled, "You answered all of my questions." He slowed and stopped. "I don't have to agree with your interpretations, but you have answered everything. I appreciate your time, cadet." And then we were at his door. "Please keep all of your concerns quiet during the inquiry, if you please." He opened the door. "Thank you, and have a good night, Reynoldi." He nodded to Ben, "Good evening, Williams."

"Sir," Ben said with a quick nod.

And the door to Bradley's quarters closed, leaving me in the hall with very protective escort. "Well?"

I blinked, wondering if part of this was a test. "He just asked me some questions. Nothing bad, nothing good. Just stuff." I started walking and Ben kept in step. "It felt like he was just making sure...," but I stopped thinking aloud. *Like he was making sure he wasn't implicated.*

"Making sure he understood your concerns?" Ben asked as we went through the halls towards the Commons.

I couldn't trust my voice, so I just nodded.

With my mind rewinding the details of the Bradley conversation, it took me a moment to realize where Ben had steered us. I couldn't help but smile. "New butterflies?"

Ben shook his head, but led the way. Once we were in the Pollination Room, he guided me to the little work area where we usually hung out. He took his usual seat, and I took mine. He set his data pod down and gave me a funny look.

"What?" I couldn't help but ask, and he wasn't his normal calm.

He cleared his throat, and then again. He sighed heavily, then met my eye. "Do you know why no one had invited you to the pond?"

I licked my lips and looked down while I nodded. "Phil's snooping. And then something happened."

He scooted closer. "Do you know what happened?"

I didn't know how much Ben knew. How much he wanted me to know. I decided to play innocent. "I just was told we weren't going because something happened. I heard Phil found a door's metal shim." That much was true, so I wasn't lying. But the guilt of hearing more, made me look down.

"There's more," he started and cleared his throat again. "There was a night, a night you sent me messages. A night you panicked, and I didn't understand why until later. Some went to the pond, and said something had been left there." He waited until I was looking back at him. "They found a...a body."

I couldn't breathe. I just blinked and searched his face. I had to pretend I didn't already know this. "A what?"

Ben pursed his lips. "I was still upset with everything that happened after seeing Ian at your door, and what you had said to him." He puts up a lone hand to ward off my interruption. "I was walking, working everything over in my head." He looked at me. "I do better when I'm walking, sorting through facts and timelines as I move." Ben waved off whatever he was about to say, then brought his hands together as he focused on them. "I was up on the upper level, not far from here, one most cadets never go on, and had left my data pod in my room. I heard voices, and came around the corner." His face went funny, more shifty than normal, like he was seeing what happened all over. "I stopped, and backed up so no one would see me."

Ben turned and looked at me. There was something so odd in his gaze. "Bones. Bloody bones, like a skeleton." He forced the air out of his lungs. "Cadets were moving it out of the inner door, by the oxygen generation station?" His tone asked as much as his look did. "I have been thinking of all that you have seen and reported." He reached for my hand, so I let him take it. "Jess, I think you are in danger."

I looked down and swallowed as both bits of information settled on me. Ben had said my name. First time since Valentine's. And he did so with a warning for my safety.

But my paranoid side launch its own counter attack. How do I know he isn't one of them, seeing what I know? What if he's setting me up? What if he is trying to get me to share information as to who told me what I already shared?

Then rational Jess railed my insecure, scared self. He never asked who had told you about the pond. He's just volunteering information.

"Jess? Plebe?"

And back to that name again in less than ten seconds.

"Hold on," I said as I put up a finger. I ran through what he said again. Then I looked at him, really looking him in the eye. "I need to know if I can trust telling you things, Ben. That you won't shut down and take off like you have before." I swallowed the lump growing in my throat.

He apologized and said he was concerned for IDEA and her

cadets.

I had no one else I could turn to. The directors knew my concerns. It was time to show some faith in the guy who made my heart crumble, and I was praying that my heart was as smart as my head, if not smarter. "I came to you that night with the directors because I heard something. Then I found something. And your messages were cryptic. I was afraid for you. I was reaching out for help."

"What? What did you hear? What did you find?"

I swallowed. "I heard those muffled calls for help, and laughter." I tried to gauge Ben's reaction before I added. "And blood." The memory and the guilt of literally and physically flushing bloody evidence stopped me from saying something he might not like to hear. "I had to know that you were okay," I said as I looked at his hand still holding mine. "I was afraid you were tied to whatever was happening in that room." My eyes lock with his. "I'm not supposed to talk about it. Forshay warned me about talking about it. And tonight, that was in part why Bradley wanted to see me."

Ben did his shifty eye thing, his face tight. When he looked at me, he tried to smile. "I understand everything from that night now. But I didn't send you anything that should have caused you alarm. You need to know that I am not like that."

And right then, I did. I trusted him, or I sure hoped I did. "I know. So, when a message from you came with my name, you understand why I was concerned? I was thinking someone had used your device like they had with that student who I saw floating outside my window. Someone has been covering all of this up." And despite all the warnings given to me, "And, I think it's Phil. Maintenance-guy-Phil."

Ben nodded. Then the nod turned into a head shaking.

"What? You think I'm wrong?"

His shaking went back to nodding.

"You're not making any sense," I said as I pulled my hand from his.

Ben looked me dead in the face. "Phil wasn't moving the... remains."

Oh? Hmm. Well...but, "Who was there?"

Ben squinted as he said it, "Like I said, it looked like some cadets. I didn't really see them very well. I was pretty far away. And I couldn't hear them as they were keeping their voices low." Ben rubbed his face. "But there were three of them. "

"Looked like cadets is not cadets, Ben," I said. I sighed. "Do you realize what you are saying? That cadets are involved in a serious cover-up, including murder and desecrating a body? That they have power over the powers that be in IDEA."

Ben shoved away from me. "Never mind." He shook his head. "Forget I said anything."

"How can I?" I slapped a hand over my mouth, then jerked my head side-to-side. "I have seen things I cannot forget. Done things I regret." I reached for his hand, but he was reluctant to give it. "If you say it's cadets, because *you* saw something, I have no choice but to believe you." He looked at me for assurance. "I believe you."

Ben nodded and wrapped his hand around mine. "I'm worried about you."

"Why?"

Ben stared into my eyes. "Because if I'm right, you have already shared your time in the interviews and the body floating past your window with your friends, and people talk. It's how they found that lady's remains in the fish tank, remember?"

Oh crap. I swallowed. "I didn't share a lot with that group. Mostly, I shared with just you."

Ben cocked his head. "Me? Are you sure?"

I nodded. "You were my witness in case something happened to me."

"Just me? No one else?"

Warning bells dinged in my head, but I swallowed anyway. "I have it all in my journals, but yeah, just you."

"Please tell me you have your journal password coded?"

More warning bells, and lights. "Of course." Fear made me test a theory, "And I think someone tried to get to my journal." At Ben's sudden look of shock, I continued, "So I changed my passwords on my device and set up another one for my entries."

"Good!"

And he didn't ask what they were, so the sirens dulled...a lot.

"Be careful, plebe. I don't want anything bad to happen to you."

"I don't want anything bad to happen to me either, I assure you!" I released the breath I had been holding. I smiled at the worried look on Ben's face. "At least I'm not the only one who has seen things. That makes a few of us now." For a moment I hesitated in the blunder of announcing more witnesses.

But Ben only commented, "Good. The more who see odd things, the better. *They*," he emphasized, "can't keep getting away with doing things like this."

I could only nod in agreement.

"I can take you back to your room now," Ben announced.

His instant change of subject made a thought popped in my head, so I asked, "Do I make you nervous, Ben?"

Ben did his shifty-eye thing. "I allow myself to be nervous around you."

"Why?"

He looked me in the eye, "I don't want to mess anything up."

I lifted my free hand and touched his cheek. "You are so sweet." Then I removed my hand. Leaning forward, I gave him a quick peck on the cheek while he pulled back in surprise. The result meant I mostly missed. I blushed and looked down in my now empty hands. "I'm sorry."

But then he tilted my face and his lips were on mine.

Okay, totally not *sorry.*

Log-in: JessReynoldi18851
Date/Time: 25 July 2202/2200hrs
Subject: Confidant

It feels so much better around here knowing I have a confidant, someone I can share everything with. Even better when he decides we can, make me blush, snog. He's only pulled me into his lap a couple of times when in the Pollination Room while we discuss a possible future after IDEA. I know he can pretty much have the pick of his career options, and I may too, but there are times I wonder if this is just some "college fling."

Hard to believe that so much has happened to change my life forever. I feel like I have grown up more than I ever thought possible. I thought I was mature when I was interviewing for this academy. So much has altered me, and I still have three years to go.

John asked me about coming back to the Hatchery before all the new plebes arrive. I said I would love to. To be honest, I didn't think Hope would recognize me. Bonds. I'm learning more and more about what they really mean.

ENTRY END

I hold an excitement I haven't felt in weeks. As soon as the door opened, the intense heat and peep, peep, peeping brought a huge smile to my face. Hearing my name, I turned to see John with a basket of chicks to transfer to the feeder section. I quickly pulled on a harness tray combo and started extracting chicks like a pro. "Some things you never forget," I said as I cast a look in John's direction.

He only smiled and reached for more puff balls in need of feathers, and food. When his tray was full, I followed, even though mine wasn't. "Missed you around here." He started depositing chicks into their new area.

I nodded. "Missed it. External maintenance is run, run, run and then extremely cold and quiet when you're outside. This is the complete opposite." I continued transferring the like moving peeps.

John only nodded and worked his tray. "Which task did you like better?"

After a few seconds I shrugged. "I like them both. I love the seeing of life happening here, despite what happens to the meat birds. And I really liked the excitement of the external runs and buddy system."

"Minus runaway venting oxygen tanks?"

I raised my eyebrows at him, then laughed. "Minus stupid venting tanks. Yeah."

When John was done with his tray, he helped me finish with mine. "Bet your wondering why I asked for you to come here today."

I shrugged. "You told me you needed some help. I'm qualified." Then I looked at his face. "That was it, right?"

John rested an arm on the cage. "Have you brought anyone in with you? I mean, ever?"

My mouth did the goldfish gulp. "What? No. You told me I couldn't. I even had my friends ask for a tour, and they gave me grief when I said no." My excitement in coming kept dulling with every syllable. "Why would you even ask that?"

John regarded me a moment. "I believe you. I know that we have worked together most of you shifts. I am asking for two reasons. One, there has been some odd door activity lately. Unsecure lockings and I have to ask." He held out his gloved hand. "Key card."

My jaw dropped. "Are you serious?" At his nod, I fished through my protective garment to pull out my card and hand it over.

He motioned for me to follow.

While I did, thoughts about Phil screwing with me came to mind. "If this about my turning Phil in, I'm going to be pissed. If he set me up...."

John put up a hand and kept walking. He went up some stairs that I hadn't ever been on before, and it took us to an office filled with computers and monitors. John went over to a computer and scanned my card and typed in something. Within seconds dates and locations polled and aligned next to another report. John traced the lines for several dates and locations from one screen to the other. Then he handed my card back. "Sorry. I had to double check."

"You could've just asked. I reached over his shoulder. I was working external these days. And here," I pointed to the June 8th date, "that was when I was getting the snot beat out of me by a broken oxygen tank external side." I indicated other dates, "Infirmary visits. Director visits." I shook my head. "Wow. I come here to help and am ambushed." I put my card back into my suit's pocket.

"Cadet, please understand. I had to be sure. There have been a few...intrusions here. And when chicks started disappearing..."

"Wait! What?"

"You can understand that we have to check with every member of IDEA who has had access.

"Did you check with Phil? Did you scan his card?" I felt the heat in my face while I felt it in my voice.

John cocked his head. "Phil?"

"Creepy? Stalker? Maintenance guy? Phil. Has access to every place here." I whirled around for effect. "Phil. The guy who gave me access to the Hatchery when he swiped my card," I fumble to bring it out again, "that day with Director Bradley."

John frowned. "I know Phil. We've been friends for years. He'd never come here."

"Oh?" My voice raised in disbelief. "And why's that?"

"He's vegan. He hates the cages. Besides, he's allergic to the feed." John just shook his head twice as he thought.

My jaw dropped again. "What?"

"Someone stole four chicks. All deformed. And chick feed." John stood and faced me. "That's why I was thinking it was you."

"Why would I steal chicks and some feed?"

John pursed his lips. "I wondered the same thing. Then your Hope came up missing. Except she's a laying hen now. Someone took her right out her nesting cage."

I stopped breathing. A wave of dizziness overcame me. "Wait. What?"

John kept his eyes on me and repeated that Hope was gone.

"Someone was taking the crippled chicks?" I sank to the floor. "Someone took Hope?" A numbness filled my limbs and made them unresponsive. But my mind was rampaging through thoughts and memories like a thundering herd of wildebeest. "Someone took Hope." My eyes found John. "Oh crap. They are coming after me."

John asked me to explain, but I was too busy trying to gain function of my resistant limbs. I needed to go to someone for help. I struggled to my feet and blinked at John, "It wasn't me. The person who did this is trying to get to me."

"What do you mean? How so?"

His face was so innocent and I remember how much faith he had put in me. I spilled everything about the first body, to the concern which landed me a chance to work in the Hatchery. I also told him my suspicions about Phil's involvement.

John had listened to all that I had to say with quiet interest. But when I told him of my allegations, he became angry. "It was you!" He stepped away from me. "Phil has been on staff with IDEA for a dozen plus years. He came here after his wife died of cancer, and both their kids committed suicide due to the inability to deal with the stress." John put a hand over his mouth, probably realizing he was giving too much away. Then he turned back towards me. "And he's in quarantine because of you."

I blinked at the tone. "I...I'm sorry. I think it's him." I turned my head side-to-side as I replayed my conversations with Forshay and Bradley. "He has access to everywhere. He sees everything.

He snoops the halls at night. He's looking for...." But I couldn't finish without implicating my knowledge of the pond.

"Rule breakers?" John supplied.

I nodded. "Yes! He accused me of stuff to keep me off his trail."

"Cadet!" John cleared his throat. "It couldn't have been Phil who took that chick you feel for."

"Oh? How do you know? Maybe he has been pretending to have allergies or whatnot." Okay, that sounded weak even to me.

John scowled, and I missed the old John more than ever. "Phil has been in quarantine awaiting a formal investigation and trial back on Earth. I have lost two hens since he's been locked away. The last time was yesterday." He turned to the screen. "But according to here, you were in lecture when the doors mysteriously opened without a chip card. Then someone accessed several hen cages until one was opened. The one," he turned towards me again, "that had Hope."

My mouth went dry. I was thinking. My mind was just tidal wave after tidal wave. "Is she dead?"

"I don't know. There's no carcass that we have found."

I nodded, mind still racing. "Someone must have known about her. I showed...showed pictures and videos of her." My eyes hit his. "Oh my god. It's one of my friends. One of my group. Or one of their friends." I rubbed my face. "I want to go back to my room. Especially since you don't really need me."

John informed me I could, but let me know that my room was currently being checked for Hope and evidence of her care. "Fine. You won't find anything, since I didn't take her."

He finally let me leave. And it was more than just being able to leave the Hatchery that had me shaking and wanting to curse a blue streak. Someone had taken Hope. Someone was posing as my friend, and clearly wasn't. Someone had access to everywhere. And it was someone close to me who had seen the videos of Hope and knew of my time in the Hatchery.

The question was which one.

As I stripped the sanitation garment off, I made a list of everyone who had seen any pictures of my time in the Hatchery, and any of their friends. Primary and up-close and personal friends were: Tori (who felt jilted by my not letting her go to the Hatchery), Bryce (who constantly mocked my chick chore), Ellie (who was supportive of my chore), Kim (who seemed more worried about being the next victim), James (my Head of House, Chain of Command and all-around good go-to guy), Ian (the surly disappointed, yet savior), his friends Adams and Jackson (both casual attendees at the dinner table), and Ben (my shifty-eyed beau).

Then there were all of their known acquaintances. Ian, Jackson, and James had their little Male Bonding Gang with the other few guys I didn't really know. There was that kid, Marshall, who gave grace that first meal and that I have run into a couple of times. Freaking Cecile, who with her gaggle of cronies, was often seen with James. A few of Ellie's friends, but none of their names came to mind, just faces. Adams, Lincoln, and...gosh, a few others. Some of the guys on my external maintenance teams.

I had to document all of this. I had to write down all the people who knew of Hope and their connection to me.

By the time I had myself locked away in my quarters, my list had about thirty people, and their reactions to me, and to Hope. There had to be a correlation. Once I had my list, I wondered who to give it to. I had to forward it to someone, in case something happened to me.

I decided to not send it to anyone whose name was on the list. I struggled with who to give it to. Chain of Command dictated James and then his upper. But there was a connection to

James, and I wasn't sure who to trust. Ben was on the list, so I couldn't, in fairness, forward it to Ben. Tori, though she had shared about the pond and the skeletal remains, may not also be trustworthy.

I sat and thought. Then I decided. I started typing, talking as I did, "Dear John, I don't know if this will help you. I compiled a list of everyone I have spent time with, and how they knew about my Hatchery duties, and of Hope. Someone recently told me that they were worried about me...that he thought he had seen some cadets do something. I want to trust him. His name is highlighted. But the ones with asterisks are all people I have shown videos and pictures of my time in the Hatchery and of Hope. The rest are their acquaintances, or mine. I don't want to go to the directors, as both know how I have led the charges against Phil. If I am wrong about him, which you think I am, then I am sorry. And I don't know who to report this all too, depending on the Chain of Command. But if someone is corrupted in my list, who is part of my Chain, I need a confidant." I exhaled loud. "I chose you. If something happens, there is a trail. My dad said to always cover all your bases." I thought a moment, "Please let me know if you find anything about Hope." Then I put my name to it, and hit send.

Seeing the time, I set my data device down, and showered.

When I came back, I had a response from John. "Okay, cadet. I will start my own, quiet inquiries. If you hear anything, let me know."

I set my device down and looked out my portal. Several seconds of blackness ticked by before a calming glimpse of Earth passed came into view. Nodding at her continued presence, I decided to call it a night.

Log-in: JessReynoldi18851
Date/Time: 9 Aug 2202/2247hrs
Subject: Opportunity

So, today we all had to watch a video about transitioning to the next stage of our academic life here at IDEA. During the video, we were reminded that we all had been plebes at one point, and just like others looked out for us, we were to look out for the newcomers due in next week.

At the end of the presentation, certain data pods chimed to life with messages about new responsibilities being assigned to some of the cadets. Mine chimed with a message to see Director Forshay.

ENTRY END

    I pressed the call button outside Forshay's quarters. Then I rubbed my sweaty palms against my pants.
    Forshay opened the door and smiled. "Cadet Reynoldi. Thank you for coming." Then he held the door open wide so I could enter. Once I was in, he closed the door, and indicated for me to

move deeper in. "You know the way."

I turned and went to his office and took my usual seat.

Forshay pressed the button on his desk which opened the cabinet doors to reveal the encased, illuminated sculpture behind him. While the doors opened and set, he sat in his big chair. "So, Cadet? How do you think things are going for you?"

Unsure of his question, I asked him to clarify.

He moved his hands in the space around him. "Are you feeling challenged enough? Do you have any career change thoughts we should note?"

"No, sir. I'm still happy with my choice. I'm learning more than I thought I would," and I swallowed the lump growing in my throat. It surprised me that there was one. I hadn't felt nervous around him in months. "Sir? What is this about?"

Again, he smiled. "You are still in the top of your academic courses. You are working," he looked down at the data device before him, "in both the Hatchery on occasion, and asking for continue, yet limited, duties in external maintenance." His lifted his eyebrows seeking my agreement. Once he received it, he peered at the information again. "I'm in need of aide, as part of student tasking, I was thinking you would gain a lot of valuable information on maintaining records and order." He leaned way back in that chair, allowing the sculpture to glisten behind him like a crown.

I looked into my lap and thought of the opportunity he offered. It would be a very prestigious position on my resume. It would teach me more hands-on about the paperwork side of an installation.

But I didn't want to give up working with the peep, peeps. I needed to find Hope and whoever took her. I hadn't heard anything back from John yet, but I was hoping to find out something soon. John didn't tell me he needed me in the

Hatchery though.

Then there's the adrenaline rush of the external maintenance tasking. It was phenomenal, though I had only been asked to go twice since the accident. But in those two times I hadn't seen any actual hull breaches to support the loss of a student into space's void. I was told that all hull breaches were always contained to prevent further liability, so maybe which accounted for something.

And, of course, there was the oddity of missing persons and the cover-up by whoever was the guilty party. Perhaps I could find out more as Forshay's assistant? Perhaps I would be able to find something in the paperwork to show a trail?

Decisions. Decisions.

"Cadet?"

I looked up at Forshay and quickly tried to coordinate a coherent summary of my thoughts. "Sir, I am honored that you would consider me."

He nodded, "And?"

I worked the inside of my cheeks. "Would I be required to give up my other taskings?"

Forshay leaned even further back into his chair as he thought, fingers steepled and tapping themselves as he did so. "Perhaps it wouldn't be necessary, but," he caught my look, "it would be advised. Is that the reason for your hesitancy?"

I nodded and held my head high. "I find the two tasks I have vary and offer me differing stress relief. I also want to make sure I don't overwhelm myself so I can maintain academic consistency."

Now Forshay worked his cheeks while he regarded me. After several seconds, "If you aren't interested, you only need to say so, Cadet Reynoldi." His tone was cold and dry, and his eyes mirrored that.

"Sir, you misunderstand me," I said as I tried for tactful

words. "It would be an honor to be your aide. I was just trying to make sure I weighed all my options. Isn't that what you would expect of me? To consider all my training opportunities?"

His eyebrow raised in silent question at my comments. His lips became a fine line. After several long seconds, he looked back at the data. "If you want to consider all your options, would you rather by a House Aide?"

"Like Cadet Bennett?"

"Precisely."

After a few seconds weighing the benefits of being House Aide, always on-call, still reporting to Forshay and the rest of the Chain of Command. "No, sir. I don't think that would be a good fit for me." I sighed and took a deep breath. "I accept the position of your teaching aide. I only ask that I still have an opportunity to assist in the other areas if I am needed there, and my time permits."

Forshay tapped at his desk while he regarded me. "Done," he said abruptly. "Duties commence tomorrow after your last class. Report here after chow and be prepared to stay late."

Log-in: JessReynoldi18851
Date/Time: 11 Aug 2202/2337hrs
Subject: Internship begins

I am so exhausted after this evening. I reported to Director Forshay's shortly after dinner. When I arrived I had a list of my duties and responsibilities presented to me in a folder. Several pages, including a "how to" guide, were inside.

It was a blur of information. I took lots and lots of notes.

Not sure this was a good idea. Not sure I will have time for anything else.

I can't help but wonder if maybe that's intentional?

ENTRY END

My device chimed announcing a message. It's the third time since after nine that it has gone off, and I dare not check it. Every time a notification went off, Director Forshay acted like he was waiting for me to answer or check it. I was beginning to think it was a test, and decided to just ignore every message sound while we were in his office.

After the main rundown of responsibilities, he showed me his list of incoming plebes. He showed me how the computer system had already been set up for each cadet prior to their departure from Earth. He asked me to assign them to a list of House Aides based on class schedules, ranking of specializations and scores, and personality tests. He said he need the breakdown by tomorrow afternoon so he could give the list to the perspective House Aides tomorrow evening after dinner.

He left me in his office so I could work.

Five hundred cadets. I had to place fifty cadets with one of ten cadets. That didn't seem like it would be too hard, but I wanted to make sure I didn't miss anything important in the assignment to their House Aides.

I ran through the list of ten new aides for the incoming plebes. I was shocked to find Tori's name in the midst. James remained on the previous aides list, but as already assigned to the group I was in. I didn't recognize any of the other cadets taking in newbies, so I quickly drafted a chart to help me look at an incoming cadet's numbers versus those of the potential House Aides. It took me over two hours to make a chart that I liked and thought would work.

After that, placement quick of the incoming plebes went quick. My chart worked like a dream, and I sent a copy of the chart design to Director Forshay and to myself for future use. I also sent him and blind copied myself a list of which of the five new aides were to receive which new plebes.

As I stood up and worked out the kinks that had somehow manifested themselves on my person, I checked my messages.

One was from Ben asking me to message him when I was done. I responded that I had just finished and was going to message Director Forshay to see if I could leave yet.

One was from Tori asking what I was doing. I sent her a message that I was now Forshay's aide and helping assign her new plebes. She messaged back with an immediate, "Does it give you a picture? Hook me up with some hot ones, would ya?" I couldn't help but chuckle even though I didn't respond.

And the last was from John saying Phil was to be extradited from IDEA when the shuttles departed. Guilt ate at me, and I couldn't think of anything to respond with, so I didn't. I knew it had been suggested that it would happen. I knew that all the evidence pointed to Phil. I knew that Phil had stressors that could cause him to lash out. But it was John's belief in him that made me feel bad.

After several seconds, and still no word from Director Forshay, I let myself out of his office. As I made my way through the halls, I saw some of the guys I didn't know from Ian and James' group walking in my direction. All of them had smiles on their faces, until they saw me. Two of them almost maintained the smile. One scowled, and then blew me a kiss as the group of three passed. I couldn't help but swallow the huge lump in my throat and put my head down as I booked it to my room. Before I opened my door, I checked down the hall, both ways. The three weren't anywhere to be seen.

Three guys.

Three cadets.

The conversation Ben and I had a couple days ago replayed in my mind.

Three cadets were moving remains.

I looked around me again before the door secured me safely inside my quarters.

Paranoia.

Fear and paranoia.

James and Ian wouldn't hurt me. *Right?* But that doesn't mean that their cohorts wouldn't, right? Or were they just being guys? I mean, they only know me via Ian and James, so they don't need to be nice. Two of them were smiling. Only one wasn't. Maybe they were just walking down the hall?

And this *is why I was not destined to be a pysch major.*

I quickly toss my data pod on my cot and go to my portal to look out, hoping some of that nothingness would ease itself into my mind and soul. After several passings, I decide to take a shower and start my homework.

When I am done, I work on my journaling and bring up past things and reread them. I highlight different dates in a separate file so I can quickly bring them up if I need to later. Then I decide to transfer them in chronological order.

Looking at everything, the evidence is still against Phil.

With a shake of my head, I turn out my lights and crawl beneath my covers. After several long minutes, I finally turn on my side and allow the Sandman to visit.

Log-in: JessReynoldi18851
Date/Time: 17 Aug 2202/2207hrs
Subject: New arrivals

Seeing the new plebes as they went around on their tour reminds me of how much has happened in the past year. Not just the oddities, but the growing and the chores, and the maturing. I am definitely not the same Jessica Reynoldi as I was a year ago.

I didn't even realize that my birthday had come and gone with all of the stuff going on. It was kind of nice to not have a lot of attention on me, especially because of the odd things that happened early in the year.

As Director Forshay's aide, I was present when the graduated Firsties were offered their diplomas and offered assignments from different companies or by military outposts. I teared up watching some of them receive phenomenal opportunities that no one would get unless they attended IDEA. I made a great decision coming here.

Despite the rush and chaos of the shuttles arriving and the departure of the graduates, I was in the corridor when Phil was escorted into the shuttle to await proceeding back on Earth. He looked dazed and confused. Still. After all this time.

ENTRY END

I smiled as I witnessed Tori's new plebe group passing a hallway down past the loading docks, heading off to the closet medic station and on to the Coop. She had practiced her tour with me twice yesterday, so I knew she was only about ten minutes into her actual tour.

Hard to believe that a year ago it was her and I taking our first tour. I cringe remembering my laughing too loud, trying to get James' attention, and then seeing what I had looked like when the tour ended. Good grief. Just one, incident-filled and action-packed year, ago I was a plebe.

A smile came to my face as I remember Ben's nickname for me for the past year.

So much has happened.

I have changed.

And since Phil has been locked away in isolation, no further incidents have been reported. At least, not that I know of. But I am constantly busy with the duties assigned to me as Director Forshay's Aide. I know that this year, sometimes I'll have to report before breakfast for a meeting that I need to attend, or be called late at night for other such duties. Already my little schedule is filled, and Ben asked if I could stylus him in here and there. Crack me up.

John still hasn't had any luck finding my hen. It breaks my heart, but I have to admit that she was probably already killed. It wouldn't be easy to hide a chicken this long. I just don't understand why anyone would do it. But John has allowed me to continue assisting him, and help train the cadet from Bradley House who is taking it on as his chore. Cadet Cody Jorgensen is now John's primary assistant, and I remain only as an alternate.

But it was hard watching John stand there as Phil was escorted to the shuttle to be taken back to Earth. John had called out to Phil in support, but Phil's dazed look and shock ate at my conscience. After Phil disappeared through the shuttle bay, John turned and held my gaze for a full three seconds before he headed back towards the Hatchery.

"Problem, cadet?" Director Forshay turned back to look at me.

"No, sir."

He lifted a brow and held my gaze.

I dropped mine.

As the bay doors sealed, I watched while Director Forshay authorized clearance and departure on the keypad by the shuttle doors. My heart thumped painfully wondering if I had been correct.

I kept thinking that was important.

It had to mean that I had accused the right person.

It had to be that justice would be served.

It had to be Phil.

Didn't it?

The lights blinked and the sound of the clamps releasing resound in my empty heart.

As Director Forshay introduced a man who will be replacing Phil, I extended my hand and offered a half-hearted smile. I think Forshay said his name is Bob.

After being dismissed, I head off to my quarters, not wanting to become part of anyone's tour of IDEA. I take off my class As and take a quick shower and change into my comfy sweats, deciding to wait to put my uniform back on for chow.

Tonight we will be back to assigned sections for chow until the plebes learn their sections and the rules.

My data pod chimed, and I head to my desk to retrieve it.

It's from Ben, asking if I can spend some time in the Pollination Room with him tonight before classes and chaos resumes. I cannot help but smile as I said aloud as I typed that I would love to. Ben had started calling me his Trekker. I still tag him with Genius. A part of me wondered what it will be like when I still have one more year to go, and he's off and doing his own thing.

Try not to think about it, Jess, I scolded myself.

After grace was given, I looked about. It was easy to pick out the plebes. Man. Had we looked that out of place and obvious our first day?

Tori briefed our on how the tour went, who the loud mouth was, and who she thought was hot, or not. Typical Tori, but she has grown on me, so I couldn't help but laugh and shake my head at her.

When dinner was done, I watched how some of the new cadets were checking out the Donut and I got lost in remembering my own times looking at that sculpture.

"Hey Trekker," came Ben's voice from behind me.

I slowly turned with a smile across my face. "Hey Genius." Then a thought comes to mind. "Please tell me you aren't giving away any notes to the plebes this year."

Ben does his shifty eye thing, but smiles. "Nope. Not interested in any plebes this year." Then his eyes stay steady, and on me. "Maybe some Trekker needs some notes?" He put out his hand to show me a small note all folded discreetly before he took my hand in his. I felt the piece of paper shift into my own hand as he led me towards our own little sanctuary, own little Eden in space, with a smile on my face.

Ian stood in the hallway and watched us approach. He worked his jaw and met my eyes. I offered him a timid smile and he nodded. Part of me hoped we wouldn't have a confrontation. Part of me knew this was the only thing he would do. He backed out of our way with a cordial, "Evening."

I smiled. "Evening, Ian." Ben nodded and kept moving us right along.

When we reached the Pollination Room, Ben steered me to our little desk area and sat down. I sat next to him and opened the little paper note. A ring made of braided grass or stems was folded inside and almost fell. I looked over at Ben's shifty-eyed face, "What's this?"

"Something. For you," he said as he out a hand underneath mine to make sure it didn't fall and get lost in the grids beneath our feet. "Kinda...uhm...kinda like a gift."

I raised my eyebrows, "'Kinda like a gift?'"

Ben nodded and reached for my hand, "Kinda like a gift. And kinda like a promise."

I felt tears sting my eyes. "A promise?"

"I'm going to try and keep you safe, Jess. I'm not interested in anyone else and hope...," he took a deep breath, "...and hope you'll be mine." He looked positively adorable in his insecurity.

"I *am* dating you, Ben," I teased.

He smiled that tender smile I rarely get to see. "I know. But… it's like a promise to be true to you."

I smiled and put my head on his shoulder. "And I will be true to you too."

We stayed amongst the flowers and butterflies for a few hours, talking about "what ifs." When it was time for us to head back, we went, hand-in-hand, flora ring on my finger, and both of us playing with it. At my door, he gave me a kiss that made my toes tingle, and a look that made my face blush. With a brush of his lips against the back of my hand, he backed away to allow the door to close.

I sagged against my wall, smile wide across my face. I could die happy right now.

Log-in: JessReynoldi18851
Date/Time: 31 Oct 2202/2348hrs
Subject: Second Halloween

I am better prepared for this year's Spook-trek-ular activities. Not only am I not plagued by "fresh" images of a body, but I have a date for the festivities tonight. Ben said he was going to be my Prince Charming since I was his Cinderella. I laughed so hard, but was just moved at the same time.

I have been helping John in the Hatchery. Still can't believe Hope never turned up. I have given up on anyone every finding her alive at this point. I just don't understand who took her. I mean, I kinda understand why, if he/she/they were trying to get to me. But don't you think they would have done something about it by now if they had?

Tori is giving me a run for my money this semester. The plebe she's kinda seeing is all about reputation. I have really had to step it up a lot, which has made time with Ben more about academics and growth than flirting. Personally, I think it's making our bond stronger.

ENTRY END

The call button is activated outside my door, and I rushed the few steps to open it. There he stands. Ben, pale yellow rose in his teeth and arms outstretched, and eyebrow raised in question. "Well?" he asked between his teeth and the rose.

I stepped up to him and took the rose from his mouth. "Definitely Prince Charming."

He gave me a quick appraisal of me in my skirt, since I don't usually wear my knee-length cadet skirt as part of my uniform. "Wow. Hello, Legs."

I smacked at him playfully, "You've seen my legs before, Genius."

"Yeah, but...not in a skirt." He offered me a gentleman's elbow and escorted me down the hall to the Commons where music reverberated and lights danced. Tori and Kim each took turns stealing Ben from me a couple times when their "dates" didn't take to the dance floor.

One of those times, Ian stepped up and asked for a chance on the floor with me. He put out his hand like a gentleman would, and after a quick glance at Ben and Tori twirling around, I accepted. He led me to the floor, acknowledging Ben with a terse head bob, and kept his distance appropriate while we danced to the current ballad playing.

"So? What happened to 'there's no Ben and I?'" Ian asked with a soft smile.

"Guess, I was wrong," I scrunched my shoulders.

Ian nodded and spun me around in a fun, playful dance, no other words until the song ended. "You should wear skirts more often, Jess. You have nice legs." He raised his eyebrows in appreciation.

I dropped a mock curtsy, "Thank you. I will take it under advisement." Ian turned to walk away, "And thank you for the dance."

He turned to look at me briefly.

"And for saving me on the external run," I blurted out.

He rubbed the back of his neck, "Yeah, no problem." Then he smiled and backed away with a mock bow. "Evening, Jess."

I watched him leave as I remained on the dance floor. Part of me felt bad watching him leave. Then I noticed some of his buddies follow him out of the Commons. One, the one who had blown me a kiss in the hallway a couple months back, turned and looked back at me across the distance.

An arm came around my waist and I leaned into the guy who holds me. "All good?"

I smiled over my shoulder at Ben, "Yep."

After almost an hour filled with more songs, there was a commotion by the entrance to Forshay House. A cadet stumbled into the Commons, bloody gore all over his outfit. People laughed and make appropriate "eeww" sounds as he staggered in. He held his right arm tight against his side, left hand holding it tightly, possessively. People turned away at his costume and antics, how he bumped into them, but it just made me do a double take. The guy was really into it. And he didn't mind that he was getting their clothes and uniforms dirty. H just kept pleading the people around him for help, shaking and then began to cry.

Ben had already dismissed the behavior, trying to get me onto the floor for the fast-paced boogie that came from the speakers.

But I can't stop watching the upset cadet. "Wait, no." I pushed Ben away and moved a little closer to the guy who was holding his red-stained side. Then I see, his exposed wrist is running blood, not just covered in it, due to his hand is gone. "Oh my god!" I pushed through the people and rushed to his side. "Hey!" My eyes meet his terrified, lost ones. I grabbed his protected arm, to see if it's a trick, but he has pushed it into his side so hard to try and stop the bleeding, and his other hand is clamped tight like a tourniquet.

His eyes were wild as he pleaded, "Help me! Help!" And he tried to step closer, but instead he collapsed in my arms, knocking me to the ground. His blood flowed from the missing hand and a wound in his side.

The blood curling scream I hear is my own.

With a quick flip, I moved from underneath the unconscious cadet and took off the belt of my skirt and tightened it around his sliced wrist. Then I ripped open the tear in his shirt and found a long, deep gash where blood and a smelly green substance mingled and was pooling in his abdomen. I whipped off my shrug coat and used it to apply pressure to his wound, all the while calling for help.

Ben checked the cadet's pulse. Tori came to my side and tried to help me stop the bleeding while other cadets activated the emergency alarm. Kim was on her knees panting in shock. Others were crying while they watched.

I didn't let up on the pressure as I looked at all the blood around us. There was a lot and it trailed from where he had entered. I held my uniform in place while the medics arrived and addressed a better tourniquet but did not remove my belt from its current location. When the medics told me it was okay, to let go so they could work, but I had to be pulled back by Ben.

I stared at the four medics working on the young cadet. Then I looked back at his face. I didn't recognize him. As they worked, his eyes were slightly open, but he wasn't blinking. I swallowed the sick feeling in my stomach that grew with ever second he didn't blink.

Another medic hustled up with small device called a kardiokix, like a smaller version of the old defibrillators used to jump start a heart. When the medics all pulled their hands, we heard the whine and ping of the kardiokix as it tried to revive the cadet.

It was so quiet, I realized that the music had been stopped at some point, and that the regular Common's lights were up. Again and again the soft whine and ping of the kardiokix echoed, and I looked around the room at all the faces of all the witnesses.

How many people had this young cadet touched and pleaded with before I made it to him? Before I realized it wasn't some prank in bad taste. Even now, some of the spectators were looking at the blood on their clothes and the realization was sinking in. Most had their hands over their mouths as they watched in grim disbelief.

I looked back to the cadet on the floor, then down at the blood all over my hands and clothes. I felt bile continue to rise in my throat, then all went a foggy black as I felt myself falling. Hands tightened on me, but I was still going to the floor.

Log-in: JessReynoldi18851
Date/Time: 1 Nov 2202/0137hrs
Subject: Overwhelmed

He died.

ENTRY END

I came to with gentle pats to my face. I saw Ben's worried face and Tori's tear-streaked one. With a flailing of arms, I sat up and looked around. My eyes find a sea of faces and hear the voices of lots of people talking. One of which was a medic who shined a tiny bright light in my face.

Peering through the pinpoints, I looked to see the other four medics are moving a body, his body, with my shrug coat over his face. His handless arm hangs from his side, my belt still wrapped around it, dragging along the floor as they move.

After the medic told me that I could try to stand, Ben helped me to my feet. As I stared at the blood on my hands, I noticed my little braided ring was seeped in blood. I turned towards Ben's face, my hand near his face showing him. I had no words.

He gently took my hand in his and removed the token of his affection at my dazed look.

I blinked at the loss of it, at what just happened.

Shock.

The word is hushed around me.

I'm taken to a medic room where Ben sits with me on a cot under some dimmed lights.

I replayed it...it...over and over. His pleading for help. His eyes when they met mine. His panicked voice. His blood. His unblinking eyes.

He died.

"I tried to save him." I heard my voice, like it was a distant recording playing across the room. "I tried to save him."

Ben whispered things to me, and I cannot remember what they were.

People come in and ask us questions.

Tori came in and Ben left.

Kim came in and sat in silence before she left.

Ben came back and Tori left.

I heard voices, and heard my responses like I was listening to someone else.

Blink.

His panic.

His blood.

"Why do you always seem to find trouble?" Ben's voice was

in my hair, and he kissed my forehead.

"I tried to save him," I heard my voice again.

Someone asked me more questions, but I only stare straight ahead. I'm not sure if I answered them or not.

Ben told me they were going to help me get some rest. He tried to help me lie down, but I didn't want to. I just sat there.

I felt a sting, and I swung wildly. Ben grabbed my arms, and held my hands. When he was sure I wasn't going to hurt anyone, he gently touched my cheek. Again, they tried to reposition me.

"I tried to save him," I echoed my thoughts.

"I know," he said.

And I started losing consciousness. He was holding me as I did.

Log-in: JessReynoldi18851
Date/Time: 11 Nov 2202/2142hrs
Subject: Findings

Following the incident with the Halloween dance and...Cadet Paulson (that's what his name was), I was interrogated. He had been from my own house, and I didn't even know him, but my interrogations were more intense with my previous history with mishaps here.

Chip cards were read and analyzed. It just doesn't make any

sense. His card said that he had been at the dance the whole evening and not ever coming from Forshay House as the majority of us testified that we saw.

I knew that it meant that his chip card had been taken, like before.

But the official story I read on Director Forshay's desk when I was doing my aide duties. It said what they announced earlier today, and what they had been theorizing since it happened. They said it was an accident.

ENTRY END

Tori ate silently next to me during breakfast and lunch, just like she has the past few says. She sits by me in two of our classes. Tonight she did the same, just plopped her tray down and gave me a brief look before she started eating. She talked me into an extra session in the UV room before dinner. Tonight we both were having a simple salad with a tuna salad sandwich half. It's tasty, I know, but it's still hard to choke it down. But I have to or she's going to say something. I know she'd prefer I'd do things as if it never happened.

But it did.

The official report was that Cadet Paulson must have gotten his hand caught in a door and incurred additional injuries trying to free himself in his panic. But I knew that the deep gash I had seen was too straight to have been an accident. The cadet's hand, indeed, been severed, but more precise than accidental tearing. The investigation may have come to the conclusion that this was an unfortunate accident. But I knew in my gut that it had been intentional, and he had somehow managed to escape.

And I knew who had been with me at the dance. That helped me narrow down my list of suspects. With Phil not present, it was obvious that I had been wrong about him.

Houses were separated during the investigation, like before. I don't really remember too much of the day following the... incident. But I do know that Ben has messaged me quite a bit. I know that Tori and Kim are worried about me...and everything else. And through it all, I make sure I know where my data pod and chip card are at all times. My chip card is no longer in a pocket, but inside my bra. I have clipped my data pod to my new belt. Super paranoid, yes, but I am not sure what other precautions to take.

We cadets have found ourselves talking in whispers amongst ourselves. We don't make any new friends with the new plebes, and for that I feel bad. They don't have any of the excitement and desire that they did when they first arrived here. If some of them had made some friendships in their first few weeks, then maybe some of us uppers are still talking to them.

Personally I haven't had any time to make friends.

When I am not doing my assignments, working on my duties as aide or helping on external runs or with the influx of chicks, I am found in my quarters. I have been going over notes and hunches. I have looked up detective novels and read them for ways on how to solve this series of mysteries. The one thing I learned from reading all of them, it's never the obvious guy. That's the one who always takes the fall first. The other thing I have learned is that I must have missed something previously... because it usually looks so obvious by the end of the book. But I am determined to solve this case. To protect the rest of the innocents.

Tori interrupted my thoughts, "Hey? You okay?"

I looked over at her concerned face. "Huh?"

"You zoned out there," she said. Her sad eyes look into mine. "You doing okay?"

I offered a small smile. "Yeah. I'm okay. Just still thinking."

"They still want you to talk to a shrink?" She lifted her juice in mock salute to the nickname that still lingers for psychiatrists.

I only nodded and played with my salad. Then, again seeing the spot where Ben's woven ring used to rest on my finger, I set my fork down and picked up my half-eaten sandwich.

"You going to go?"

I shook my head to indicate negative while I took a bite. I chewed slowly, deep in depressed thoughts. Took another bite, and repeated.

Tori set her near-empty glass down beside her tray. "I've gone. It's not horrible. It's just the computer program. You can select either a male or female voice." She grabbed her own last bite of her sandwich. "My shrink sounds *hot*."

I couldn't help it. I coughed up while I laughed. I offered her a slow head shake and smile while I looked first at her, then around the room.

Cadets were mostly sullen, but others, the plebes were starting to talk more amongst themselves. Some cadets were already finished and waking up to put their trays away. I glanced at the floor as they walk by, and...what the heck?

I quickly jumped up and grasped at the object dancing away on the draft caused by people moving. I could hear Tori calling my name, but I was on a mission. After several snatches, I finally had it, cupped with both hands. I stood up and saw a sea of faces. Some I knew, others I didn't. All were watching me. Carefully I peered in my hand to make sure I still had it.

I did.

Then I looked around to see who had been walking through. To see who this might have been clinging to. Then Tori was at my side. I just looked into her face, and back into what I had in my now closed hands for fear of losing it.

"What is it? You okay, Jess?" She placed a hand on my shoulder.

My eyes must be wide as saucers, and I could only nod. "I have to go. Can you take care of my tray for me?" When she nodded, I told her that I will talk with her later tonight. Then I turned and hustled from the Commons, hands cupped before me as I negotiate between tables and cadets. I looked around briefly, knowing I have caused a scene. Most of those who know me watched me depart.

I moved through the halls, making my way as fast as I could to my door. As soon as it opened, I was stepping through so it could close. When it did, I hit the lock with my elbow to prevent it from opening again. Then I made my way to my little bed, and on it, I released my captive.

A lone feather.

I stepped back, holding my breath. It was the same color as Hope, but lots of the chickens in the Hatchery or Coop were of the same tawny color. I reached for my data pod and decided to take pictures to make sure it document it. Then I sent a picture to John with the message, "I found this floating along the floor in the Commons tonight at dinner. Did your cadet have Hatchery duty this afternoon?" I released my breath after I hit send.

After a few seconds, John responded. "No. He was ill." I read the words aloud, wondering what this all meant.

Then my device chimed again. "Where are you?" It was from Ben.

I messaged him. "In my room."

After a few minutes, the call button for my quarters sounded. I messaged Ben, "Is that you?"

"What?" came back his response.

"Outside my door?" I typed back.

"NO. Be right there."

I held my breath and squeezed my device. I jumped when it chimed again.

"Jess? Are you still in your room? I buzzed, but no one answered." It was John.

I looked back at the feather sitting still on my cot, unlocked the door, and opened it.

John stood there, device in hand, and upon seeing me, exhaled loudly. "You're here."

"Jess," Ben's voice called from down the hall.

I waited for him to come in too. Then I closed the door and locked it once again. When I turned around, both Ben and John were looking at the feather. Ben was confused.

John looked at me, then at Ben. "Does he know?"

I could only shake my head.

John nodded and pulled out a small bag. "Commons, you said?"

"Yes," my voice squeaked out.

John carefully picked up the feather and put it in a bag. "I have to check and see if this is a poultry one, or if it's from something else. Have to be sure." He offered Ben a cursory glance. "I'll get back to you." Then he strode to the door, hit unlock as he stashed the feather inside his pocket, checked the hall, and disappeared as the door closed behind him.

"What was all of that about?" Ben asked.

I turned to face him and released another deep breath. "A few months back, someone took some chicks and hens. Hope is gone. Dead, probably." I licked my lips. "John told me I wasn't supposed to let anyone know. They were checking into it."

Ben did his shifty-eye thing he does when he's percolating over information. When he finally looked at me, his eyes were clear and intense. "So someone is watching you."

It wasn't a question. It was a statement.

All I could do was nod.

Log-in: JessReynoldi18851
Date/Time: 24 Dec 2202/2150hrs
Subject: Holiday Blues vs Holiday Cheer

Now that I know someone has been watching me, I strive to make myself even more invisible. I have asked to be removed from the external runs, saying it takes too much time from my homework to attend the weekly or monthly meetings. I also was removed from Hatchery duties so as to not arouse suspicion. So, now I am only Director Forshay's aide.

Ben kinda likes it. Says it gives us more time together. He finds every second he can to watch over me. He escorts me through the halls as often as his duties and our schedules allow. It makes it so I don't see many of the others. Ben says we can't trust anyone else until they find out what is going on.

And tonight is Christmas Eve. I'm reminded of last year, and how much has changed, and continues to do so. But this year, I refuse to be cooped up in my room.

And let me make sure I make something very clear, smart guys really do know how to kiss.

ENTRY END

We leisurely strolled through the halls after a fantastic dinner, hand-in-hand. I had hoped we'd be going off to the Pollination Room to get away from all the loud caroling and obnoxiousness that I used to love to be a part of back home. But Ben was leading me, long way around, to the Solarium. That would work too.

Time seems to have changed. Every day has been a blur without events. Classes come and go. Ben has worked hard to help me maintain my high class ranking by quizzing me and finding new ways to retain the information, since I'm not a photo like Tori or a genius, like the ninety-some-odd percent of the other cadets here. He has been very supportive.

Hard to believe it's been a year-and-a-half since I have known of him. It seems like he's been with me for so much longer with everything some of us have been through. It makes me wonder what the next year-and-a-half will bring before he gets his choice of an assignment.

As we near Director Forshay's office, I saw the door open, and we could hear Forshay giving someone a stern warning. James backed into the hall, and almost right into us. His look was sour and made him totally unattractive for the first time in...well, forever basically. He shot us a dirty look before he gained his composure and wished us a Merry Christmas as he passed by us. I couldn't help but look backwards over my shoulder at his brisk departure. Then as the door closed for Forshay's office, I couldn't help but wonder what he had done to have needed a visit this late.

I must have mused it aloud, because Ben offered, "Perhaps it was about the festivities and the plebes who I had heard were feeling homesick."

I smiled at my guy's comment, glad I wasn't a House Aide like James and Tori, and continued right alongside Ben.

When we reached the Solarium, Ben led me to what I jokingly have called "Our Bench". It was deeper in the Solarium so passers-by wouldn't see us, and it was fragrant and beautiful, especially when IDEA dulled the ceiling lights to simulate dusk, like the ship did tonight. Once there, he offered me the bench, and he took a knee. My heart was pounding so fast and loud, I had to read his lips to make sure I heard him properly.

"Jessica Reynoldi, when all of this is over, will you be mine?" His eyes shifted slightly. "I love you." Then he brought out an origami box of paper which looked like it had notes written on, and gave it to me.

I blinked hearing the words he had said. I looked deep into those shifting eyes I used to feel uncomfortable around. He had never said those words to me before.

"What?" I teared up and carefully took the box from his trembling and offering hand. Or was it mine that was shaking? I wasn't quite sure. But I lifted the little lid to peer inside, and gasped. Carefully I dumped the little flora ring out into my hand and set the box down next to me on the bench seat. It was braided much like the first one he gave me, but this time the weave had a little more substance to it. "Oh, Ben! You made me another one?"

"Of course," he said. But then he looked a little uncomfortable.

Okay, so I know that I'm a dolt and sometimes, usually, very socially awkward, so I just sat on the bench in silence looking at the new ring, while Ben looked at me. After several long seconds, he cleared his throat and stood up and backed away, shifty eyes in full chaos. "What? What is it? Ben?"

He turned away and scratched at his head. "I...I...," he stammered.

Then I realized that he had not only asked me a question, but had told me something very important. Holding my woven ring very carefully, I stood up and went before him. I put my hand up so he can see. "I love you, too, Ben." When he met my look, I couldn't help but blush. "Can you help me put this on?"

His eyes shifted before his gaze did. Then he put the ring carefully on my hand where the other one used to be. When he was done, he offered me a small smile before he kissed me.

I don't know how long we stood in the Solarium next to our bench, just kissing and groping each other. But I do know we were watched. I know this because I heard something before I heard footsteps leaving the shadows near us. And when I quickly pulled away, Ben and I both had the same look on our face. The one that said, "Who was that?"

After several tense seconds, Ben grabbed my hand and reached for the box left on the bench. He handed it to me and said I could read it later. His posture said he was nervous, so I decided to try and read it now. I carefully undid the origami folds to review not just any notes, not even assignment notes. They were love notes. Ones he had never sent. And in the dim light, it was super romantic. I couldn't help but place my hand on his heart while I read them.

Yep, I was mush in the palm of his hand.

After more snuggling and cuddling on our bench, and many "I love you" whispers, we decided it was time to head back. As we neared my hallway I could hear a commotion, and my joy and happiness became dread in my gut. Cadets were lining the hallway and some turned and started whispering as I approached. Ben squeezed my hand as we continued.

"What is going on here, cadets?" I heard Forshay's voice boom off the hallway walls. He approached from the other side of the hall, so I could see him from across the distance coming through the throng as Ben and I continued towards my quarters.

As another cadet moved, I stopped short. Feathers. Feathers and blood were everywhere. Some of the feathers were still even attached to a wing that was propped up against my door. A decapitated hen head lay next to the wing.

Dear God in Heaven, was it Hope? But I knew it wasn't because this bird was more white than tawny. But it had to have been one of the birds Johns said was taken. But did he, she, they know if it was Hope or not? My eyes scanned the crowd, looking for the perpetrator or perpetrators who had done this. I remember my criminal books said that the person or persons who always came to the scene of the crime to witness the reaction of the victim.

The victim.

Oh no. It's a warning.

I'm next.

Ben held my hand tight while I took in everyone looking at me. Faces both familiar from classes and from those I believed were my friends. Tori and James were standing there, trying to keep the halls quiet and calm, like good House Aides. I saw some of James' and Ian's friends who looked sick. Then I saw Forshay's reaction as he watched me. I slowly turned around and found Bradley moving his way through the crowd, telling cadets to move aside, only to stop at the scene, then look at me. Then he looked over my shoulder. I tried to see what or who he was looking at, but by the time I turned back to him, Bradley was talking to Ben.

Bradley and Forshay started barking directions, telling cadets to line up against the wall for questioning. Bradley brought out his device and soon some maintenance staff arrived. A short while later, so did John. Some of the medics arrived to check for shock and treat people if necessary. But this time, I don't have shock.

I have anger.

Rising anger and a strong sense of vengeance.

Log-in: JessReynoldi18851
Date/Time: 9 Jan 2203/2355hrs
Subject: Possible Discovery

Part of me should feel bad, but I don't. I found something when working in Forshay's office tonight. At first it didn't hit me, what I had seen.

Now? I think I understand something...but I'm not quite sure what it means yet. Or who is behind it all. So I'm enlisting some help.

ENTRY END

I pressed the call button on Tori's quarters and wait. She opened her door and smiled seeing me there. "Jess! This is a surprise!" Then she looked behind me. "Hi Ben."

I kept my face straight. "Hi. Do you have a minute?"

Tori allowed us both to enter. Then she hit lock when I asked her to. She took a seat on her cot next to me while Ben sat at the chair by her desk. "What's going on?"

Ben spoke for me, seeing I wasn't able to talk at the moment. "Tori. Jess thinks she has discovered something important about some of the incidents that have happened since the two of you arrived at IDEA." I noticed his eyes shifted before he continued. "I'm here as a witness because we think she's next."

Tori's eyes went wide. "What do you mean, 'next'?"

I held her gaze. "I think you know what I mean." I cleared my throat. "You both witnessed things, things that I didn't, and...I think you two need to share first. So that we are all on the same page." Tori and Ben look confused, so I prompt. "The pond." I licked my lips. I faced Ben, "Tori and..."

"Don't say anyone else's name," Tori interrupted, hands up before her in her urgency.

"...another cadet," I gave her a look, "saw what you did...the remains," I pointed towards Ben, "before someone moved them out of the pond."

Ben and Tori glanced between each other and their own hands. Ben had known what I had shared before about the stripped bones in the pond, but hadn't known who it was. His normal eye-shifting was accompanied by the splaying of his fingers across his knees. Tori worked her cuticles as the seconds ticked on.

"Oh, for crying out loud," I said as I sat next to Tori. "I saw a body float passed my portal window when we first arrived. I helped discover that staff member's skull in the fish stock tank by the Solarium. I was sent odd messages about the pond, after the incident that you," I pointed back to Tori, "found." Then I sat up straighter, "And I was in Bradley House one night when I hear someone crying, like he was begging for his life, and then someone laughed. I found blood outside that same room where he had been pleading." I brought up my data pod and started showing Tori some of the pictures that Ben has seen. I continued through both of their outbursts and questions, "I think someone broke into my room and tried to access my data pod on at least one occasion. I was assigned to multiple chores, and one of them involved chicks."

Tori's eyes go wide. "Please tell me that the mess...oh...the head...wing. When I asked you before, you said it wasn't Hope. Was it?"

I shook my head and continued, "But I think it was a warning." I advanced through some of the pictures on my device until I got to the ones from Director Forshay's office. "I took these pictures, and I know I shouldn't have, so I don't need a lecture, on the findings. I have been going over and over my journal, trying to see if I have missed something. I'm hoping tonight, the three of us can find out if there's any correlation that I haven't been able to come up with."

Ben took out his own device and added, "And then we should

also factor who we know who has access to all of these places." He inclined an eyebrow, "Including who could have had access to the janitorial closet on that night when you heard the pleading and found the blood."

Tori leaned forward. "So? What you want...what we're really going to be doing right now, is look at the investigation and find what they didn't?"

I nodded and put up my crossed fingers. "I hope so."

She grabbed her device. "Okay. Let's do this." She pulled her hair away from her face. "So? Where do we want to start?"

I frowned. "I guess we start with our arrival at IDEA."

For the first hour or so, we were working on how the cadet was put on the wrong transport to IDEA. Ben generated models to emphasize how a body should have been expelled from the shuttle bay areas, versus how I say it was seen that night. Then it was to what the report showed. Ben reminded me what Director Forshay said about passing the information onto the investigation. But I don't see any mention of the cadet's trajectory or spin velocity of IDEA versus other possible scenarios, and let them peer through my images. Because it took so much time, Ben suggested that I send both him and Tori respective images so we can all look at them on our own time. After only a few seconds, I sent both of them copies of the pictures. Then I sent them the photo of the blood outside the room that night months ago.

Close to midnight, Tori's call button sounded, startling all three of us. Tori motioned for us to move while she quickly backed out of what we were working on and deadened her device's screen.

I did the same. When I looked over at Ben, he had some notes before him from his mentoring class. Then I watched the door open.

"Evening," Director Forshay's voice echoed in the small room. "I was needing to check," he poked his head in further to see us, "...and yes they both are." He brought out his data pod and sent a quick message. "Needed to see if cadets Williams and Reynoldi were here like their chip cards indicated." At Tori's wave showing him inside, he stepped into her quarters. "Studying?"

"Yep" I said at the same time that Ben answered with, "Yes, Director Forshay."

He nodded. "All good then. Just with a bunch of chip cards in one room, this late, I needed to double check."

I offered a simple smile but no comment.

Ben made a show of checking the time. "Oh my! It *is* very late. Ladies, we'll resume where we left off before Director Forshay came." Then he hesitated. "When do we want to continue the mentoring?"

Tori clicked and spoke up first, "I could use all the help I can get on that subject. Being a photo doesn't help with theorization."

Ben nodded. "Tomorrow night then? Same time? Same place?"

Tori and I glanced at each other.

"Sure," I said.

"Unless I get called on a House Aide call," Tori added. "Maybe we should just make it Jess' room, just in case?"

We all bobbed our heads in agreement, then looked towards the doorway where Forshay still filled the space. Quickly, I started grabbing my paper notations and hooked my device on my belt. Ben started doing the same, placing his own device on top of the small stack of papers filled with his scrawl. Then Ben and I tried to duck past the Director as he moved out of the way just enough. When Ben reached for my hand, Forshay told us he would escort me back to my quarters.

At my door, Ben told me to hold his lecturing notes in my room so he wouldn't lose or misplace them and handed them to me. Then he gave my free hand a quick kiss, and started moving down the hall towards the Commons and his side of IDEA.

Forshay stood at my door while I watched Ben leave. "Theorization?"

I turned and looked at my House Director, while I fought to keep my voice and face casual. "Yes. We were talking one night and with Tori and I going into the same field, and Ben...Cadet Williams being a mentor and so knowledgeable in so many academic things, he said he'd spend some of his free nights helping us on that...and other things if we need."

His eyebrow lifted and he changed his focus from me to Ben's departing back. "Ah. Cadet Williams does have a knack for mentoring. Or so I am told."

I tried a small smile, hoping to be dismissed.

"So what were you working on tonight?"

I couldn't prevent the crease in my brow while I fought for some words, "Speculation versus scientific findings."

Forshay's eyebrow lifted even higher. "Really? Interesting." Then he offered me a quick good night and started down the hall the direction of the Commons.

After gaining access to my quarters, I locked the door. I sank onto my cot with the release of the breath I hadn't realized that I was holding. Then I pulled up my notes on my device and started perusing Ben's hand written ones. I frowned at a phrase written at the top of one of the pages. It said: Type of student? IQ versus studying?

I never took Ben for someone who thought of others in that way.

My device chimed with a message from Tori, asking if I made it to my room okay. I told her I had and was going over the notes

Ben had left with me. She asked if Ben was still there. I said that he had left, and the brief conversation I had with Forshay outside my room in case we were questioned. She agreed that it was good to have our stories straight. I called it a night and told her that we'd see her tomorrow.

Then I sent a quick message to Ben, asking if he made it to his room yet?

After several long minutes, I finally received a response from him. He said that Director Forshay had followed him all the way to his quarters, without a single word.

"Odd," I said as I typed and then hit send.

"Very," Ben sent back. Then he wished me sweet dreams and told me that he'd see me tomorrow.

Log-in: JessReynoldi18851
Date/Time: 31 Jan 2203/2302hrs
Subject: Possible Breakthrough

It seems so trivial, what others take for granted. I never thought who I was or what kind of a student I was would be the reason for me being singled out. But then again, I have seen things that I wasn't meant to have seen.

Today, after about three weeks of meeting, ten times total, I think we have the why.

History always seems to replay itself. Why do people have to think of others as having more of a right to live than others, or a right to study at the place of their choice?

Yes, I am sure we have the why. But to be sure, I asked Tori to invite someone else in to our little study group.

ENTRY END

I opened the door to my quarters to see Tori and Kimberly Hess. I smiled and allowed them passed me while I checked the hall for witnesses. Seeing none, I let the door close and hit lock. It may have felt like we were conspiring against the others, but I thought we have good reason.

Kim looked so confused at the three of us sitting as we have for the past few weeks in my quarters. Ben sat on the floor with notes all around him. Tori took up most of my bed with her form. I maneuvered to my desk and took a seat in my chair. "Tori, make room," I scoffed.

"Oh, yeah. Right," Tori said as she scooted to make room. "Here ya go."

Kim carefully sat down on the edge of my bed, looking at all three of us in turn.

I cleared my throat. "I bet you're wondering why Tori asked you to come." At her nod, I kept going. "Our first semester here you said something, something like you didn't want to be next."

All the color drained from poor Kimberly's face. Her lips parted while her eyes danced from person to person. "Oh my

God." Then she bolted for the door.

As it was, Ben was in her path and stopped her. "Whoa, whoa, whoa."

I jumped over to Kim. "We're not here to kill you. We're here to ask you some questions." I took a step back. "I swear. That's it."

Ben let go of Kim and put his hands up in a show of innocence. "Help us find out who is doing this. Please."

Tori patted the bed next to herself. "Come on, Kimmer. After what we have seen, you had to have known we weren't the only ones who have seen something."

Kim paused, then looked at Tori. "What is going on?"

Tori blurted, "Jess has seen things. Pretty much since week one. We," she indicated the three of us, "feel something is very wrong with IDEA. And we think we know why things happen, but want to have someone else look at what we've come up with. Since you were there with me that night..."

"Tori!" Kim's eyes darted to Ben's.

"...you're already part of it, so it's easier to ask you." Tori waved a hand to dismiss Ben's being present on something they had previously agreed would never be discussed. "Oh, he's seen stuff too. It's okay. Well, not okay, but he's okay."

So we jumped right in and took turns about different things in the time line we constructed. We even showed her some pictures of documents and the photo of the blood in the hall. She carefully went over the notes we abbreviated for her.

After nearly an hour, she put up a hand. "So what exactly are you wanting me here for again?"

"Why?" I asked. "Why did you say that you were afraid to be next that night in Forshay's office our first semester?"

She blinked and blinked again. She took a deep breath. "Because they told me I might have a mild case of space illness. I think it's because I heard something in a hall one night after we first arrived." She swallowed before she began again. "It was very late, and I was lost. I had already left the medic station for insomnia and must have made a wrong turn. I was using my data pod to search where I was versus where I was supposed to be versus where I thought I was. I stopped at a corner, trying to get my bearings. I heard...I heard someone pleading for his life." Her eyes went dull. "I peered around the corner and saw that staff member who died walk up to the group of cadets, trying to break it up. She...she didn't even have a chance. They pounced on her while two still held onto the crying cadet. Her blood was everywhere by the time they turned back to him." She blinked a very times in rapid succession. "Then they stabbed him in the stomach. They covered his mouth while they stabbed him...over and over. One guy, I still don't know his name, he licked the knife and said that it tasted like rare steak." Her eyes dropped as she remembered. "He cut the trapped cadet's sleeve off exposing his arm. Then the cutter put his knife into the arm of the cadet who was trying to call for help, and the knife went from shoulder to elbow." She blanched with the memory. "A huge chunk of meat just hung there." Her eyes found ours. "He cut it off! He cut off the muscle off that kid's arm! I couldn't believe what I was seeing. It was so bizarre. Then he cut a smaller chunk of it off and put it in his mouth!" Kimberly closed her eyes as if it would help her erase it from her memory. "He *ate* it. He *ate* it while this cadet watched himself being eaten. Then, the cutter took chunks of the muscle and gave it to each of the guys there. They laughed as they...they *ate* him."

We three sat in stunned silence.

But she wasn't done. "I backed up around the corner and took off running. I was going to get help. A few corridors later I ran right into Director Forshay. I...I told him I had seen something and that I needed him to see. But before I could tell him what it was, he had some message come up on his device. He looked at my name tag and told me to go to my quarters immediately, that he would check in on me in a bit to find out what I had seen, but he had a situation somewhere he had to be." She cleared her throat. "He dismissed me, so I went to my quarters and waited. The next morning I was called into his office. I hadn't slept yet, and was still freaking out. When Forshay opened the door, I was told that James was there as witness, so none would claim misconduct had happened."

"But I am alone with Director Forshay in his office all the time," I said.

Tori made a snort sound, like the very breath was taken from her. "We're supposed to be present for one of our cadets. Or someone else is. That's to protect them or the cadet from possible assault or...yeah, misconduct or whatnot." She shook her head, "Maybe you just didn't see James there? Or maybe now since you're his aide?"

I thought back. Several times, James had been leaving Director Forshay's office when I was let in. Ben had been with me one of those times. I reminded Ben of that.

"Regardless," Kim was still talking, "I just told him I hadn't been able to sleep. I didn't get any further before Forshay turned to James and announced how I needed to be taken to the medic station immediately for space illness confinement. Now you know what I saw way back when. Now you know why I said what I had, and why the remains in the pond freaked me out." She shifted on my cot. "I was told that I had early signs of space illness when I went to the medic stations that first week. I didn't even have to take a test. I was just prescribed some sleeping aids. I thought that my telling Forshay was written off as such. Even with all the interrogations that followed, it was noted in my record as to my having space illness."

Tori leaned over and put an arm around Kim's shoulders. "I'm sorry. I'm sorry they didn't take action. I'm going to find out why they didn't."

Kimberly Hess, the bubbly girl I wanted to hate when we first arrived, sat with tears rolling down her cheeks. It made my heart drop in my chest. Licking my lips, I added, "I'm sorry, too. I should have reported what I saw that night. But I was freaking out. I was showing possible signs of being sick. And I didn't get a good look at their faces." She swallowed hard. "I was just afraid and kept being told that I had space illness."

Ben stood up and stretched, his eyes doing their shifty-thing. "You said that it was a group of guys?" At Kim's nod, he added, "How many?"

Kim looked off to the side, remembering. "Five."

I try to picture any group of guys who hung out a lot. At once, I picture the swooping side-to-side from the waist, arms locked over each other's shoulders, chanting guys. James, Ian, Jackson, and a few other cadets from Bradley House. But their numbers were six to eight at any given time. So, I'd have to keep my eye out for a different group like that.

Tori just shook her head. "What I wouldn't like to give to see who has who in the House breakdowns."

I put up my left hand. When everyone looked at me, "I have that." I quickly open up the necessary files on my data device. "Director Forshay had me assign all the new plebes to each of you new aides within his House."

Tori's laughed, "And how did you do that?" Then she sang out, "Eeenie-meeenie, miney-moe?"

"No," I rolled my eyes. "I had access to all the current aides profiles and those of the incoming plebes. So, then, all I did was create a chart which helped me place them. Pretty easy that way. I even forwarded the chart to Director Forshay so he could see what I did and keep it on file if he liked the template. He had to approve the placements anyway, so I thought he could see why I did what I did."

Ben's eyes shifted quickly, "And what did you do? How did you sort them?"

"Well, here." I forwarded the list and then the chart I had used to each of them.

Tori looked through the names of each of hers. "Huh."

"What?" I asked.

"Oh, nothing. I just hadn't realized how many of my cadets a non-photos. That's all."

I frowned. "Why does that make a difference?"

Tori smiled, "For me it doesn't." I could tell she was advancing through the list by the way she moved her finger over her device. "Hey! The one that died at the dance isn't from our House."

"I know," I said as I started my own perusal of the list.

Don't you find it odd that all of them were from Bradley's House?" Tori asked as she keeps scrolling. "And that they were... well, maybe." She changed to a different image and started to read the information before her.

"What? What is it?" I asked before Ben and Kim chimed in.

"That first cadet," she looked at Kim, "the one you saw get attacked. He was a non-photo. His selection scores reflect that too. The second, missing...and presumed the one found in the pond...also a non-photo."

"What does that have to do with anything?" I couldn't help keep the defensive tone out of my voice.

Ben quickly rummaged through his notes. "And that last one, he was a non-photo." His eyes landed on me. "Jess. You're a non too."

My voice cracked as I said, "You're saying someone is targeting, that these other cadets are targeting, non-photos?"

I glanced at each of the faces in the room. Tori, photo. Ben, genius-slash-photo. Kim? At my look, she offered a small smile and said she was a photo. *Crap.*

Tori blurted, "But it's not as obvious with you. You retain lots and study hard. You gave yourself away that night way back when at dinner. Some make it very obvious that they aren't photos."

"Does that mean that the non-photos don't deserve to be here?" I snapped. "I think if we make here, it shows how much better we actually are!"

Tori mumbled an apology.

But Ben countered with, "And maybe that's why nons are being singled out and eliminated. Someone may be feeling threatened."

After a few more uncomfortable minutes, we adjourned, agreeing to meet in a couple days to see if we could come up with any other ideas or theories. Part of me knew we probably weren't. In fact, I was having a feeling in my gut that they were right.

So, not only was I a non-photo. I had also seen things I shouldn't have, been where I wasn't supposed to be, and reporting like I wasn't allowed to.

Ben came up off the floor after Tori and Kim left, and put his arms around me, holding me from behind. "It's going to be okay, Jess."

I wished I felt as confident as he did.

Log-in: JessReynoldi18851
Date/Time: 13 Feb 2203/2355hrs
Subject: Staying Invisible

It has been hard to seat and eat at the same table as my friends. Ellie has wanted to spend time with me since Bryce has been aloof after some little lover's spat. She really isn't looking forward to tomorrow.

But maybe…I'm not the only one trying to not be noticed?

ENTRY END

Ellie sat down with us in the Commons. Then she rested her head playfully on my shoulder. "It's been so long! Where have you been hiding?"

I shrugged, effectively and carefully removing her from my person. "Mostly my room." Then I resumed eating my fruit medley.

"And with Ben," Tori added, tipping her pineapple juice glass in Ben's direction for good measure.

Ellie shook her head. "So, no wonder Ian's still a bear." At my eye roll, she continued, "He's been secluding himself. Like he's depressed or just plain pissy."

Part of me felt bad, like guilt. But I shouldn't feel bad for not reciprocating Ian's feelings. I glanced around the Commons. Tonight, as like the past few nights, Ian sat away from his buddies. Yet he was watching them, and the whole Commons. At least, that's how it looked to me.

James crossed over to our table and wished us a pleasant evening. Then he crossed to Ian, and set his tray down. Ian's head snapped up and the two talked in hushed tones before Ian stood up and grabbed his half-empty tray. He glared at James and then his eyes found mine. With a shake of his head, he took his tray to the windows to dispose of his meal.

Ellie touched my arm, causing me to jump. "Whoa! Sorry."

My eyes found hers, "What?"

Tori said that Ellie had asked me a question.

But I was back to watching Ian's departure. Then my attention was changed to the five guys all stood up together and brought their trays to James' table. I recognized three of them from the chanting, swaying and hall-passing incidents. Apparently the male bonding wasn't going so well for Ian right now.

Then two looked over at me. Then back at their trays and no one looked my way again. Was that just coincidence?

Tori reached across and grabbed my hand, and I flinched again. "What is wrong with you?"

I met her look. "You know very well what is wrong with me." I spared a quick glance for Ellie and saw her bewildered look. "Sorry. Just a little on edge lately. I wish you luck at the dance tomorrow."

Then the five guys got up and took their trays to put them away.

Five guys.

Ellie started talking about her plans for the Valentine's dance for tomorrow, but I could hardly focus on her words. She didn't seem to notice.

My eyes sought Kim's. Her look was down, into her food. Lips pressed. I kicked at her feet beneath the table and she looked around until she saw my face. She followed my line of sight and her eyes bugged and she went back to food watching. Then she met my look and gave me a slow blink. Kimberly Hess and I had just had a moment.

I continued to take in the room. Forshay sat in his usual spot, scanning the room with an air of authority. Ben had a student at his table. Bradley was sitting at his table, finger rubbing across his lips, as he checked his device. Two more cadets, different ones this time, sat next to James and bent their heads towards him. He looked around the room, and I tried to see where he was directing his gaze. When I didn't note anything right away, I turned my attention back to him in time to see him nod. The two guys got up and took their trays...with food still left...and dumped them. They started back towards Bradley House.

Why did all of these guys sit with James like that? Why did they all just up and leave without finishing their meals?

Tori kicked me under the table, gaining my attention. "You are going to the dance with us girls then, right? To make a statement?"

I licked my lips as I quickly pieced together what was happening at my table. "Sure. Girls' night. No problem."

"Ben won't mind?" Ellie asked.

I shook my head. "I can still dance with him a time or two, can't I?"

Ellie smiled and put her head on my shoulder again like a mock hug. "Thanks, Ladies! You're the best!"

Shouts from down the hall had all of the Commons attendees' immediate attention.

My heart started pounding in my chest. I scanned the room

and others were starting to stand like me, wondering what was going on. Then a young female cadet came running into the Commons calling for help.

Suddenly everything was a blur as I somehow was pushing my way through the mass of cadets. At one intersection, the wall stopped and the whispers continued. I kept pushing my way forward, needing to see. Needing to know. I kept pushing and elbowing my way, all the while anxiety turned to bile rising in my throat.

Finally I made it to the center of attention. There lay a large male cadet, unconscious and face down. As another cadet reached for him, someone scolded and said not to move him, in case it caused injuries. Some cadets took a step back while others took their place.

But I reached forward and felt for a pulse along the outstretched arm. "I have a pulse!"

I just nodded and looked over the crowd, the crime book "pointers" playing in my mind. I saw a sea of faces, swimming with both familiar and non. My glance went back on the prone figure my hand was on.

I was grateful that within minutes the medics were there, and then a stabilizing transfer board arrived. I moved back and watched as the medics worked with precision to check for injuries and then the carefully turned the cadet over to maneuver him onto the board. When they did, my jaw dropped.

It was Ian Hanson.

Log-in: JessReynoldi18851
Date/Time: 15 Feb 2203/0013hrs
Subject: Valentine's Recap

So the dance was rather lame. The holographic images were overly mushy. And Ellie kept giving Bryce the cold shoulder. I felt so bad for him that I danced with him. That made Ellie less than pleased until we convinced her to let go and have some fun. By the end of the dance, which was promptly at midnight, they were back to holding hands and kissy-kissy stuff. *Hormones.*

But I was distracted. Ben knew it. I knew it. I kept seeing Ian's body as they turned him over.

Why haven't they told us anything about his condition? Where was the investigation? Who had done this to him?

Was it because of me? Did he take some attack trying to stand up...trying to protect...me?

One can hope.

If he did...I am thankful. And I owe him.

ENTRY END

"What are you thinking about?" Ben said as he walked me to my quarters.

"Honestly?" At his nod, "Ian."

Ben slowed down and gave me a look. "Ian? Why?"

I shook my head and reached for Ben's hand again. "It's not like that."

Ben stopped altogether and tried to pull his hand.

So, unceremoniously, I drug Ben the rest of the way to my quarters. Once there I began my thought rant. I began with how Ben didn't have a need to be jealous of Ian, or anyone else for that matter. I told him how I still felt indebted to Ian for the tank incident. I went on about wondering if Ian was part of the cult we were speculating was being organized on IDEA.

"Jess," Ben began, "He's been a part of that group forever...at least as far back as there was a group."

I asked Ben to explain what he meant.

Apparently, but not surprising, Ian had always been the jock-type. That didn't surprise me. Nor did how the news worked with the image of the team-support-arm-linking-and-swaying. But that Ian hadn't ever dated or shown interest in female cadets, that Ben could recall, did. I don't know why that struck me as odd and... moving, but it did. *Ian wasn't a player.*

Ben also told me how Ian had ridiculed him, almost to the point of bullying, when they first arrived. The stories weren't nice. And they were few. I hung my head lower with every tale as I gained a different view of Ian's past, and how it morphed the man I had come to know.

The criminal studies and novels started replaying over Ben's voice as he continued. Ian was admired. Ian had bullied someone...or someones. Ian wasn't always nice and cordial. I recall the time when he went cold and distant, and almost vicious when he was outside me quarters last May.

Wow. Had it been almost a year already?

Okay, so now I have missed a bit of what Ben has been saying while I did my own reflections. *Does that make me a horrible person? My not paying attention to his personal stories? The ones that have obviously mattered? Crap.* I sighed.

Ben paused, "Am I boring you?"

I slapped my hand over my mouth. Then I uncovered it to say, "No!" I shook my head and placed my hands on my hips. "I get it. I do. But he saved me. Ian saved me. Even when he knew I wasn't interested in dating him."

Ben pursed his lips. "So you want to believe him to be a good guy? Even after all I just told you?"

My shoulders slumped. "I don't know how to explain it." I put my hand up while I talked. "I know that criminal studies say it's the likable guy. I know that Ian helped me. I know that he told me he was more interested in the person versus the body." I shook my head. "I want to believe that the guy who saved my life that night on the run is a good person. No. I *need* to believe it."

Ben continued to look at the floor. When he did look back at me, there was an emptiness that filled his gaze.

I felt it hit me like a tidal wave. "Ben. Stop. I know that look. I'm not interested in Ian." I took his hands in mine. "I'm not. There is *no* need for you to be this way."

Ben bobbed his head gently. "It's just...Ian's so...so different... from me."

"Yep," I agreed. "And that's why I prefer you." I brought his hands to my lips and kissed them. "I love you."

He wrapped his arms around me, almost crushing me to his chest. "I will do whatever it takes to keep you safe, Jess."

I snuggled in for a few minutes until he pulled back to give me a kiss. "I just wish there was a way to let those back on Earth know what was going on."

Ben made another face. "Let me see what I can do on that."

Though I knew he couldn't help me on that, I smiled up at him and stepped close enough to activate my door. "I wish...but I know you can't. Goodnight."

He gave me a quick peck on the check. "Lock your door, Jess," Ben said as my door began to close.

Just like that, the smile left my face and fear started to take its place. I was nodding at Ben as my portal secured. After it shut, I hit the secure button wondering if Ben would double check. I leaned against the cool metal and breathed. Within seconds, I felt and heard the pressure of the door being checked.

I took a step from the door knowing it had to be Ben...making sure I was safe.

I went to my data pod and starting researching possible ways to transmit messages back to Earth. I couldn't find anything. But I knew that giving Ben the idea, he'd find a way.

Log-in: JessReynoldi18851
Date/Time: 10 Mar 2203/2201hrs
Subject: Vigilance

Ian's still in isolation and we are not allowed to visit. No one has given us any updates despite some of us asking. It makes me wonder if he is still alive, or if he became a victim of the cannibal cult on IDEA.

I wonder how much he knew of their behaviors and activities. I know Ian can be tough and gruff, but he had saved my life that night on the external maintenance run. I can't help but think of all his sweet mannerisms when he was thinking we might be an item. It makes it hard to think of him as a bad guy. But quite a few of the criminal scenarios show that people seemed hood-winked by the guilty. Most never suspected the criminal.

I just want to see if Ian is still alive. I want to ask him questions.

And Ben thinks he has found a way to send a message back to Earth. He says he can't, but he has asked me to have a meeting with John. He said something about testing someone's theory.

ENTRY END

I have asked to talk with John this evening after dinner. I let him know that Ben and Tori will be with me. We waited in a side room to see if John will come under the pretense of studying should we get any visitors coming to check on us. Ever since that one night when Forshay came to verify we were all safe, our little group has had numerous "check-ins".

The call button to the room sounded and Ben got up to check. He let in James, who smiled as he looked at us. "Hey guys. What is this? A party without me?"

Tori smiled and battered her flirtatious eyes, "Didn't you get the invite?"

James shook his head.

Ben resumed his seat and grabbed his data pod. With a brief smile at James, Ben offered that he was tutoring us.

James frowned half of a second. "Tutoring? Jess, I can see. But Tori? She's a photo."

Did I just hear that? I glared at James. "Hey! What's that supposed to mean? I'm still number one in my course."

James put up a hand as a form of apology. "I didn't mean disrespect, Jess."

My look told him that I didn't believe him. Not for a second.

Tori harrumphed and tossed me a quick comment about non-photos being hyper sensitive.

I knew she didn't really mean it. I knew she said it as more of a way to cover her tracks, and not show favoritism, as we didn't know who was out to get the nons, like me. It didn't make it any easier to have her say it though, so I gave her my disgruntled look.

James muttered his apology again and said that he was to check all doors and small gatherings because of the Ian incident and other concerns that had been brought up.

How I bit my tongue I have no idea.

Tori nodded and said that she was to make rounds later tonight and hoped everyone would be studying like we were, otherwise she'd knock heads.

The image of Tori getting physical made me laugh.

Bryce popped his head in through the door. "I recognize that laugh. Hey Jess." When he saw Ben and Tori, he address them too, asking if we were going to watch Ellie play some wallball. When we said that we had some studying to do, he bobbed out and promised to cheer loud enough for all of us.

Tension broken in the room, James just asked us to be careful and told us all to have a good night. As he stepped out, he asked,

"What are you studying?"

Ben said, "Hydroponic subsystems on varying terrains" while Tori said, "Stuff."

Then I realized James was looking at me for clarification, "Stuff about hydroponic subsystems on varying terrains." Seeing James' eyebrow lift, I shook my head. "Finding out about underground waterways and ecosystems, maintaining their integrity while allowing for the expansion of human life. Since Ben's been working on plant species and other things that influence Tori and my course, we've been discussing how some parts of our courses interact and differ." I don't even bother to look at my conspirators. "It's actually pretty interesting. Maybe you *would* want in invite."

James frowned. "I think I have my hands full at the moment. But, have fun." With that, he closed the door.

Tori let loose a huge sigh of relief.

Then the door popped open again and James peeked in. "When is the next meeting?"

I looked at Ben, "When are you available again?"

Between the three of us, we negotiate and agree, with James as our witness, to meet again in a week. Part of that reason was because we have been for some time. Another part was knowing that James was on watch during this time, so not likely to be able to join.

James made a face. "Huh. I probably will be on hall patrol again. If I'm not, I'll let you know. Maybe I would like to hear what you guys talk about."

Tori smiled sweetly, "You just want to hang out with Jess and me. Admit it."

James shook his head and backed out again, chuckling.

I exhaled loudly, "That was a bit much. How much more of this sneaking around can we get away with?"

Ben nodded and gave me a steady look before his eyes began their shifty-thing. "It's like we're being targeted. Every time we are in our little meetings, someone comes along. Every time."

Tori leaned forward. "It's because someone knows we're onto them."

A few minutes later the room's call button sounded again. Ben went to the door to check it. Then he opened it without a word, and stepped aside. In walked John, his device in hand. He met my eyes. "Cadet."

We talked for over an hour. It was informative. Phil had been interrogated and given several lie detector tests, and passed them all. When I asked how he knew all this, he assured me that there were links for certain staff that allowed them access out of IDEA, and back to Earth.

My throat had gone dry. It was true. Ben said he thought there had to be a way to call for help. "Can you please...please... tell Phil that I am sorry? I probably won't be available to do it myself." I felt my voice start to crack, so I swallowed a couple of times. "We have some more information that I didn't have when I wrongly accused Phil. I retract my accusation. If that helps him now, and I hope it will, please pass that on." I blinked against the tears in my eyes. "I had been fooled."

John only looked at me through narrowed eyes, brow furrowed. "What do you mean?"

Ben offered what he had seen in detail. Tori did the same. We also had Kimberly's anonymous testimony.

John reluctantly took all of what we offered him, his eyes empty, distrusting. When the conversations came back to me, John looked at me expectantly. "And what do *you* have this time around?" His words and tone were rightfully and terrifyingly accusing.

I shrugged, feeling hurt. "I have nothing. I have only this

speculation on a cult having been formed here. A cult that had working knowledge of Phil's accesses and capitalized on that. I think that this group of cadets were able to trick people, myself included, into accusing Phil to lead anyone off their scent." I bowed my head, "That and the knowledge that I trust you." My eyes met his. "I trust you to help us find these people and to help us stop them."

"And why the change of heart against Phil," John challenged.

I shook my head at the list growing in my head, but luckily Tori and Ben came to my rescue. They even mentioned the fowl decapitated remains at my quarters, Tori was much more animated and sincere sounding, so I never needed to speak up. They barraged him with information, and John took plenty of notes. At least it seemed like he was taking notes.

When both Tori and Ben were done, John gave me one last opportunity to share.

"Help me," I pleaded. "We think I'm next."

John's face changed. His features pinched. "I will do what I can." With that he got up and excused himself from the room.

Tori turned to Ben when the door closed. "How long will it take for you to know if it worked?"

Ben offered his shifty-eye smile. "I expect a message any moment."

Log-in: JessReynoldi18851
Date/Time: 13 Mar 2203/2049hrs
Subject: A link

Apparently, it may be possible to send a message back to Earth. Ben thinks that Ellie has found a way to get messages to Earth by piggybacking off messages from staff members. My hope is that: 1) Ellie and Ben are right, 2) John doesn't find out, 3) John doesn't get into trouble, and 4) I can submit my concerns and confession of erroneous accusation to free Phil, all without dying. But before I can submit, I have to have something substantial. Yes, I have statements from Kimberly, Tori and Ben. But I need to know who.

So many cadets are involved now. Maybe that will protect me.

And when, if, I get the chance, I also have to send an apology for wrongly accusing Phil. I can only hope he forgives me.

ENTRY END

Tori held my hand as I took a deep breath, then exhaled. "Do it," she whispered against the tension in the room.

I looked at Ben, who only nodded.

I reread the message one more time.

To whom it concerns,

Please forgive me for my earlier accusation of a maintenance staff member, Phil Macke. I believe everything was staged for him to take the fall. Oddities have continued even after he was removed.

We need help here on IDEA. Attached are testimonies from other cadets of both houses and of differing seniority. We believe a cannibalistic cult has formed here. Students are missing. I have even attached a photo from outside one of the rooms where I stumbled on something. I believe one staff member and at least three cadets are dead because of this group of individuals. There may be more.

We jacked into a secure line in an effort to transmit this information to you.

Please, send help.

Then I had my contact identification number and name. Attached were four testimonies, the blood in the hall, and a couple of entries, to include the most recent Halloween incident.

That was it. Sure, it was a lot. But would it be enough?

With one more look at each of the two tense faces in my quarters, I linked it to John's line using the codes Ben had secured. Then, holding my breath, I hit transmit.

I blinked as I watched the screen change from "sending" to "sent" in just a second. My heart started pounding in my chest and I suddenly felt dizzy. "Oh my God. I did it." My device fell from my hand onto my lap. "Heaven help me. I did it."

Tori rubbed my back. "No. Heaven help all of us. We're all sitting ducks up here."

Ben reached for my hand. "It's going to be okay. We built a solid case. They have to take notice."

I merely nodded, feeling a sense of numbness take ahold of me. "Okay. Okay." I could hear myself say it, but I didn't know why I was. Part of me felt relief. Another part still felt anxiety over everything. Part felt just tired...past done. "Okay." I gently squeezed Ben's hand, then offered him a timid smile. "We did it."

Log-in: JessReynoldi18851
Date/Time: 20 Mar 2203/2049hrs
Subject: Test...Test...or Tested

I received a transmission from Earth. Short. It said that my concerns were documented, as well as the breach of security that we were able to discover in tapping into a staff member's secure line. I have decided to let only Ben know.

I don't want Tori or Kimberly to start sending messages home and blowing our only chance.

ENTRY END

Log-in: JessReynoldi18851
Date/Time: 21 Mar 2203/2049hrs
Subject: Witness...again

Oh my God. I don't know how much longer I can survive. The past few weeks have been a blur of trying hard to blend in and keep my head down. I have to hope that all the documentation is going to save us...me...but I doubt it.

Especially now. I...I think I have sealed my fate. So, I have come straight home and locked myself in. I'm lucky I even got here.

It was an accident. Lord, *please* let it have been an accident and NOT what I think it was.

Heck, who am I trying to fool. It was definitely what I thought it was.

Crap. Dang.

Because it was...and I'm really next. Not just worried I am. Doomed, I am.

ENTRY END

I put my ear buds back in and focused on the tasks before me. Despite my best efforts, the little wireless things kept falling out or getting caught on things, like my loose hair, while I was working. I grunted while melodies rocked my mind. It seemed like this night was never going to end.

I had been asked by Directory Forshay to assist an instructor in the preparations for an upcoming lab, tidy the back storage room, and take the recyclables to the center. It shouldn't have taken as long as it had. Just ensure everything was sterile, labeled properly, and that cadets were assigned into groups with items for everyone. Simple enough. I should have been done over an hour ago. But, as I have been trying to not make waves and go unnoticed, I didn't really care how long it took. I just wanted to be sure I had done everything right. I didn't want to anger whoever was out there ready to get me. But I also didn't want to miss anything while completing this task, hence screw up and get noticed even more.

I know I missed evening chow again, but if I knew Ben, he would have commandeered something from the Commons to tide me over until breakfast. Or we'd go to the Shoppette and make a date of it. I sent him a quick message saying that I was almost done.

After going over Forshay's list one more time, and taking about fifteen minutes to do so, I sent off another message to Ben saying that I was finally done, and asked where we were going to meet up. I was guessing he was going to tell me the Commons, so I shut off the light as I backed out of the storage room. With the music blaring in my ear, I turned, arms full of supplies, my chip card, and my data device. As I crossed the room, I heard the chanting I have long associated with that arm-swaying group of guys. I turned off the light as I passed through the door, and allowed it to lock behind me.

Then I froze, momentarily, at the sight before me.

Red.

Red puddles and drops.

Red swipes and smears on the walls and floor.

All placed where I would see as I left the classroom. Staged.

Off to the side stood seven guys. I recognized some of them were part of that group. Not James, and not Ian yet as he was still recovering, but that cult watched me, linked arm-over-shoulder, swaying while they chanted. No one else was around, so I bopped my head as if to music and kept my eyes half-shut, playing innocent.

The pause in between the songs playing on my device allowed me to listen while I carefully stepped down the hall. This is what I heard:

We come to meet.

We come to eat.

We've chosen our "someone not special."

Not special at all, to see.

We meet; we feed.

Oh my God. Where's Ben?

I kept my eyes downcast as I looked at my device and made my way through the hall, waiting, no, praying for my device to chime. I pretended to not notice anything gross and unusual while I listened to my music with half-closed eyes. I just pretended that I hadn't seen anything while I tried to swallow the lump rising in my throat. With steady steps, eyes focused on my device, I was walking away alone. I met the looks of a few of the other cadets who were in neighboring halls but didn't recognize anyone with whom I could confide. I shot a quick glance behind me and found them, following.

Circling.

Like vultures.

I'm in trouble.

I made cheery comments to people in the halls, drawing attention to myself. I was hoping that it would create some distance between the cadets and myself.

As I continued to hustle to my room, I realized that I had always seen them, from the very beginning, with every oddity I found. Kimberly had seen some cadets attack that plebe when we first arrived. I had heard and seen them, with James and Ian, before I found the blood I had taken for the result of a nosebleed. So many times. So many instances.

All this time I had mistaken it for male bonding. Ha! I was a naïve fool! It wasn't camaraderie. It was the very idea of cultish. It was perverse. It was my innocence thinking IDEA was a safe place.

I checked my device again as I quickly crossed the empty Commons. Nothing. Where was Ben?

Another look over my shoulder proved that I was still being tailed, but only by three. That made me wonder where the other four were. The fear of a trap ahead had my sprint the rest of the way to my quarters. I heard the hustling and minor commotion behind me and I knew that they were in pursuit. But as soon as I got into my room, I was hitting the close and lock on the door. I stared at the door as it started to move...in what seemed to be in super...slow...motion. Or was it my panicked mind?

As the door slid home, I slid to the floor. I jumped as a loud bang sounded on the metal, but I didn't cry out. After several seconds I realized that I had been holding my breath.

I looked down at my device, wondering why Ben hadn't responded. Part of me feared something had happened to him before I had left the storage room. Needing someone's help, I tried to reach out to Tori. And then I tried Kimberly. And Ellie. And James. And Bryce. And finally Director Forshay.

For a few hours I tried to reach out for help. No one responded.

Panic ate at me. Was everyone dead? Was everyone who knew me being picked off?

My mind went into full chaos as paranoia sank in. I wondered about the gore that must be happening beyond my locked door. I wondered how long before they broke in. Or would they starve me out? A million scenarios played over and over and over in my mind as tears streamed down my face.

I am going to die.

Log-in: JessReynoldi18851
Date/Time: 21 Mar 2203/2205hrs
Subject: Testing me

I stayed the whole day in my quarters. I only had water from my sink. No food today. I don't dare go out. Is this how they got everyone? Starve them out? I'm not going to leave. No way.

I hadn't received a single message. I even tried the secure line trick to get John or Ben. Nothing. Until just a few minutes ago.

He is blocking my messages. He has been made aware of my accusations. He is angry...not just upset.

I was so blind. I should have seen it. I trusted falsely.

I am doomed.

ENTRY END

I kept going over and over conversations. And how much he had been interested in me.
Dumb. I was so dumb.

I've been the picture of naïve.

Log-in: JessReynoldi18851
Date/Time: 22 Mar 2203/2003hrs
Subject: The HALO, the CROWN

He is coming. I know it. His video message said to prepare myself. The image of him sitting there, like some kind of medieval king on his throne, made me cry out in outrage before I was able to get a grip.

All the messages showing blame are queued and ready to transmit, if he would just not have blocked me.

What to do?

ENTRY END

I went over my journal entries again. It had all seemed pretty insignificant, but all those times…it really wasn't. Looking back, it all was right there in front of me…and the others.

I also realized that James had to have been the one who had taken Hope. He had held the door open when he had run into me that time leaving the Hatchery. He must have placed a shim and gone back in. He was my House Aide, and had so much access to me. He had been in the arm-swaying group with Ian, at my door with Ian, and with the ones before Ian had been attacked.

How dumb and naïve I had been. How trusting. I had been completely fooled but the masks they had worn.

No longer.

Log-in: JessReynoldi18851
Date/Time: 22 Mar 2203/2122hrs
Subject: Paranoia

I'm smarter than this. I mean, I made it here, to IDEA.
So? What am I missing?

I don't want to just die here. Not trapped. Not by the cult. Not like this.

I'm finding my paranoia is my worst enemy. My door is locked. He can't just come and get me. Can he?

Of course, the janitor's closet had been accessed without a key? How did he do it? He has to have some sort of master key...or shims. He would know about the shims, wouldn't he?

And why haven't my friends come to try and find me? Try to check on me? Are they really dead? Or am I just...that cut off?

ENTRY END

I can't sit down anymore.
All I have done is pace.
Then I sit, only to get back up and pace my small quarters.
I got so stir-crazy that I even did sit-ups and push-ups, to mentally prepare myself for the battle I knew was coming.
Dumb. I'm not a fighter. I'm not athletic.
Not dumb. I have figured this out. I have uncovered his cult and crimes. I have found a way around him.
I only needed to live long enough to...well, live.
And that was going to take a miracle...and more sit-ups.

Log-in: JessReynoldi18851
Date/Time: 22 Mar 2203/2241hrs
Subject: I think I found a way!

I can't believe that I didn't think of this sooner. I piggybacked a message back to Earth via his messages to me. I was hoping that he didn't know how Ellie had shown Ben, and I had done it. Just that it somehow had happened using John's line.

I did it. I took all of the entries that had anything to do with him... others who know...and I piggybacked it through *his* message.

Take that!

It was so satisfying to watch all the files go from "sending" to "sent". I don't have that panic or numbness like I did back on the 13th. I feel excited and rebellious.

Dad, I sure hope you got the message and that they can show you everything. I'm not sending these so he can't see an extra transmissions.

Wait...what's that?

Oh crap. I need help. They are here!

I am going to try Director Bradley via piggybacking on *his* link. I don't know if it will work on IDEA, or just to transmit off.

Someone has to be able to help me.

ENTRY END

I tried the secure link piggybacking again as I sent a message to Director Bradley. It was brief and frantic, asking him if he got my message, to check on Ben and please come to my rescue. I forwarded all my entries on as well. I watched the two messages switch from showing as "sending" to "sent", and let the tension in my shoulders go.

Then I went to get the metal shim I had used to when I had sneaked off to the pond and tried to wedge it as hard as I could to create more friction and tension between the door and the metal framing. I stood on it to force it down deep in the crevice. Then I stepped back.

I looked at my reflection and cringed. I looked scared and exhausted. I didn't want to go out like that. No way. So I went to my closet. And like I did when I first arrived here, I teared up as I geared up. I put on my nicest Class A uniform and put on my shrug coat. I zipped up my calf-length boots and quickly did up my hair in a tight bun. I wanted to portray the professional image of IDEA's cadets when they came for me.

With a quick glance back at my reflection, I nodded. Then I looked for anything in my quarters that I could use as a weapon. In that, I didn't do so well. More flexing and ready-stances were easier to accomplish.

Log-in: JessReynoldi18851
Date/Time: 22 Mar 2203/2245hrs
Subject: They are here

I can hear voices. I think they are working on opening the door. Someone is pushing on it. I can see the metal shift minutely. They are going to force their way in!

Oh crap.

I'm afraid.

Ben? Help me? *Please? Please come save me!*

ENTRY END

Log-in: JessReynoldi18851
Date/Time: 22 Mar 2203/2258hrs
Subject: "Goodbye"

I can hear the door move even more now. It won't be long before Forshay and his cadets are in.

I should have seen this coming because of all the times I was in his office. He sat there, on his throne, crowned by his IDEA sculpture. His message said he shouldn't have been stuck working with less than perfection. He didn't think he should have to work with Bradley on anything. That it had been so easy to manipulate those with space illness into doing the horrible acts, like it was a game. And he added to not hope for someone to save me.

I'm going to stop typing and try and work against them. The shim I placed has moved about an inch. The voices are getting louder, more excited. They know they are almost in. If I don't put up some more resistance, they will be in here shortly. I don't know how to stop them. I don't have anything else.

Wish me luck.

But it if this is my last message, I went down fighting.

ENTRY END

Start TRANSMISSION/SEND

I locked and then shut off my device. Quickly, I placed it at the bottom of my undergarment drawer. With a quick look at my determined reflection, I noted the dark circles under my eyes. Taking a deep breath, I pushed with everything I had to hold the door in place or towards where it should be if closed. Within moments, my sweaty palms became another adversary and I cursed my fear. I quickly wiped them on my dress pants and put them up again, straining against the slightest shifts I felt go against my efforts.

It didn't make sense. How come know one stopped them? How come no one was coming to my rescue?

I could hear a voice come through the edge where the door was about to have clearance, "Calm down, cadet. We'll be done with this."

Fire rolled within me. "How can no one see what you are doing?" I shouted back.

I heard him chuckle. "It's okay, Cadet. We'll have you free in no time."

That's how. It was to look like they were rescuing me. Like I was trapped or stuck in my room. Then what? I would be carted off to some medic station like Ian? Or to some quiet, out-of-the-way room to be...*no*! Don't even think about it!

Like every heroine I had ever read about, I braced my nerves and readied myself for the attack.

Then more voices sounded. The door stopped being worked. I quickly wiped my hands, ready to apply resistance as best as I could. Grunts and shouts. I pressed my ear to the metal door and then looked down at the poor-excuse-for-a-weapon I had at the ready. I abandoned the position of door holder, and snatched up the metal hangers in a death grip from hell. I swallowed the fear and tension that kept choking me, and primed myself to swing if the door moved open even one more inch.

For several long minutes the sounds of confusion and mayhem, or was I hoping it was some sort of a rescue mounting, leaked into my room.

Then silence...eerie and just as intimidating as the sound of people trying to break in.

Then someone banged on the metal. I jumped. Then the banging sounded again. Three solid bangs. A voice called, "Cadet Reynoldi?"

I didn't answer. I didn't recognize the voice through the

metal build of my door. Instead, I flexed my grip on my hangers... and waited.

The door shifted hard and fast about two inches, and then was forced open. I started my first swing of my weapon with everything I had in me.

And Director Bradley dodged it just in time.

I stepped back, apologizing. Faces of other cadets, some I didn't know, loomed. I panicked. Had I been wrong? I raised my weapon again.

"Jess!" Tori's voice rang through the air as she pushed her way forward. Tears were streaming down her face at the sight of me. "Jess!"

I choked back a sob and my body shuddered.

"Cadet?" Director Bradley put up a hand in defense. "You're okay. You're safe." He didn't advance in any way. "You can put your weapon down now."

But I didn't. My eyes were still taking everything in. James was on the ground with three cadets holding him, his face an angry mask with a sock in across his mouth, and tied behind his head. Forshay was unconscious on the floor with two staff members tying him up. The male cadet who was part of the cult, who had blown me a kiss, was being hauled off by three brawny cadets and a staff member. I blinked as the rest came into focus. And my arms started lowering my hangers. "It's over?"

Director Bradley nodded and then motioned for Tori to come forward. She ran up to me and I started crying as her arms came around me.

Log-in: JessReynoldi18851
Date/Time: 23 Mar 2203/2012hrs
Subject: "I'm saved!"

I made it.

I can't believe I made it.

I lived.

And now, for answers.

Jealousy is the worst kind of illness. Jealousy ate at Director Forshay for the number of geniuses, photos and semi-photos that Director Bradley had. Also, the knowledge that the sculpture in his office was bronze was a constant reminder and reflection of his lower standing on IDEA in Forshay's sick, twisted mind.

When James had first arrived, showing signs of space illness, Forshay was afraid to lose one of the few photos he actually had, and had helped hide and treat the illness with other cadets suffering, as he himself did. The control and trust and secret they all shared created a bond that became more twisted. Especially morphed by those with space illness manifesting as mental illness, resulting in the first kills, the cadet and staff member. When they realized what they had done, they had called their confidant for guidance. Forshay had helped hide their crimes...while orchestrating the later monitoring of my accidental findings.

Forshay had kept me under his thumb and watch shortly after James had mentioned my possible space illness symptoms.

Director Bradley had begun some investigations on his own, but hadn't been able to figure out who the master mind was. He had noticed the male bonding group, and started noticing a correlation to their sightings and the mishaps...but nothing had been conclusive. He had been able to ask Ian what was going on, and Ian confided in certain things. Bradley also notice oddities with accessing certain areas, or private meetings, even with some of the cadets from his house, and was documenting everything. When my message came through earlier, he had briefly scanned the message, and went to find Ben for confirmation.

Finding Ben unconscious in his quarters, Bradley had called his trusted House Aides and members of staff to the Commons for a quick rescue. Tori had seen him and addressed the concern for my door still being locked and no messages from me. It had been her second attempt to report her concern for my safety, and Bradley had told her to come along, but to stand by, ready to help or to run and report using a secure line in his office if things went wrong.

Ben had been taken to a secure medic station. It was the same one Bradley had put Ian in while he worked on his investigation. Both were recovering and awake. I am told I will get to see them tomorrow.

Concerning Ian, he had never participated in any cult-like incident. He was just some jock who partnered up with the guys in the gym and different teams, and the camaraderie just grew. When he had suspected something was wrong, that something was going to happen to me, and he threatened to protect me, unknowingly from this friends, they had tried to take him out. The innocent cadet from Bradley House had been put under Bradley's protection during the investigation.

All for his jealousy. The green monster of spite and anger.
The director with a master key and codes for accessing rooms.
The one with a bronze crown suspended in his office like a
second-hand trophy.

> Long may he pay,
> King of Illness and Jealousy,
> Director Forshay.

Am I a little bitter? Sure. Wouldn't you be if you almost died?
Were almost eaten?

But I'm safe.

My parents better be proud.

And me? I think I am ready for bed. I'm exhausted. This has
been a long couple of days.

Goodnight, Mom.

Goodnight, Dad.

ENTRY END

Start TRANSMISSION/SEND

Did you enjoy this book?

A different adventure begins with ANOTHER DAY SERIES:

Another Day

Another Time

Another Place

Another One

Follow me on

Facebook - http://www.facebook.com/jodiemswanson

Twitter - http://www.twitter.com/jodiemswanson